Buffy relaxed a[...] enjoying the n[...] aware, always aware, that the heart within his chest did not beat.

The only true physical warmth between them came from her. *If wishes were stardust,* she thought, *we would sparkle together forever.*

"I won't leave you," he said, and she could tell by the tone of his voice that no amount of bickering would change his mind. "I'll be close. Always."

She pushed back, but still gripped his arms. "All right," she finally said. "Close is good. But *don't* interfere, no matter what happens." Her fingers gripped his cool forearms, feeling the strength in the muscles. "How did they do it in the old days? If I fall, you can be my . . . second?"

He smiled tightly. "Your champion?"

"Always," she said, and meant it. She smiled back. "You'll always be in my heart, you know. If she beats me, then you can step in and take her down where I didn't. And if . . . " Her voice broke for a second, then smoothed out as she found the courage to say the words

[...] worse comes to worse and I fall, Angel, make sur don't . . . come back. I don't *ever* want to come back."

Buffy the Vampire Slayer™

Available from ARCHWAY Paperbacks and Simon Pulse

Available from POCKET BOOKS

BUFFY THE VAMPIRE SLAYER™

TEMPTED CHAMPIONS

YVONNE NAVARRO

An original novel based on the hit TV series created by Joss Whedon

POCKET BOOKS

LONDON · SYDNEY · NEW YORK · TOKYO · SINGAPORE · TORONTO

First Pocket Books edition March 2002

POCKET BOOKS
An imprint of Simon & Schuster
Africa House
64-78 Kingsway
London WC2B 6AH

www.simonsays.co.uk

The text of this book was set in Times.
Printed in the United States of America.
2 4 6 8 10 9 7 5 3 1
A CIP catalogue record for this book is available from
the British Library
ISBN: 0-7434-5031-0

For
Alexa deMonterice
Hey, Red.
This is what by now . . .
fifteen years?

Acknowledgments

A big round of thank-yous to Lisa Clancy, Howard Morhaim, Nancy Holder, Chris Golden, Weston Ochse, Martin Cochran, and my friends and teachers from the Degerberg Martial Arts Academy in Chicago—Dan, Jill, Rick, Lucilla, Raynay, Angela, Julie, Dennis, Charles, Gary, Jaime, Oscar, a whole bunch of other great people from there, and, of course, Fred Degerberg.

Chapter 1

"IT HAS BEEN AN EXCELLENT DAY FOR TAKING IN MONEY,"
Anya said happily.

No one heard her, of course, because the Magic Shop
was empty. Giles had left a half hour ago, something
about getting ready to play that guitar of his in a café
somewhere tonight. She thought it was endearing that a
human as old as he was would still sit in and try to sing
in front of others. It didn't bother her, but the rest of the
gang seemed to find it somehow embarrassing. She
didn't understand why—actually, she didn't understand
the entire concept of being "embarrassed" at all, especially because of someone *else's* behavior. *People are
responsible for their own actions, aren't they? Why,
then, should what someone else does humiliate you?*

The Magic Shop was cool and quiet on this early No-
vember evening, sales good but down from the mad
Halloween rush at the end of last month. She loved this
place, with its warm, golden lighting and shelves filled

with everything from trinkets and harmless potions to weapons that could kill huge demons if a person knew the correct phrase to add, a pinch or two of the right herb and dried lizard parts. It was so beautiful here, and safe—most of the time, anyway. With the exception of being with Xander, there was nowhere else Anya would rather spend her time. That Giles was finally entrusting it to her care, to count the money in the register and lock everything up, just made it that much more special.

She finished the day's accounting and put the money in the safe, then quickly ran a feather duster along the fronts of the display shelves, making sure the place looked spiffy and clean. A final check to make sure the back door was locked, and Anya picked up her purse and headed out. When the front door was securely locked behind her, she turned and—

No Xander.

Darn it, he was late again. What was it this time? Probably some skanky vampire or lesser demon—she loved Xander, but sometimes Anya felt like he put everything in Sunnydale before her. Why couldn't *she* be the number-one thing on his priority list? He was such a typical male, like a thousand others she'd cursed through the centuries.

Okay, maybe Xander wasn't *that* typical. After all, she would never settle for such normalcy, never tolerate the sort of mistreatment she'd avenged for others. He treated her exceptionally well, in fact, and he'd made it clear he loved her, and he was great in bed if not unaccountably embarrassed when she told everyone about that. And there it was again, that "embarrassed" thing: men were supposed to be proud of their prowess at sex, weren't they? So shouldn't he be wanting her to shout it on the hilltops?

Anya sighed and took a couple of steps off the sidewalk so she could check both ways on the street, but there was still no sign of Xander's car. Back on the walkway she paced nervously back and forth. It was a beautiful fall night, a little cool with a light breeze rustling through leaves that were changing colors. It was also deserted, and she wished Xander would get his act together and pick her up on time for a change. Of course, he would just tell her she should have waited inside, and he was probably right. For God's sake, she felt like a walking appetizer standing out here.

Anya heard a footstep behind her and whirled to see a guy coming toward her on the sidewalk. "Stop right there," she snapped. "What are you doing?"

The stranger froze and stared at her, his expression confused. "Uh . . . walking on the sidewalk?"

She crossed her arms. "And where do you think you're going?"

His baffled gaze turned irritable. "No offense, lady, but I don't think that's any of your business. Last I heard, this was a free country."

Anya frowned at him, then relaxed a bit. He was young, early twenties, and dressed nicely enough in a blue plaid shirt and a yellow sweater vest. He even had little round glasses. The whole look was vaguely reminiscent of Giles. He looked a little nerdy, and she didn't see any grave dirt clinging to his shirt collar. Besides, no self-respecting young man would be buried in yellow, so he must be okay. "Sorry," she finally said. "I guess I'm just jumpy."

His frown softened. "I can understand that. Waiting for someone?"

Anya nodded, still a little wary. "My boyfriend is picking me up."

"Looks like he's late." He glanced around. "Would it make you feel better if I waited with you?"

Anya considered this. "Well—"

"Tell you what," the guy interrupted. "Let's not."

Anya blinked. "Not? Not what?"

"Wait." And he morphed into a vampire.

"Oh, why are women always *right?*" She swung her purse and hit the dirty beast on the side of the head nearly before his change was complete, acting on pure instinct. He yelped in surprise and staggered sideways, giving her the two-second opening she needed to run. She didn't get far; the dress, the purse, the shoes—the entire look-like-a-woman thing that she'd really come to enjoy—they were really a huge disadvantage in a fleeing situation.

Anya heard him catch up with her before his wrinkled-up fingers closed around her wrist, screamed at the same time she flailed wildly with her pocketbook. He flinched away from the blows but didn't let go; instead he managed to catch her purse by the strap with his other hand and yank it out of her grip. He tossed it aside without looking in it.

"Hey!" Anya protested. She pulled backward, trying to think of something that would stall for time. Surely Xander would be here any second. "That's got my money in it, and my lipstick!"

"Where you're going, you won't need it." The vampire grinned at her.

"You should brush your teeth more often. They're really yellow. And you've got horrible breath." He scowled but didn't let go, then he began to drag her toward a clump of bushes about twenty feet away. "Let me go!"

"Be quiet," he barked. "You're dinner, remember? Food shouldn't talk."

"Neither should vampires."

Both Anya and her attacker jerked in surprise at the new voice, low and silky, unmistakably feminine. The creature had been intent on carting her off to a nice, private spot, and Anya had been just as intent on not going; neither had realized there was a young woman trailing after them. She was tall and pretty, dressed in a sort of pseudo-poverty/punk style and sporting spiky strawberry blond hair with dark roots that reminded Anya of the way Oz had once worn his. Her dark eyes were rimmed with kohl Goth-fashion, a stark contrast to her pale skin and colorless lips.

Rather than let Anya go, Tooth-Boy jerked her around and reached for the newcomer. "Oh, goody. An appetizer!"

"Hey, *I* was supposed to be the appetizer!" *Wait,* Anya thought as she tried vainly to pull free. *What am I saying?*

The new girl didn't back away. "What's up with the food references?" She grinned as the vampire's hand locked on to her arm. "Besides, I really think you've ordered off your last menu."

He stared at her, then at the hand he'd folded around her wrist. "Hold it, you're not—"

Before he could finish, the redhead grabbed him by the bangs and yanked his head forward, slamming it against hers.

He howled in pain and Anya found herself suddenly free. She stumbled and fell, then scrambled over and snatched up her purse as the vampire and her rescuer began solidly pounding on each other. Bag in hand, Anya backed away and watched, fascinated despite herself. She ought to run, but still . . . blow for blow, it was obvious the vampire, not the girl, was tiring—at one point the young woman laughed out loud, as though this was nothing more than a darned good game.

No fool he, the vampire knew when he was outmatched. He turned tail and tried to run, but the female stranger was having none of that. Her hand zipped forward and grabbed the back of his shirt collar, then she hauled him backward, hard.

Right onto the point of a stake she pulled out of the pocket of her army pants.

The bloodsucker disappeared into the traditional cloud of dirty dust, but the redheaded-girl hadn't let go of the stake. Anya's rescuer pulled her arm back, spun the stake in a move that could only be called Western-movie, then pocketed it. Finally she clapped her hands together to rid them of the vampire residue.

"Wow," Anya said, stepping forward. "That was great. I can't thank you enou—"

"Where is Buffy the Vampire Slayer?" the girl demanded, jerking around to face her.

Anya stopped short. "She's, uh, not here."

"Do I seem blind to you?"

Anya swallowed. "Well, no, obviously you're not."

"Then answer my question."

"Well, I don't know where she is, exactly right this minute. I mean, it's not like she gives me her social calendar, then checks with me if she makes last-minute changes to it. She could be anywhere, there's at least a dozen places she could be. . . ." Anya was faintly aware that she was babbling and backing away from the woman at the same time. Her elation at being saved had undergone an instant metamorphosis into fear; there was something wrong about the stranger, who was matching her retreat step for step, something *really* off. The tone of voice, her expression—no, Little Miss Fighting Machine here wasn't blind, and she wasn't an old friend of Buffy's, either.

"You're really starting to annoy me," the redhead said. "If you don't tell me where she is, I'm going to rip your eyeballs out and use them as marbles."

Anya tried to laugh and succeeded in only sounding panicked. It was just her luck to get rescued from one nighttime-nasty by another who turned out to be just as sinister. "Oh, there's no need for that. If you want marbles, we have them in the Magic Shop. We have eyeballs, too. Nice ones, in fact, blessed by a cabal of—"

"I can *smell* you," the young woman said suddenly. Her nose wrinkled in the air. "There's something different about you. What . . ." Anya's rescuer narrowed her eyes. "Why, this could be . . . priceless."

Anya risked a glance behind her. There was maybe twenty feet between her and the girl, and she was almost to the bushes. But really, what chance did she have fleeing from someone who could fight like this vampire-killer had? It'd be like trying to get away from Buffy. Still, there was that distinct alarm-thing going on in her head, the one that was *screaming* at her to get the heck away right now.

"Oh, that's me," Anya said with fake exuberance. "Priceless! Just ask anybody." Something familiar worked its way into her hearing then, that very particular *ping* sound that came from the engine of Xander's car. It had always aggravated her before; now she couldn't have been more grateful.

"Ask *who?*" the stranger sneered. "Your family? Been gone awhile, haven't they?"

Anya's eyes widened. How could this woman know anything about her family? "Who are you, anyway?"

The woman grinned and reached for her. "You'll never know."

But Anya had already started to run in the other direction, toward that now-comforting *ping*. She could see his headlights about a half block away; at the same time she heard her former savior's pursuing footsteps, the welcome sound of Xander's engine going abruptly full throttle filled her ears—such a dutiful boyfriend, he'd seen her running and was now intent on coming to her rescue. It seemed she would be saved—hopefully—twice in one night.

"Hey, I'm not done with you!" the woman yelled.

Anya didn't bother to answer—she needed every bit of air to keep running. This woman was faster, stronger, and far more brutal than she, and her only escape was going to be to get to Xander before she was gotten *to*. For a long moment her entire world was reduced to one small thing—Xander's headlights—then she felt the redhead's fingers brush the back of her dress.

She opened her mouth to scream, and Xander's horn blared obnoxiously. The sound startled her, but not as much as the woman chasing her. That one-second pause was all Anya needed; when Xander stood on the brakes and came to a squealing stop next to her, she clawed the door opened and leaped inside.

"Drive away!" she gasped and slammed her elbow down on the doorlock. "Really fast—really *now!*"

The woman skidded to a stop on the passenger side of the car and punched at the window; Anya let out a scream as the lightly tinted glass next to her dissolved into a lacy pattern of bulging cracks.

Xander floored the accelerator before another blow could follow. "What the hell was *that?*" Anya heard him asking as she was pressed back against the seat. He clutched the steering wheel as storefronts and parked cars whizzed by, his gaze darting to the rearview mirror to make sure they weren't being followed, that the woman hadn't suddenly sprouted wings and taken to the air. In Sunnydale one couldn't rule out anything. "Who *was* she?"

Shaking, Anya twisted around and stared out the back

windshield, but her attacker was already out of sight. "I don't know, but I think she might be a friend of Buffy's." She looked back at Xander. "Or maybe an old enemy."

Celina, as she was calling herself these days, watched the woman she'd saved and the dark-headed man speed away, then slipped into the shadows between the building and the bushes. A minor disappointment, nothing more, and she had long ago learned not to let frustration influence her decisions—that way lay nothing but disaster. Still, it was too bad they'd escaped; she could smell something off about the pretty young thing, knew that scent meant that while she looked human, might even *be* human now, once she had been something quite different. Ties to the nether realms like that could never quite be erased. She could have gotten much information from that one but the girl had gotten lucky and escaped.

But not for long.

Chapter 2

"AND THEN," ANYA SAID TO FINISH HER STORY, "XANder pulled up and I jumped in the car. I barely escaped with my life." She turned and gave her boyfriend a brilliant smile. "Just like in the movies, Xander rescued me!"

Before Giles could comment on that, Willow raised an eyebrow. "Are you sure you're not exaggerating? Maybe that woman just wanted to talk to you some more."

"Have you by chance seen the passenger-side window in my car?" Xander's face was red around the edges. "If that's how she shows she just wants to 'talk,' I'd hate to be on the receiving end when she starts yelling."

"She broke the window," Anya added. "Right next to my head." She glanced over at Buffy, who was listening intently. "She punched it like you punch the hanging bag in the training room. And when she fought that vampire, she was just as fast as you, too."

"And then you drove away?" Giles put in.

Xander slouched back on his chair. "If you consider

driving away as a synonym for flooring the accelerator and praying that the car doesn't die, then yes. We drove away."

"Interesting." Standing behind the Magic Shop's counter, Giles took off his glasses and polished them absently. "All that strength, but you say she wasn't a vampire?"

Anya, looking fully recovered from the evening's adventure, puttered happily among the inventory. "If she was, she didn't show it, even when she was chasing me. Besides, she killed one to save me. Don't they usually just share?"

"I wonder why she wanted to know about me," Buffy said. "She sure doesn't fit any friendship slot in my memory bank."

"With friends like that . . ." Tara shuddered and left the familiar sentence unfinished.

"And she wasn't very nice about asking, either," Anya said, sounding irritated about the encounter all over again as she rearranged a few items. "That's why I decided not to tell her."

Giles nodded. "A wise decision, Anya."

Anya tilted her head to one side. "You know, I think she had an accent. Kind of European, I think. There was something . . . *wrong* about her. Something way scary." She shuddered.

"You mean more than the normal bloodsucking-fiend kind of scary?" Tara asked. Her eyes were wide.

Anya nodded vigorously. "Way more. It was like the time when I granted a wish for this girl who wanted her cheating boyfriend's head to explode the next time he looked at his new girlfriend except that she didn't tell me that the new girlfriend was her own *sister,* and so when he—"

Xander cleared his throat to cut her off. "So, Oh-wise-Council-one," he said to Giles, "who do you think she is? A vampire?"

Willow sat up straighter. "Hey, maybe she's another rogue slayer, like Faith." She looked suddenly alarmed at her own words. "I mean, here she comes and beats up on the vampires but doesn't turn into a vampire herself, and then she wants to know all about Buffy. What else could she be?"

Tara looked at Willow nervously. "Doesn't the current Slayer have to die before you get a new one?"

"Generally, yes," Giles answered. "But there have been exceptions to that rule because of circumstance. Kendra, for example, was called the instant Buffy died, but then Xander resuscitated Buffy. Since Kendra had already been called, we ended up with two."

"And Faith was called when Kendra was killed," Buffy added. "So we still have two."

Silence settled over all of them as they contemplated this. It was Buffy who finally voiced what the rest of them were thinking but were too reluctant to ask. "Giles, you don't suppose something happened in Los Angeles, do you? Because I'm obviously still oxygen-enabled, and for another slayer to exist at the same time as me—"

"—that means someone killed Faith," Xander finished for her.

More silence, as each of the gang who had dealt with Faith wrestled with their feelings. So much of the legacy that Faith had left them was tainted, but even so, her being in their lives had left bits of good, too—a life saved here, a moment of laughter there, for Xander an introduction into manhood. Sometimes the lessons, as when Buffy had learned to trust in Angel's love for her, weren't so apparent or easily understood, but they were there nonetheless, insights into the results of a life lived on two sides.

"I'll call Angel," Buffy said. Her expression was grim. "If he doesn't know already, he'll be able to find out."

Willow shuddered. "Prison—it's just an awful thing. I mean, think about how it must be, stuck in there day and night, with killers and thieves and who knows what else, unable to leave for years and years."

Xander pushed his sleeves up, decided he didn't like them that way, then pushed them back down. "Faith *is* a killer, remember? That's why she's in there."

"But she's not invincible," Giles reminded him in a low voice. "She can die just like any of us."

"Which would mean another slayer," Willow said.

"There are other possibilities, too," Giles told them. "Other dimensions, parallel universes, opened portals—"

Anya had moved behind the counter to stand next to Giles. "Someone always seems to be monkeying with the fabric of time," she said. "And it always backfires."

Willow frowned slightly. "You aren't exactly the one to be pointing fingers about that."

"Well, you certainly shouldn't. You're the one who had a double that kept popping in and out like an unwanted relative at Christmas. I—"

"And whose fault was *that?*" Willow shot back.

Sitting on the other side of Tara at the table, Spike had been silent so far; now he dropped a heavy book on the tabletop, and the *bang* was loud enough to make them all jump. "Can we get back to the here and now? Or would you all rather take your chances on getting pounded into the bloody concrete just for being palsies with the Slayer?"

Xander scowled at him. "Say, aren't you supposed to be in a dank and dirty crypt somewhere?"

"There's no reason to get insulting," Spike said defensively. "I try to keep my digs clean, thank you very much. And I have my ways of getting around in the daytime hours if I have to. I'll be okay."

"Enough, already. As much it pains me to agree with anything he says, Spike's right." Buffy stood and grabbed her purse. "I have to go pick up Dawn. When I get her home, I'll give Angel a call and get the scoop on everything Faith-related in L.A."

Giles straightened his glasses. "I'll make some discreet inquiries among the Council members, see if I can find any references that might be helpful. Sometimes they can be a wiley bunch, so I'll search a little behind the scenes, call in a few markers, and make sure they'd not hiding anything from me."

"It wouldn't be the first time," Buffy said darkly.

"No kidding," Xander agreed. "What can we do?"

Buffy glanced over at Anya, who seemed to be fiddling way too much, even for her non-stop-shop tendencies. Nervous energy, probably driven by leftover fear. "Why don't you take Anya home?" she suggested. "She looks a little freaked."

"Outrunning a psycho-woman with superhuman strength will do that to a person," Xander said. He pushed to his feet and looked at his girlfriend. "Ahn, what do you say we go home, maybe order a pizza and watch a vid?"

"Yes!" Anya's voice was a bit too loud and bright. "That's an excellent idea. Pizza is good. I *love* pizza." The gang looked at one another. The shop could theoretically be open for another couple of hours or longer; for Anya to leave the store during any potential moneymaking time confirmed how wigged out she still was.

"Okay," Xander said amiably and steered her toward

the door. "We'll check in with you guys tomorrow. But definitely give us a ring if you need emergency disaster demon-aid."

"Will do," Giles agreed.

"I'm out of here, too," Buffy said as the door closed behind Xander and Anya. "Dawn's doing an extracurricular thing tonight, some kind of science-project thing, and I want to make sure I'm there when she gets out of school. Let me know if you find anything." She left Giles already searching through his books, and while Willow and Tara dug their noses into papers they had to get done for classes, their presence in the Magic Shop was enough to let Giles know that both would pitch in with the search if he needed them.

Closing the door behind her, Buffy cast a last glance over her shoulder, a little envious in spite of herself and her resolve to make the best of the way things had worked out. She missed college and the schoolwork— even the classes she'd never managed to master—and especially the bright but unreachable future that enrolling had falsely promised. She'd tried so hard to keep a tight grip on that little imaginary slice of the universe, but time and time again she'd been taught that in the scheme of things, she was next to nothing—an ant beneath the boot heel of something so great and vast none of them could really comprehend it. The reminders of that were all around her, particularly in the absence of her mother and the presence of Dawn, how the way the younger girl felt like a part of her life when Buffy knew she'd hadn't been that at all.

And now there was this stranger, someone new in Sunnydale and looking for her. Who could she be? It wasn't like Buffy hadn't made her share of enemies in and out of the nether realms since she'd moved here, but she was pretty sure she'd remember someone with punked-out reddish hair and fighting skills like Anya had described. The girl sounded too with-it to be some kind of demon kicked up from Hell and sent to take her out—those were usually recognizable no matter how hard they tried to hide behind a store-bought set of high fashion.

Maybe Anya had simply overreacted, misinterpreted the stranger's intent until the visiting dudette had gotten frustrated enough to run after her. That thing with Xander's car was probably nothing more than a lucky—or unlucky—smack in just the right pressure point on the glass. Anya's savior of last night was likely nothing more than someone who'd moved on from Sunnydale High before Anya had come into the picture, which would explain why Anya hadn't known who she was. They'd figure it out . . . but she'd call Angel later tonight, just to be sure. Buffy wanted to think as positive as anyone else, but doing that around here could get you killed. After all, this *was* the Hellmouth.

Celina moved easily through the streets, following the streetlights until she came to the main section. It was so bright here for a weeknight evening, and crowded and noisy, as if the residents thought that bunching together would make it safe. Not hardly; Sunnydale was infested with the undead—something else she could smell, literally, on the air currents. The scent of them drifted around her like dead memories wafting out of an ancient catacomb.

Walking among the humans, she took care not to pass too close to the shop windows, mirrored doors, or the windows of parked cars. Over the centuries since her change she had adapted so many times, evolving with the world around her. It was said that man was the most adaptable creature on earth, that the species could change to fit its environment like no other. Celina had done just that, ultimately learning to walk like an American teenager, to talk like one, to dress like one.

She found an ice-cream shop that wasn't crowded and was free of pesky reflective surfaces. She bought the largest coffee-flavored slushy drink they had, then carried it back outside and sat cross-legged on the sidewalk to watch the people and traffic. She'd seen so much, but they were different here in Sunnydale, California, more accepting of a darker side of existence that they had no idea survived, almost like there was something in their subconscious minds that handily tuned it out. Maybe it was an evolutionary thing, a switch that had flipped to keep them sane when they'd seen things they couldn't explain or accept.

Celina grinned to herself and sucked greedily at the straw.

If only they had a clue . . .

Buffy was waiting when the last of the way-smart science-project pack straggled out of the doors at Sunnydale High, and the look on little sister's face—embarrassment, anger, dismay—almost made her turn and walk off.

Almost . . . but not quite.

Dawn was everything to her now, her whole world. Everyone else had someone or something: Giles had his Magic Shop, his books, and an occasional surprising romantic excursion that made Buffy secretly envious; Xander and Anya had each other, likewise with Willow and Tara. Angel had his agency in Los Angeles, Riley had the Initiative or whatever that group was calling itself now that Professor Walsh's little underground dream team had disintegrated. Whatever it was that kept him from coming back to her.

Buffy had lost so much. But she still had Dawn.

"Hi," she said and dug up a cheerful smile. Dawn only looked pained as the two or three girlfriends who'd been walking down the steps with her glanced warily at Buffy and hung back. "What are you doing here?" the younger girl asked testily. "I was going to go to the Espresso Pump with my friends after we got through with the project."

"I was close by and I realized you were getting out, so I thought I'd meet you." *Lame, lame, lame.*

"Buffy—"

"I thought we'd go to the mall," Buffy said quickly. "A little shopping, some really greasy fast food with buttered popcorn and a movie for dessert." It was a fast-thinking bribe, and both she and Dawn knew it.

"I have homework," Dawn said reproachfully. "You know I have to be careful to keep up my grades."

Buffy didn't say anything for a moment as resentment flashed through her at the memory of the school principal telling her that Dawn would be put into a foster home if they decided Buffy wasn't taking proper care of her. Dawn wasn't even *real*—what right did they have to do that?

No, I mustn't think like that, Buffy reminded herself. *She's my sister and she is real—she's standing right here, looking daggers at me for making her feel like an eight-year-old in front of her girlfriends. In her place I would be looking at me the same way. Yeah, it all feels pretty real to me.*

"You're right," Buffy said. Dawn's eyes widened in surprise, and Buffy thought how pretty she looked, with her long dark hair shining in the glow of the dozens of street lamps outside the high school. "So we just quick-shop. Then I'll whip us up something à la microwave at home while you hit the books." She gave little sister her best smile. "How about it? I'll buy you a new fall sweater."

Bribery again, but after all, Dawn *was* a teenager. In the end Dawn waved goodbye to her pals, and she and Buffy strode happily in the direction of Sunnydale Mall.

Chapter 3

ANYA FELT BETTER, A *LOT* BETTER, ONCE SHE WAS AT home. The apartment was like her little slice of safety—nothing bad had ever happened to her here, no demon had ever darkened her door, no vampires had ever been invited inside. Not even Spike had crossed that threshold, and if she had her way, he never would—this was a Monster-Free Zone, and darn it, she intended to keep it that way.

"So," Xander said once they were inside. "Pizza with all the gooey, cheesy, heart-clogging accoutrements?"

"No."

He blinked at her from where he'd been standing by the kitchen counter, telephone in one hand, delivery menu in the other. "No? But I thought we agreed."

"I changed my mind."

"But—"

Anya frowned at him. "Is there a problem? Women change their minds. It's an expected thing—in fact, songs have even been written about it."

Xander put the phone back on the receiver and tossed the menu aside. "There are some things you could avoid about being human, you know. Poor stereotypes being one of them."

"I want to cook."

Xander's eyebrows shot up. "As in—"

"Prepare a meal using foodlike ingredients and kitchen utensils. People do it all the time."

"You aren't just any 'people.' "

Anya folded her arms, her expression obstinate. "I do *not* want pizza."

"But I clearly heard you say you liked pizza." Xander's hand inched toward the delivery menu. "In fact, I have witnesses, other people with ears."

"I do like pizza. But not tonight." His hand paused. "Tonight I will fix Sloppy Joes and baked potatoes."

Xander gave up and shoved his hand in his pocket. "I don't think potatoes are usually served with sloppy joes. That's usually more of a french-fry thing."

Anya pulled a skillet from one of the cabinets, then found a can of Manwich Sauce to go along with a package of ground beef from the freezer. "I don't know how to make french fries," she told him. "But I *can* microwave a potato as well as the next person." She frowned again. "Is that unacceptable? Should I be taking a cooking class or—"

"Baked is fine," Xander said hastily. "Fine and dandy, yes, sir."

"Good," Anya said with finality. "And we will do laundry."

"We will?"

"Yes." From the look on Xander's face, she could tell it wasn't the way he'd envisioned spending the evening. "I feel like being domestic tonight," she finally said. It was the best she could come up with as an explanation. "It makes me feel good."

For a second he only looked blank, then he understood. "Hey," he said, coming over and putting his arms around her. "Don't worry, okay? That woman—she has no idea where we live, doesn't even know your name. You said yourself that you'd already closed up the Magic Shop, so she probably doesn't even have a connection there. You're home, and safe, and with me. Okay?"

Anya inhaled, then made herself relax. Xander was right, of course. Hadn't she just thought about how this apartment was a Monster-Free Zone? "Okay," she agreed.

"Tell you what," Xander said. "You start the sloppy joes and, uh, baked potatoes, and I'll take the dirty clothes down to the laundry room."

"All right." She glanced over her shoulder anxiously as he headed toward the bedroom. "But take a stake with you—it's dark down there, and it's a public place!"

"Definitely not going wood-deprived," he called back. She heard Xander rummaging around in the other room, then caught the sound of the front door closing firmly behind him.

She was bored.

"What to do, what to do," Celina murmured to herself. Keeping things interesting—that was the trouble with immortality. She didn't understand how other vampires did it . . . or maybe she did. They had that whole socialization thing going on, banding together like little gangs of bloodsuckers, always hatching some plot or another to unleash chaos on the world, destroy this part, kill all the people in that part, open up this other dimension and let all the oogitty-boogitties out. And they were always getting their undead butts roundly kicked, too, if not by whatever Slayer happened to slaying at the time, then by someone else. Do-gooders abounded: ex-Watchers, demons who didn't like their own dimensions, those annoying little white witches—there was even that vampire with a soul out in L.A. She was going to kill him someday.

But that would be then, and this was now. For tonight's entertainment, Celina decided a great place to start would be away from the bright and busy central area of the town. The darker parks definitely had more to offer the hungry, restless vampire, and the pickings there would be safer. Not that she was afraid—she wasn't—but she'd learned long ago that the humans were a lot less likely to miss the lowlifes in their society than they were to misplace Ma and Pa McCarthy on their way home from evening church services. She'd gotten wise through the decades and learned to steer away from the temptation of the careless and oh-so-easy teenager out after curfew; those were much sooner missed than the motorcycle freak or the budding drug user. Those were easy to spot by their smell. She knocked them out and dragged them off to somewhere nice and dark; when they woke up, she did the vamp change and let their own fear generate the adrenalin that flushed away the last of the drugs. Yummy little snacks once they were all cleaned out.

Despite its small size, Sunnydale wasn't much different than anywhere else. In fact, she caught an immediate two-for-one special when she stopped in a scuzzy bar called Willi's Alibi Room and sat down with a couple of dealers who smelled of living somewhere else. Where? It only took Celina a moment to decide it was Monterey, a small city of about a hundred and twenty-five thousand people through which she'd drifted once or twice over the decades. She talked to them like old friends first, finding out that these guys were looking to sell off a shipment of stuff they were claiming was cut with dried ogre and fire demon's blood. It was a mix that the clientele around Willy's would find exceptionally interesting, but in reality Celina could tell their blow was almost nothing but red chalk powder. How foolish humans and demons alike were spending their money on stuff like that when everyday life was so sweet in its natural form.

The two guys, both in their mid-twenties and drug-free themselves—they would never put these chemicals in their *own* bodies—liked her. Celina gave them lots of dark and sultry smiles, knew how to walk the walk and talk the talk. They thought she was a player, a smaller-time dealer than themselves who wanted to spread their particular brand of powdered pseudo-joy around Sunnydale. To further the illusion, when they named a price Celina counteroffered, knowing they'd be instantly suspicious if she agreed to their first demands. A little bantering back and forth, but it wasn't long before an agreement was reached.

She didn't have the money on her, of course, and they hadn't expected she would. Instead of the usual arrangement to meet later, she slyly suggested they take her "home." She had the cash, they had the flash; with a grin that held a lot more meaning than they realized, Celina told them that at her house, they could wrap up the night with a nice meal.

Foolish, useless humans. They never learned.

She left their drained and forever dead bodies to rot in a ditch at the side of a dirt road a half mile out of town.

Grinning to herself, savoring the lingering taste of the meal, Celina drove their car back into downtown Sunnydale. Too bad she couldn't keep it, but there was just nothing low-key about the flame-red Mercedes convertible. Her jazzed-out hair and the fact that she had no problem riding around in the chilly night with the top down was apt to make her stand out even more. In the end Celina parked it a couple of blocks away from a nightclub for the younger set called the Bronze and left it there. Just for giggles, she left the keys in it; whatever short-brained lout stole it would probably end up trying to explain the two bodies once the local cop-shop got wind of them . . . and they always did. Normally they might not make a stink, but these two boys probably had rich parents back in Monterey, lawyers or doctors or dentists *oh, my!* Had it been a runaway or a vagabond, even the cops wouldn't have cared. *How much more of an indication is it that you mean nothing in the world when no one even notices when you're gone?*

But enough of the bleak thoughts. Her appetite didn't stop at blood, and there was more fun to be had here in Sunnydale. You just had to know where to look, and Celina was pretty sure she had it figured out.

The Bronze was clearly the town's hot spot, and she quickly blended in with the crowd around the exterior of the club. Inside and out, the place was packed with teenagers and young adults . . . and a whole lot of other beings that would scare these timid little humanoids right out of their collective skins if they only knew the truth. Vampires, demons, werewolves just waiting for the cycle of the moon—why, this town was a regular Grand Central Station for the Netherworlds. She'd heard it rumored that a Hellmouth was here; obviously the stories were quite true.

There—two of them, both obviously thinking they had the Bloodsuckers Anonymous look down pat. To Celina they might as well have had big, blinking arrows above their heads—*"Stake Me Now!"* would've been appropriate, or maybe a neon bull's-eye on the chest sur-round by the sparking proclamation of *"Pointed Wood Goes HERE!"* They were too slick, too suave, and way too nice for any self-respecting member of the female human race to believe.

But, of course, there was always the dumb blond.

After dumping the frozen hunk of meat into the skillet and setting the burner on low, Anya scrubbed a couple of potatoes and set them aside for microwaving. There were two or three glasses in the sink; not enough to bother with the dishwasher and her hands were wet anyway, so she decided to give them a quick wash. The whole domestic thing was having the desired calming effect on her. It was like leaving all the nastiness of the real world behind and retreating to her own safe little fairy-tale world, a place where she and Xan—

Pain zinged up her forefinger and hand.

"Ouch!"

Anya jerked, then gasped when the water running over the top of the glass came out red below it. There— the glass had broken when she'd shoved the sponge inside it, a large triangular piece separating itself cleanly from the rest. The new edge had caught her on the first finger of her right hand and sliced right to left almost to the bone up to her knuckle as she'd turned the sponge. Now there was a gaping, painful wound, and she was bleeding all over everything.

She dropped what was left of the glass into the sink. The rest of it shattered, but she didn't notice as she stumbled backward, surprised at the quantity of blood against the white porcelain, shocked by its *redness*. Sure, she'd been bruised and banged up before, once badly enough to warrant a trip to the hospital and an arm sling. But this, this was *wrong,* there was so *much* blood.

Pain was throbbing all the way up her wrist now and the crimson liquid of her own insides seemed to be everywhere—in the sink, down the front of the cabinet where she'd instinctively pulled back, filling her other hand when she automatically cupped her lacerated finger.

Anya found enough sense to grab at the roll of paper towels hanging next to the refrigerator and left a trail of blood as she did so. Her heart was pounding as she watched her blood soak through the wad in no time—was she going to die here? Bleed to death, just like that, with no warning or anything, before Xander could even get back up from the laundry room? What about all the things she'd planned to do? She wasn't ready to die, not yet—

Joyce Summers hadn't been, either.

Suddenly, with about as much subtlety as a freight train, the concept of Anya's own mortality hit home. She sank to her knees on the kitchen floor, didn't even feel the *thunk* of bone against the linoleum. She *was* going to die, maybe not today from this cut finger, but someday, and Sunnydale being what it was, she probably *wouldn't* be ready for it when it happened. All too clearly the memory of those chilling hours in the aftermath of the death of Buffy's mom came back to her, punctuated by the words Anya's had blurted out, hard evidence of her own fear and confusion—

". . . there's just a body, and I don't understand why she just can't get back in it and not be dead anymore, it's *stupid!* It's mortal and *stupid!*"

She was just like Joyce, a human. A *shell*. She, Xander, Buffy, Willow—that's all any of them were, fragile shells containing some sort of elusive force that animated them, kept them going as walking, talking human dolls. And one of these days, they would all die and, just like Joyce, be gone forever.

Kneeling there, Anya clutched tightly at the paper towel wadded around her injury. It was sodden with blood, bright and beautiful where it dripped against the white floor, a crimson sign that seemed to scream to everything in the universe that she, too, would eventually die like everyone else.

When it happened, what would it be like? Would it hurt, be boring, or lonely? Would she even *know* when she was really and truly dead? Death was the ultimate unknown, something more dreadful than anything Anya had ever considered. She didn't have the answer to any of those questions, and the lack of answers left her feeling terrified and overwhelmed, more afraid than she'd ever been before.

And all she could do was kneel there, bleeding and shuddering with pain and fright, until Xander came up from the laundry room and found her.

The blond came out of the front entrance with one guy on each side of her, her arms hooked through the vampires' and clearly oblivious to the fact that the skin against hers was the same temperature as the round steak wrapped in the local grocer's case. Laughing and giggling—*twittering* actually—she was basically making an embarrassment of her entire gender. The whole display made Celina want to slap the girl, but she was more interested in the bloodsuckers. The vampire part of her had been satiated earlier thanks to the two dealers.

Funny how the vamps always paired or packed together once they made it through the initial survival period; they seemed to know instinctively that most of them would never succeed on their own. Oddly enough, at the same time, it was as though immortality cheapened life, that "too much of a good thing" concept where instead of appreciating whatever they'd been gifted with, the recipient soon began to take it for granted. They got careless about where they went, reckless about their victims, way too overconfident. One of the things that had intrigued her since she'd first seen it was skydiving, and that was a prime example. Celina couldn't try it herself (no one skydived at night except for the military), but she had read up on it; one of the most interesting facts had been that newbies hardly ever had accidents because they were so careful about everything (translation: *terrified*). It was almost always the most experienced, the crackerjacks who came in for speed landings at up to eighty-five miles an hour under smaller canopies or waited too long to pull their chutes who got killed.

Just like the vampires.

These two, for instance. In full view of everyone they sauntered out the main entrance with a girl on their arm who was well-dressed enough to probably be the daughter of some local town official. The charm bracelet on her wrist was real gold, as was the heart-shaped locket around her neck; half-carat diamonds twinkled in her ears. She smelled like money and power and connections, and that made her a bad, bad choice. Typical; as with most young vampires, it was all about them. No thought for their race or the other vampires who needed to remain hidden in the town, no inclination to look at what effect their actions might have on the bigger picture.

Celina's mouth twisted in derision, then smoothed out. It wouldn't do for them to see by her expression that she thought they were idiots. No, that wouldn't do at all.

She moved gracefully into step beside the one on the left. "Hi, boys."

The one nearest her glanced to the side and saw her. He started to grin, then it faded when he instinctively knew she was like them. "Screw off," he said out of the side of his mouth as he kept walking. "We're not into sharing tonight."

Celina ignored him and followed as they began to steer the girl toward the alley at the side of the building. The girl, chattering happily with the other vampire, took a couple of steps, then noticed Celina. "Hi," she said. "My name is Cathy. Are you friends with Bill and Walter?"

Celina grinned at her. "Sure. We're *old* friends. I could really give you the goods on these two."

Bill—or maybe it was Walter—stopped short. "Why don't you go away?" he snapped. "We didn't ask you to join in."

His tone of voice made bouncy little Cathy also jerk to a halt. "Hey," she said, looking from the two guys to Celina. "What's going on—join in what? Why can't she come along? I thought we were going to the movies."

"Only if you want to watch yourself die," Celina said calmly.

"What!" Shocked, Cathy yanked her arms free and stepped back. Celina's bluntness took the two vampires enough by surprise so that they didn't hold on.

"Oh, yeah," Celina continued. "In my circles we call guys like these two 'Bloodsucker Boys.' " She stepped closer to the taller of the duo and grabbed him under his chin, moving too fast for him to get away. Five fast steps and she'd propelled him backward and back around the corner into the alley. "They'll do things to you that you can't even imagine," she said darkly. She glanced over her shoulder at the staring teenager. "Better run home, little girl. As fast as you can."

Cathy's tolerance for fear was obviously on the low side—she turned to head out without a second warning. The other vamp tried to grab her, and Celina lashed out with the toe of her boot, hard and sharp, into the heavy muscle of his thigh. He yelped with the pain, but any thought of giving chase disintegrated. "Oh, *man*," he complained as the three of them watched Cathy scurry off. "Bill, she ruined our dinner!"

At least now she knew which was which. Bill was the tall one she still held by the throat, Walter was shorter and had the more weasel-like qualities. He was also a whiner under pressure.

"Let me *go*," Bill snarled. Feeling benevolent, Celina decided to obey, but not before adding a little push to the release. Bill tumbled onto his backside, then was on his feet again in an instant. "What the hell do you want?" he demanded. He brushed the alley grit off the seat of his khakis. "What, you can't find your own food to play with?"

Celina gave them a sugary-sweet smile. "My name is Celina. I'm a vampire slayer."

"No way," said Walter, squinting at her. "Vampire, yeah. Slayer? Not in this lifetime."

"Exactly," Celina agreed.

"Uh-oh," Bill muttered. He started backing away from her. Loyal friend that he was, it was painfully obvious Walter was going to have to fend for himself here.

"What?" Walter looked from her to his retreating friend. "Hey, where're you going? We can take her!"

"Use your brain, moron," Bill hissed. "You hit it right on the mark—'not in this *lifetime*.' A slayer is what she *used* to be, before—"

"I became a vampire," Celina finished serenely. Walter made a sound in his throat that sounded vaguely like *gleep,* but before he could flee, she leaned over and grabbed him by the hair with her left hand. Bill had turned and was already running at full speed, but it didn't help him. One of her stakes was in her hand without a second thought, then it was sailing through the air like a short, deadly spear. It caught him in the center of the back, right where it was supposed to. After all, she'd had several centuries to practice.

Walter tried to pull away, but he had died as a young man with a nice thick head of hair; he'd have been luckier to have male pattern baldness, because all those locks gave her plenty to hold on to. Celina yanked him back and forth a few times, liking the way he sort of rag-dolled in front of her, arms and legs comically flapping around. Still, that was funny for only a few seconds. She got bored so easily nowadays.

"So," she said cheerfully. "What shall I do with you?"

"How about you let me go?" Walter squeaked. "We weren't going to kill her, honest. A little snack—"

"Spare me the snow job," Celina said, then halfheartedly jammed another stake into his chest.

"Owwwwwwww!" he screeched.

She blinked and nearly let him go. "Whoops—sorry about that. Didn't quite get my target down, did I?" She slapped her fist against the blunt end of the wood and drove it deeper, enough to where it found the vampire's heart. A heartbeat later—if one could call the dried-up dead muscle a heart anyway—he joined his friend as alley dust.

Sloppy, she thought. Disgusted with herself, she pocketed the stake. She wasn't really high on the idea of torturing people, alive or undead—that was something she did only as a last resort, if she needed information about something, and the person or creature was too stupid to go ahead and talk. Who wanted to listen to all that screaming, anyway? Not her. She'd much rather—

Speaking of listening, or rather *hearing,* there was someone else in the alley with her.

Celina nonchalantly leaned over and toed the ground, as if she were searching for something, seeming for all the world like she had no idea someone was spying on her. It was dark and close in here, but she had no trouble seeing that over there, just to the left of a grouping of garbage cans, was a shadow that didn't belong. Darker than the ones thrown by the cans under the streetlight, this particular splotch of darkness had a tendency to fidget; apparently its owner was too dumb to realize that fidgeting meant movement, and movement meant noise, and noise meant he was going to get his butt discovered.

Coming up with the stake in her hand, Celina took three sprinting steps and yanked the person who was spying on her out into the open.

Not a human, a demon.

"Oh, gross," she said and pushed it away from her. Celina tended to group demons by color more than anything else, and this was one of the green ones—she'd never been good at remembering all the names and species. Yeah, a green one . . . almost, anyway, except for the brown and yellow splotchy areas across a scalp that was hairless. Well, except for the couple of spots of thin hair on each side that made it look like it had pathetic pigtails. Short and squatty like a troll, it had teeth that were kind of buckish, like a rabbit's, and six fingers on each hand. The fact that it was wearing human clothes did nothing to disguise skin that looked to have a really horrid case of acne.

Celina glowered at it. "What are you doing skulking around here?"

The thing cringed and tried to back away from her, but there was no place to go except back behind the garbage cans. Even it knew that was useless. "Nothing, I swear!" The demon's voice was kind of gloppy sounding, like it had a cold. "I was already in the alley and then you came in and kicked vampire butt but there was nowhere for me to go and I didn't want to get in your way and ruin your good time, and of course I certainly didn't want to bother you and so I thought—"

"Stop." She held up a hand to halt his tumbling words, smirking when the creature gasped for air. "Just stop."

"Sure, of course, whatever you say." The demon back-stepped, then began to edge along the wall that led out of the alley. "I'll just, you know, be on my way here, wouldn't want to cause any problems or anything, didn't actually *see* anything anyway—"

Celina thought about killing him, then just waved him away. "Get lost." He scampered out, now and then using his hands to help propel him along like an ape, or maybe one of those cool and evil little flying monkey-demons in *The Wizard of Oz.* A kill would probably be nasty, some kind of greenish-yellow demon ooze all over everything; if she got it on her outfit, she'd have to come up with something new to wear, and it would all be just a big pain she simply didn't feel like dealing with right now. Stupid creature was inconsequential anyway—not much more than a bug on the windshield of darkness. Celina had better things to do with her time.

Like find that slayer.

Chapter 4

SINCE PROFESSOR DOOM AND GLOOM—AS HE SOMETIMES thought of Rupert Giles—hadn't come up with anything worthwhile, Spike decided it was time to do a bit of investigation on his own. There were places he could go to drink and listen, just sit back and take in the info. Buffy and her little band of followers didn't know them all . . . they just *thought* they did. A perfect example of their ongoing ignorance had been when he'd dragged her over to see what lover-boy Riley had been up to in that skanky little blood-addict house—the Slayer hadn't had a clue that places like that even existed, much less that humans would pay to have vampires nurse on them like baby bottles. Spike loved her—though God only knew why—but at times Buffy's skull could be as thick as hardened concrete.

What had Giles said? Something about finding references now and again in the Watchers' journals about an unidentified murderous vampire. Bloody lot of good that did—surely it wasn't a newsflash that almost *all* vampires were murderers. That was the problem with the Watchers and that stupid Council; they thought they could solve everything by looking in their books and on their computer, but a plastic box with a bunch of wires in it was nothing compared to the real world. You wanted information, you had to get into the *experience* of it, make the connection with the people—or whatever—who had it. And Spike knew right where those connections were.

There was a new place three blocks east of the Sunnydale Armory, one that the Slayer and her gang didn't know anything about. Being so close to the Armory made it alternately risky and smart—who the heck would expect a monster bar *there?* It was only a matter of time before Buffy found out about it, of course, but in the interim the patrons enjoyed a measure of relaxation that hadn't been available in quite some time. JuJu's Catbox—the tackiest choice of names Spike had ever heard—was in the basement of an older warehouse that on its upper levels was used for the storage of small machinery parts, things like gears and screws and gadgets. No one ever needed these things at night, so the bar's owner, a weasel-faced human named Benny Speegle who paid big amounts to a number of protection demons, could give his customers peace of mind and a place to party without being bothered. At least for now.

The Catbox looked pretty much like a normal, run-of-the-mill vampire-and-demon hangout—lots of shadows and dim light, red vinyl chairs and booths. All the furniture was metal just in case somebody got ticked off and tried to stake the guy at the table next to him; having your customers dusted was really crappy for business. Spike liked to sit at the bar and sip on his drink—the only way he could get human blood anymore—and listen to the gossip flying fast and furious like it always did. Tonight was no different, and he was just starting his second glass of prime red when the short and slimy demon pulled up a stool two seats down from him.

Spike had seen the demon before, even knew his name. Dumpy or Dunphy, something like that. He was a talker, an annoying little squirt that Spike would've normally avoided like a pointed piece of wood. Tonight, however, Dunphy was just the prize Spike was after.

Dunphy ordered a drink of something noxious and glanced curiously in Spike's direction. Spike saw his chance and snatched at it, raising his glass slightly. "How're you doing," he said amiably. "Dunphy, right?"

Dunphy nodded and grinned at him, showing teeth that could have used a good scrubbing starting a couple of decades ago. Spike had barely blinked before the demon had scooted over next to him, so eager for an ear to ramble in that he sounded almost breathless. "I'm fine, fine." He grinned wider. "Though, I tell you, I think it was my lucky night, oh, yeah, my lucky night."

Spike raised an eyebrow. The guy had a tendency to talk without stopping—if he asked, would the fool run out of air trying to answer? It was an amusing notion. "Really. And why is that?"

Dunphy leaned close and Spike resisted the urge to jerk away. The creature's breath smelled like rotted fish. Just what the heck did this thing eat, anyway? "I was in this alley, see, over by that teenybopper hangout with the metal name—"

"The Bronze."

"Yeah, that's it, the Bronze. So anyways, there I was, minding my own business, checking around for a freebie meal or two by the cans—"

"That would be the *garbage* cans?" Spike asked dryly.

"Whatever. You wanna hear my story or not?"

Spike tipped his glass again and glanced at the demon over its rim. For a long moment, he let his features slide into vamp-face. "I'll wager you aren't going to stop me now, are you?"

"Right. So I'm bending over and checking out this find, see, it looks like a good one, some leftover fried Mandarin fish from the Chinese place—"

At least that explains the decomposing fish breath, Spike thought.

"—and these two vampy dudes coming strolling past the alley. They got this girl with them, a human. Pretty little thing with blond hair and them big girly blue eyes, but really, dumb as a rock, if you get my drift. I mean, what kind of brain-dead dipstick do you have to be to take a nighttime stroll with two vampires—" The demon glanced nervously at him. "Uh, nothing personal or anything."

"Whatever."

Dunphy swallowed. "Yeah, right. So anyways, they look like they want to bring her into the alley proper, then up comes this other babe. Now *she's* hot, okay, she's got this whole dyed redhead thing going, that black stuff outlining her eyes, nice tight outfit on top to go with an army getup on the bottom." His grin widened at the memory. "Make even a demon look twice, you know? I can really get into that whole military thing, the camo and the boots. So anyways, the blond's got nothing on her, serious competition, except the newcomer ain't interested in a catfight."

"No kidding," Spike said. He started to ask a question, then cut off the inhalation that he needed to get the words out. Dunphy's drink had arrived, and even the bartender was holding his breath when he served it. Pink chud pureed with a mixture of hundred-year-old whale oil and rotting toad's liver. Guy really had some taste.

As it turned out, Spike didn't need to prod the demon to keep the tale going strong. "Yeah, so instead this red-headed chick proceeds to tell the bubbleheaded blond that her two party boys are going to kill her, you know? So airhead takes off—probably the only smart thing she's done all year—and then the redhead further proceeds to kick some major vampire ass."

Spike was sitting up very straight now. "Punched 'em around a bit, did she?"

The demon laughed, the sound like iron beads rolling around inside a wet coffee can. "They shoulda been so lucky. She dusted them, man. Like *that*." He snapped his fingers, and Spike noted there were six on each hand. "They might as well have been nothing—neither one of 'em ever got a finger on her."

Spike frowned at him. "So you're telling me this girl killed two vampires?"

Dunphy stared at him blankly for a moment, then realization shone in his eyes. "Oh, no—she's no human. She's a vampire herself. I mean, no human could fight like that, she had to be a vampire, killing her own kind." He should his head in wonder. "Yeah, whoever heard of *that?*"

Spike rubbed his chin thoughtfully. "So, they were talking about what before she wasted them?"

Dunphy took a long pull of the disgusting liquid inside his mug. It left a sludgy-looking green coating on the inside of the glass and Spike didn't want to think about what was going on inside the creature's mouth. "Beats me. I wasn't listening, just trying to sneak the hell out of there before they noticed me. They could've been talking about the weather in Macedonia, for all I knew." He glanced at Spike from the corner of one watery eye, and he looked vaguely proud. "I was mostly trying to do the possum thing, but she caught me going out anyway, after she hammered those other two saps into eternity."

Spike sat back and regarded Dunphy. "And why didn't she kill you?"

Dunphy shrugged, then straightened the collar of his shirt. "Who knows? Maybe she liked what she saw—"

Spike had had enough. He reached forward and grabbed the nasty little demon by that same shirt collar, hands crossed over each other. He rotated his wrists like he was looking at a watch, and the shirt collar came together in a viciously tight choke hold. Dunphy's eyes bulged.

"Somehow I don't think you're being quite straight with me," he said. "And since vampires and demons don't socialize much, there must be some other reason."

Dunphy gagged and Spike let up a little, afraid the putrid mini-beast would yark on him. "Okay, okay— don't be so touchy! She said I wasn't worth killing—are you happy now? Does that make you feel better?" Dunphy took advantage of Spike's loosening grip and yanked away, straightening his shirt again and sending the vampire what Dunphy probably intended as a murderous look. Spike thought he just looked comical. "Jeez," Dunphy complained. "Try to tell a good story in a bar and what do you get? Manhandled by some skinny, bleached-out bloodsucker who looks like he hasn't had a good meal in years."

That did it. He'd never been known for his patience anyway, and now Spike let himself morph into full vampire mode. "I'm feeling that way right now," he growled. "Want to help me fix that?"

Dunphy blinked, then grabbed his drink and took a step

back. "You don't scare me," he said, but he sure *sounded* scared. "Your kind doesn't like the way I taste anyway."

Spike sneered and pushed him away. "I don't even like the way you smell."

"Hey," snapped the bartender from a few feet away. "You two zip it up or take it outside. I don't allow fighting in my place."

Spike started to retort, then realized that the man was slapping something against his palm. How convenient— it was a two-foot length of wood with both ends sharpened into points. "He was the one who got all bent for no reason," Dunphy complained. "He—"

"Do I look like Judge Judy?" demanded the bartender. "You know what, he stays and *you* get the hell out. You're stinking up the bar."

"Try lemon juice," Spike said snidely as he settled back onto his seat. "I hear that goes well on fish."

Dunphy grunted moistly and stood, then chugged down the last of his drink and slammed the empty mug on the bar. "Don't like this place anyway," he declared. "It's got bad clientele. Plus you can't make a drink worth a damn."

"Yeah? Well, it won't smell anymore when you're out the door," the bartender told him. "Now beat it. I ain't telling you again."

Dunphy glared at him but did as he was ordered. The last Spike saw of him was with his blotchy little head held high in the air as the door of the Catbox closed behind him.

A few feet away the bartender brought up a garbage can and shoved the mug into it using the tip of the stick. "Crap won't wash out," he told Spike. "I'm tired of having to throw out my bar glasses."

Spike stifled the urge to tell the guy it was part of the

price he paid for letting the clientele class slide. "So what have you heard?" he asked instead.

The bartender didn't look at him. "About what?"

"The warrior woman that aquarium-breath was raving about. What's the news?"

The guy took a halfhearted swipe at the bar top. "The word's around. She's supposed to be bad news, with a quicker tendency to kill than introduce herself. She hasn't been in here, but there were a few people saying she'd been over at Willy's. I called up the owner, and he told me what she looked like, said to watch out for her and don't start a fight. Says people have heard of her now and then."

"She a bloodsucker like Dunphy said?"

"That's what they say. No one's got a clue why she's showed up here, though."

Before Spike could think of anything else to ask, the guy headed in the other direction to wait on a couple of customers. It didn't matter; Spike had enough info—it seemed the whole underground was practically smoking about her. The redhead was obviously the same babe who'd gone after Anya, and there was no question she was bad news.

But why was she looking for Buffy?

That worried him. He'd heard plenty about the hell that Buffy had gone through with Faith, and while he hadn't been around or been on the weird side of good then like he was now, he didn't want Buffy to have to go through that again. She might not have the same feelings for him as he did for her, but that was the way the headstone crumbled. Until something happened to change his feelings, he had a chip in his head that kept him behaving like a good little monster, and a chunk out of his cold, dead heart that he'd given to Buffy . . . whether she wanted it or not.

Chapter 5

"Did I do that?"

Giles jumped and almost dropped the magnifying glass he was using to peer at a page in the open book he was holding in front of him. "Wha—oh, Buffy!" He frowned at her. "It's rather disconcerting to sneak up behind people like that, don't you think?"

"Sorry," she said as she pulled out one of the chairs and dropped onto it. "I didn't think I was sneaking. You must have been in brain mode."

"Yes, I suppose I was." The former librarian put down the book, then peered at her. "I believe you asked me a question without a clear subject. Would you care to rephrase it?"

"What subject?"

Giles sighed. "Did you do *what*, Buffy?"

"Oh! Yeah, that." She thought for a moment, trying to figure out how to put it. "Dawn—it's like she's having these little bouts of . . . I don't know. Trial independence or something. It's a constant struggle to make sure she's going to be somewhere safe."

Giles slid his hands into his pockets and leaned back against the counter. "You can't put the girl in a cage and monitor her twenty-four hours a day."

"I know. But it's like yesterday. She's getting ready for school and suddenly she tells me about this science thingy she's working on at school, some three-dimensional model of a chemistry formula, whatever, and says she has to stay late afterward and finish it."

"Schoolwork—"

"And then, bang! This morning she does the same thing," Buffy complained. "Only this time she wants to spend the *night* at a girlfriend's house. Can you believe? Now she's all bent out of shape at me because I said no."

Giles tilted his head. "Actually, that might be quite safe for her, assuming neither the girl nor her parents have ever invited a vampire inside."

"And what if they had?" demanded Buffy. "Without knowing it? Or what if the place is attacked by a demon, or the Punk Girl from Hell who Anya and Xander claim went after Anya?" She shook her head so hard that her hair whipped across her eyes. "No way am I taking that kind of chance."

Giles was silent for a moment. Finally, he said, "Yes, you did."

Buffy glanced at him. "I did what?"

"The same thing that Dawn's doing. Stretching—testing the waters of independence. She can't wait to try new things. It's a part of life, Buffy. We all go through it, from children testing the limits of their parents' rules to adults who push in everything from participating in dangerous sports to cheating on their taxes. She's growing up, reaching out, *expanding*. You might as well learn to roll with the waves."

Buffy crossed her arms in an unconscious gesture of protection. "I can roll just fine, Giles. I just want to make sure Dawn doesn't drown."

Thinking he might catch a glimpse of Sunnydale's mysterious newcomer, Spike dallied a bit about the town before going into the Magic Shop the next evening. No luck, though—perhaps her taste for killing had been satisfied with the two vamps she'd dusted in the alley. Her being a vampire herself . . . well, that put a spin on things. There weren't a whole lot of blood-suckers that would kill their own brethren just for gig-gles, and fewer still—Angel came to mind, but not many others—who would do it to save the life of a human. Bad enough the unknown warrior woman was on Buffy's trail, worse that she had the strength and cun-ning of a nightbeast behind her.

The lights were on in the Magic Shop, the usual gang all gathered round and yapping their little human heads off about not much. They stopped when he came in, looking at him with expressions that ranged from wari-ness—Tara—to blatant annoyance—Xander. Little Miss Ex-Demon had one hand wrapped in a white bandage that did nothing to hide the smell of fresh blood from his sensitive nose. It was best not to torment himself, so Spike decided to sit as far away from her as possible.

"Got some skinny on our out-of-towner," he an-nounced as he plopped onto one of the chairs at the end of the table. Buffy and a grumpy-looking Dawn were leaning against the counter next to Giles; if the Slayer noticed his hopeful glance in her direction, she gave no sign of it. Spike pressed his lips together and adjusted his coat, irritated as always that nothing he did seemed to impress her.

Anya was the first to ask. "What did you find out?"

Spike glanced in her direction, then frowned when the story that might be behind the bandage sank in. "Say, she didn't get you in her sights again, did she?"

Anya shook her head. "No, I cut myself on a glass."

"Four stitches," Xander announced. He sounded absurdly proud. "When she breaks a glass, she does it right."

"Marvelous," Spike said dryly and looked back toward Buffy and Giles. "Anyway, you might like to know I came across an ugly little demon who claims he had a run-in with the warrior babe herself yesterday evening. Not precisely a run-in, since she caught him playing Peeping Tom in the alley by the Bronze, but he says she's bad news." He made a show of inspecting his black fingernails, then gave everyone in the room a smug glance. "We already know she's got a taste for staking vamps, but she's a bloodsucker herself."

For a few seconds, they were all startled into silence. Then Xander muttered, "too bad she didn't run into you."

Willow shot him a *shut-up* look. "Wow, that's in the big-time realm. Any clue about who she is, a name or something that'll help us figure it out?"

Spike shrugged, then leaned forward. " 'Fraid not. But I will say this. The whole town's talking about her—"

"The 'whole town' part being *your* part of town as opposed to our part?" Buffy put in.

"Can't see how it makes a difference which *part* the scoop came from," Spike said. He tapped a small hodgepodge of old books on the table with an impatient finger. "I did a whole lot better than your yellowed old stacks of paper."

Giles reached over and pushed the books out of

Spike's reach. "You gave us somewhere to start, anyway. I'll give you credit for that much."

"About time someone gave me credit for *something*. If you ask me—"

"Word on the street might help us locate her now, but it's these 'yellowed old stacks of paper' that will ultimately tell us what we're up against," Giles said before Spike could finish. "By this time tomorrow, I'm betting we'll have a lot more information about her, maybe a callback from Angel on the message Buffy left earlier."

Spike made a disgusted sound, then stood. "I'm heading back out," he said and headed toward the door, his steps purposeful. "Piddle around all night in your books, if you like. Play with your computers, too. But the real info is out on the street, and I'm going to find it."

"Okay," Xander said, "provided we don't have a repeat of last night, you want to take another crack at being the domestic-type cook?"

On the passenger side of the car, Anya gave him a grouchy look. She might even have smacked him, except her hand was throbbing, which was why she'd decided they should head home for a while. "Not in this dimension, thank you. Or at least not this week."

Her dark-headed boyfriend chuckled. "Then how about we try again for that pizza?"

"Okay." She settled back and watched the houses as they passed, not really wanting to talk. This whole thing with the unknown woman had tired her out. No one had ever targeted *her* before—it was always Buffy, or Dawn, or the vampires. There wasn't any reason to be interested in an ex-vengeance demon, and that was the way she liked to keep it, thank you very much. It was draining on the one hand, but on the other it already seemed like it had happened a long time ago, and to someone else.

"You feeling okay?" Xander asked.

"Yes, I'm fine."

"But you're awfully quiet."

"I'm *fine.*" Okay, so that sounded a little snappish, but a girl had a right to think her own thoughts sometimes. What was it with guys sometimes trying to possess every part of a woman, anyway?

Xander wisely decided not to press the issue, and by the time they walked into the apartment, Anya felt much better. Almost human, or at least as close to that as she was ever going to feel after centuries of being anything but. It felt good to be in here, comforting and safe—or it would be as long as she stayed away from washing dishes and sharp glass. Xander, of course, headed right for the pizza delivery menu in the kitchen, then she heard him arguing with someone on the phone. Curious, Anya wandered over to hear what was going on.

"No, I don't want to come and pick it up. That's *your* job." He waved the menu around, as if the person on the other end could see it. "That would be the *'and Delivery'* part right after the words *Julio's Pizza?* No, I don't want to order a pizza from Bennie's. They have lousy pepperoni." He dropped the menu on the counter, listened for a few seconds, then poked at it. "You expect me to believe a pizza-delivery place has only one car?"

Anya tugged on his sleeve. "What's the matter?"

"Hold on a sec." Xander scrunched the phone under his chin. "Guy says they have two delivery men, one called in sick, the other one's car broke down. They can't deliver."

"Then we'll go get it," Anya said. "It's not very far. And it might even be hot when we get it home."

Xander made a face. "Yeah, that *would* be different. All right."

He went back to ordering, and Anya drifted back into the living room, thinking that the couch looked especially inviting tonight. She'd been so stressed since the night before yesterday and that ridiculous thing outside the Magic Shop, then today at lunch there'd been a run of guffawing, prepubescent boys in the store. She'd had to go in twelve directions at once trying to make sure they didn't break or filch anything, and at one point the tallest of them had tried to juggle a trio of shrunken heads. The boy, of course, had no idea that the heads he so happily tossed up in the air had once belonged to the three fiercest warriors in a tribe from a now sunken island in the Pacific. Had the pea-brain dropped them in precisely the right order (smaller one, then the next two after a three-second delay), the spirits of all three warriors would have been rejuvenated right there, and they'd all probably be dead right now.

Yes, the couch was definitely the place to be. Julio's was notoriously slow—she and Xander always ordered the extra-large supreme and that meant the pizza wouldn't be ready for at least an hour. A little catnap would be just the thing to revitalize her body and senses, so Anya lost no time kicking off her shoes and stretching out on the soft corduroy fabric. She could hear Xander fiddling with stuff in the kitchen, putting dishes away and making noises that were nice and homey, comforting. She was so tired, just forty winks, or maybe fifty—

"Anya?"

"Hmmmmm?" She smiled and clutched at the ladybug throw pillow she'd stuffed beneath her cheek. She opened her eyes a little and saw Xander crouching next to the couch. "What?"

He grinned at her. "Hey, sleepyhead. I'm going to go after the pizza. Be back in twenty minutes."

She yawned, then tried to clear her thoughts. She must have fallen asleep, but—

"Wait," she said groggily and started to sit up. "You're going to leave me here alone?"

He pushed her back down. "You'll be fine. Remember what Spikey said? Our unknown gal is a vampire—she can't come in here. Just don't call out 'come in' if you don't know who's at the door."

"I know better than that," she mumbled crankily.

"Of course you do." He patted her arm. "Back to dreamland."

Anya managed to drag her eyes open a bit. "Are you sure?"

"Come with me if you want."

She thought about getting up, but the comfy couch was addictive. "No," she decided. "But don't stop anywhere else, okay? Let other people fight the bad guys tonight."

"I promise," he said. "I'll be back quicker than you can say 'Xander, where the heck is my pizza?' "

"Xander, where the heck is my pizza?"

He leaned forward and kissed her on the nose. "Very funny."

Anya smiled to herself and closed her eyes again, felt the edge of the couch cushion dip as he used it for balance when he stood. A few moments later she heard the apartment's door close, followed by the sound of the lock *snicking* firmly into place. *Pizza,* she thought. *Yum.* She *was* getting hungry, but she was still in her work clothes. Maybe she ought to make herself wake up, get her sleepy butt off this couch and change—

Something fell over in the bedroom.

It wasn't a big sound, certainly not the noise of anything breaking, but Anya was instantly awake and on her feet. There was another sound, like a drawer being pulled out, then pushed back in. It couldn't be a vampire—a burglar? But how had he gotten inside? Had he been in here the whole time that she and Xander had been home, just waiting for when they would leave? Maybe—neither one of them had gone in any part of the apartment except for the living room and kitchen.

And what was she going to do now that Xander had gone?

The door, Anya thought. Her heart was hammering and despite all the logic that insisted it couldn't be that woman from the other night, she had the irrational fear that's exactly who it was. *I'll just slip over to it and walk right out. Easy as pie. I won't even put on my shoes.*

She sidestepped, once, twice. But she didn't make it four feet before the door to the bedroom opened.

"Anyanka."

The voice was gravelly and low, still very familiar. The terror that had been building along her nerves endings peaked for one painful second, then dissipated like burst soap bubbles. She turned. "D'Hoffryn!"

The demon smiled at her . . . at least as much as he *could* smile. Quite tall, he had mottled grayish skin below several small horns and pointed ears. His sunken black eyes regarded her, and his wide, hooked nose nearly touched his upper lip. Long wispy strands of beard rested against the black of his robes. He shuffled over to the couch and poked at the throw pillow—her favorite—she'd had wadded beneath her head. "Sleeping on a replicant of an earth insect," he said. "Cute." His attempt at a grin showed pointed, yellowing teeth. "Nice place you've got here. Very human."

Anya put her hands on her hips and glared at him. Her relief had dissipated and now she was suspicious. "What are you doing in this house?" she demanded. "You can't just waltz into someone's home like you owned the place. That's not how it works."

He frowned at her. "I can't?"

"No, you can't!"

He tilted his head. "Funny, I always have before."

"What do you *want?*"

"Ah, yes." Back on track, the demon that had gifted her with the Power of the Wish a millennia ago nodded. When he spoke, he sounded a little regretful. "It seems there's been an untimely . . . mishap with one of the current vengeance demons. I was really fond of this one, too. Got her out of India. Long black hair and dark eyes. Very pretty for a mortal and she made an exquisitely beautiful demon."

Anya felt behind her until she could sit on the arm of the couch. This whole appearance by D'Hoffryn made her wary, and she had a *very* bad feeling about this—no matter what he'd said about going where he wanted, since when did he make house calls, anyway? He usually brought people to him. "What . . . mishap?"

"Apparently she was a little too quick to grant the retaliation wish of a wronged teenage girl. She failed to note that the wording of the girl's wish was a little too broad." D'Hoffryn looked as pained about anything as she'd ever seen him. "Inexperience, really. Unfortunately she found herself included in the 'All the females in this town should just have their heads melt."

Anya nodded. "Not very smart. I'd guess her head— and the girl's—dissolved along with everyone else's."

"Like a well-used candle."

Anya folded her arms. "So what are you doing here?"

One of D'Hoffryn's horns twitched. "Obviously I've come to offer you a return to your status as Anyanka, the vengeance demon. You would take her place and become immortal again, once more wield the Power of the Wish."

Stunned, Anya could only stare at the creature while she tried to process what she'd heard. When she didn't immediately answer, D'Hoffryn gave her a crafty smile. He rubbed one dark finger along the arm of the couch, the ragged nail making a scratching sound. "I see you're surprised," he commented. His eyes glittered. "No doubt you're uncertain, too. Clearly you've made a quite comfortable existence for yourself in this dimension. But really, do you truly want to brave the instability of life as a mortal? They are so . . . fragile. A speeding car, the wrong turn of an ankle as you descend the steps—you might die tomorrow, and for what?" The demon gestured at the cozily furnished living room. "The few material comforts of a simple creature's life."

Her mouth worked, but no sound came out. D'Hoffryn was offering exactly what she'd wanted . . . when? A year ago? Two years? It all blurred together, the months and the struggles and the friends and the love—

"Why the hesitation, Anyanka?" D'Hoffryn asked, as if he knew what she was thinking. "You once begged me to restore your powers, asked me to fold the very fabric of time in order to do so. Now I offer you your heart's desire, but I don't hear 'yes' in your answer. In fact, I don't hear an answer at all."

"I-It's just a lot to take in all of a sudden," Anya stammered. "Unexpected."

"The best gifts always are."

"I mean, there are things here that I would have to take care of," she hedged.

"Things?"

"People that I'd have to talk to. I can't just pick up and leave without any notice at all. That's not the way things work in this dimension—"

D'Hoffryn scowled at her. "I sense indecision in you, Anyanka, and a lot of it tied to one mortal man. Five years ago a human male would have been nothing but a cockroach worthy only of crushing beneath your shoe. Now your entire existence, your future as an immortal, hinges on a being with a pathetically limited life span." He sent her a disgusted look. "You would throw away eternity for a creature whose life force can be snuffed out in the blink of an eye?"

"I didn't say I was throwing anything away—"

"I will return for your answer in three days," D'Hoffryn interrupted. "That should give you enough time to reflect on your surroundings and compare them to the comfort that comes with knowing you will never die." He gave her another dark, toothy smile, but he sounded anything but pleased. "Think well, Anyanka. Second chances are called such because they don't happen a third time."

There was an instantaneous singing along the surface of her skin as though all the air had been sucked out of the room for one long moment, then the demon was gone.

Anya was still sitting on the arm of the couch and staring at the space where D'Hoffryn had been when Xander unlocked the door and came in with the pizza. He started when he saw her, then set the pizza on the coffee table. "Hey, what's the deal?" he asked. "You've got that *I've-just-seen-a-ghost* look that we all know and hate."

Anya blinked and opened her mouth to tell him what had happened. At the last instant the words wouldn't come. Instead, she said, "I was just sitting here and thinking about how hungry I was."

Xander grinned. "I hope that 'I was' is really an 'I

am,' because I've sure got the cure for that." He swept a hand toward the pizza box. "Ta-da—Julio's Supreme Supremo. Delivered fresh and hot, right to your coffee table by little ol' *moi.*"

"Great. I'll get napkins and something to drink." She left him there, knowing he would start eating before she got back. Why hadn't she told him about D'Hoffryn's visit?

The answer was obvious.

Wasn't it?

Actually, it *wasn't,* and that was exactly why she'd kept her mouth shut. If she'd outright told the demon *no,* if she'd been inclined to do that, she could have blurted out the whole sordid tale and they could have had a good chuckle over it—*"Can you believe he'd even think I'd go back to being a vengeance demon?* But she hadn't said no, had she? Nor had she said yes. And right now she didn't know *what* she was going to say.

Human.

Or demon.

Puny, limited life span.

Or immortal.

Really, the choice ought to be easy. But it wasn't. Her situation had changed, become all tied up with emotions and sensations and friendship and love and loyalty and desire, all things that had meant different things back when she'd been Anyanka. To Anyanka, those things were . . . *fuel,* the stuff that fed the hatred and anger which made her very existence necessary. They were still fuel in this existence, but it was all different now, as if thc firc the fuel fed was a totally different color. Those emotions didn't make her existence necessary, they *were* her existence.

Sweet. But it was an existence that would also be very limited in length.

Could she trade immortality for a few short decades of questionable happiness? And what if she didn't even get *that* much? As D'Hoffryn had pointed out, one wrong move—a drunk driver, a misstep, even some nasty microscopic bacteria or virus—and she was history. History? Not even; as if anyone would care that a woman named Anya Jenkins lived or died. As a mortal, she was a blip in time, an unnoticed speck in the eye of existence. At least if she were a demon again, the smidgen of time allotted to her had the potential to be a lot longer.

"Anya?" Xander called from the other room. "Hey, I thought you said you were hungry. You'd better get out here before I work my way through your half of this pizza."

"Coming." She hurried out to join him, realizing she'd been standing next to the counter for far too long. The paper napkins she'd been clutching in her hands were crumpled. *Listen to him—Xander sounds so happy, so . . . sure of himself.* And why shouldn't he be? He had it all down pat—he was what he was, and provided he didn't get unexpectedly chomped on the neck, his path was pretty clear. Being human, and mortal, was what he knew and accepted and *expected.* She, on the other hand, had once been given a taste of something far more expansive.

And now, God help her, she wasn't so sure she didn't want that taste back.

Chapter 6

"Do we have any news?" Buffy asked, striding into the Magic Shop with a book-laden Dawn in tow. "Preferably of the good problem-is-all-solved kind?" Without waiting for an answer, she guided her younger sister to the table. "Homework," she instructed in a stern voice. "We goofed off enough last night. I know you have a trig test on Friday with Mr. Beach."

"Oooh," Willow put in. "And Thanksgiving's only a couple of weeks away. He gets all cranky because he doesn't like the smell of turkey sandwiches and everyone brings them. If your grade point average drops, he'll come down on you really hard after the holiday."

For a long moment no one said anything. "I know that somehow that's meant to make sense," Xander finally put in. "I just can't find the folder labeled 'Logic' right now."

"It's true," Willow insisted. "You wait and see. It happens like clockwork every year."

"Maybe it was a bad childhood experience," Tara suggested. "Holidays aren't always . . . happy experiences." The expression on her face made it clear that hers hadn't been, and Willow reached over and squeezed her hand.

Xander tilted his head. "He was probably the victim of one too many mashed-potato-and turkey-gravy swirlies."

Dawn made a face. "Ewwwww."

"Hey, you *like* gravy," Buffy protested.

Dawn tossed her hair back. "Not like that."

"Can we focus, please?" Giles interrupted. "Let's not forget there's a woman running about who's a potential killer. Buffy, any word from Angel? Can you call him again?"

Buffy shook her head. "Nothing yet, and I already tried to call. Got the answering machine a second time."

"Out saving the world like a good little private detective vampire," Xander said snidely. He looked over at Anya, but she was staring into space and not paying any attention.

"Well, I'm sure we'll hear from him soon." The former librarian pointed to several stacks of older, leather-bound volumes. "Despite Spike's comments, there was quite a lot of information to be had. My research indicated that—"

"I've been called a lot of things in my time, but never invisible," said Spike, sauntering in from the back room. "I'll thank you to look my way when you're talking about me."

"I don't believe we could get that lucky," Giles said irritably. "Now as I was *saying,* I did some extensive research today, most of it by myself." He sent Anya an arched look, but she was still wrapped up in whatever was going on in her head and she missed it. "Certain other people in the shop seem to be a tad on the preoccupied side today."

When she still didn't hear, Xander reached forward and tugged on her arm. "Anya—"

"What?" she snapped, then sat up straight when she saw that everyone was staring at her. "What?" she asked again. "What is everyone looking at? I did my required job today. I helped customers spend money, and I tended to the inventory. I don't know who this woman is or what she wants with Buffy, so why should I be concerned about her beyond that?"

Xander rocked back on his chair and regarded her. "Uh, that would be because you thought she wanted to kill you the other night. Remember?"

Anya slapped a hand on the table hard enough to make both Tara and Willow jump. "I don't even know her," she said harshly. "I'm going upstairs to dust the shelves."

"Quite the testy little ex-demon, isn't she?" Spike noted.

Giles frowned as he and the others watched Anya stomp over to the ladder and climb out of sight. "I don't understand what's gotten into her," he said.

"Me, neither," said Xander. He shook his head. "Earlier at home I brought back one of the best Julio's pizzas we've ever had, and she barely touched it. There are some moments of appreciation you just don't pass up."

"Maybe she's just tired of this whole research thing," Willow suggested. When Giles looked at her sharply, her eyes widened. "Not that *I* am, no, that's not at all what I meant." She held up one of the books and gave the former Watcher a bright smile. "Happy to help, that's me. Just call me 'Little Miss Research.' "

"Well, we can dig a bit more, but here's what I've got so far, and perhaps Willow can substantiate it on the computer." Giles rearranged the books on the table until he found the ones he wanted, where he'd placed folded sheets of paper in them to mark his place. "I found numerous references to a female vampire who's apparently attained legendary stature not only for her strength and viciousness, but because of her hatred for both the living *and* the undead. The records are sketchy at best, and there are no pictures—whoever she is, she doesn't want to be found out. Despite numerous inquiries over the years, no one seems to know her real name or when she originally lived, or even who sired her." He sent Spike a pointed glance. "I don't suppose that 'word on the street' you were going on about last night panned out?"

"Not yet," Spike answered. Unperturbed, he inspected his black fingernails. "But it will. I've got my sources. You just wait and see."

"Uh-huh. While we're waiting for *your* sources, mine—I believe you called them 'yellowed old stacks of paper'—told me that the last time our vampire visitor was sighted was in Poland nearly fifty years ago." Giles snapped the last book shut. "It's only a paragraph in passing, but back then she was known by the name *Catia*."

"So, the mystery woman now has a name," Buffy commented. "Or at least one she used a half century ago."

Tara's brow furrowed. "But where has she been since then? Are you sure it's the same person—er, vampire?"

"Now, there's the million-dollar question, eh?" Spike sat forward. "But I'll bet you it is."

It was Willow's turn to look puzzled. "But why hide her identity? I mean, vampires are all proud-and-show-offy, 'look at all the big bad stuff I've done' about the bad stuff they've done, right?"

"Not all of them," Buffy said quietly.

"I don't think we can count your ex-beau in the same league as the woman Anya had her little run-in with,"

Spike said sarcastically. "From the tales I'm hearing, this bird hasn't a shy bone in her body about killing."

Dawn had been quiet, looking very much like she was studying. Now she lifted her head. "So you guys don't really have a clue."

Buffy turned to look at her. "What?"

"You don't have a clue," Dawn repeated. "None of you. You don't know who she is, why she's here, or why she's looking for Buffy." She shrugged. "Spike says she's a vampire, but look where he got his info—from some creepy bar demon. That's stable."

"Don't you have trig homework?" Xander asked.

"Yeah." Dawn gave him a sweet smile. "And I think I'll make a whole lot more progress on it than *some* people are making on other stuff."

"You just stick to the mathematical world, and we'll stick to the monster," Xander retorted. "And never the twin shall meet."

"Twain," Willow said.

"What?"

"Never the *twain* shall meet."

Tara smiled a little at Willow and Xander, then looked up to where Anya had disappeared into the upper level. "Um, what's wrong with Anya?"

"Good question," Giles said. "Xander, you're sure she didn't meet up with—"

"No way." Xander shook his head emphatically. "Unless . . ." His eyes narrowed as his gaze found Spike. "You're sure this Catia chick is vampirized, right? I only left Anya in the apartment by herself for twenty minutes while I picked up the pizza."

Spike looked offended that his info was being questioned. "I've got it on good authority. Not just that Dunphy mope, but the bartender had heard of her as well."

"Anya's been acting bent since I got back from Julio's." Xander ran a hand through his hair. "Well, except for that crabby part in the car, but with the whole hurting her hand thing, she's entitled." He shrugged. "Maybe she's pissed at me for leaving her, but it was her idea to begin with. I wouldn't have gone if she'd said it was a big deal—plus I offered to take her with, but she said no. And everything *was* the same when I got home, all locks still engaged and thresholds uncrossed."

Dawn's head lifted from her homework. "If you're trying to do *Star Trek,* you're getting you're quotes all messed up."

"Whatever."

"She's probably fine," Giles said. "Just a bit rattled. Maybe she'd—"

"I'd like to go home now," Anya announced from the other side of the railing.

Giles actually stepped back a little. "How did she do that?"

"I'm tired and I want to take a shower and I want to go to bed," she continued as she climbed down the stair ladder and came over to Xander.

"Sure," Xander said. "Home is good. Warm, welcoming. Full of hot water, food, and—"

"I don't want to have sex tonight."

Willow grinned as Xander's mouth worked for a second. "Anya—"

"I know," Anya went on. "You told me not to tell anyone that we were going to have sex. You never told me not to tell them that we weren't." Her gaze swept the others in the room. "We're not. I think I'm supposed to say something like 'I have a headache.' But I don't have a headache. I just don't feel like having sex."

Xander inhaled. "Okay, we're out of here." Anya seemed like she wanted to add something but he was already pulling her toward the door. "Say good night, Anya."

"Good night—"

"Good night, Anya," Dawn said with a giggle, then the door closed and the couple was gone.

"Anya not wanting to have sex?" Buffy commented. "That's a first."

"No kidding," Spike said. "I thought she was the queen of—"

"I think we get the idea," Giles interrupted.

"Would you like to be vampire dust now or later?" Buffy asked with a step toward Spike. Her voice was hard.

"Okay, okay." Spike held up a hand. "I can take a hint."

"If only," Giles muttered under his breath, then he cleared his throat. "Anyway, back to the business at hand. At this point all we can do is just keep hunting for more information on this Catia woman."

"I'm going to take Dawn home and get some supper," Buffy decided. "If Angel does get my message, he'll call at the house first."

"Tara and I are going to have to scoot, too," Willow said. "We've both got papers to write tonight."

"How very domestic everyone is," Spike sneered. "I suppose Giles is going to go back to his place for tea and crumpets."

Giles lifted his chin. "It's a civilized habit you'd do well to re-embrace, Spike. It might bring a touch of humanity back to you."

"Why the hell would I want that?" Spike launched himself to his feet. "Guess I'll hit the streets again.

Someone in this group has to do something that has to do with finding out the *real* goods on Catia."

"You do that," Buffy said with feigned sweetness. "I know you can handle it. What would we do without you?"

For a moment Spike hesitated as he tried to figure out if she was serious. Then he glared at her. "You just keep on mocking me, Slayer. I don't see anyone else coming up with anything but speculation and old paper."

He stomped out as Willow and Tara stood and gathered up their stuff. "I wouldn't say it in front of him, but he's right," Giles told Buffy.

"I know." Buffy waited while Dawn shoved her trigonometry book and her notepaper into her backpack. "But I've got a feeling Angel will call tonight. And when he does, we'll finally have the help we need to get the jump on her."

"I hope so," Giles said. He followed the four young women and shut down the lights, then stepped outside and locked the door to the Magic Shop. "Because I truly despise going into a battle with blinders on."

Buffy knew it was Angel calling the instant the telephone rang.

In the beginning of her Slayerhood, what she sometimes privately thought of as her training period, she'd had kind of a problem with the whole "sensing a vampire" thing. Other slayers apparently had no trouble with it, as if they'd been born with some kind of inner toggle switch that rocked to the On position whenever one of the toothy beasts came within calling distance. For a while Buffy figured she must've been looking the other way in the Great Herebefore when the Powers That Be had passed out their equivalent of this part of the holy equipment. But if it was true that some way or another, she'd been skipped over when it came to vamp radar, then she'd eventually learned it on her own, because now she could do the sixth-senses thing—see, hear, feel, taste, smell, *and* sense the big bad vamp— with the best of the Slayers.

But this was a different radar altogether.

It was almost like the telephone had a different *sound* to it, something deeper and more resonant than the standard, bell-like ring she'd become so used to after her mom's death. She'd come to dread the sound of it in very short order; for quite a while every time she'd answered, she'd had to listen to a sad and sometimes prepared speech about condolences and how she only had to ask this friend of her mother's, most of them complete strangers to Buffy herself, if she needed anything. After a time the calls had slowed, then finally stopped; now if the phone rang it was Giles or one of her friends, and once in a great while, one of the few *real* friends of Joyce Summers who really did care if her kids were getting along okay without their mom.

It was late and Dawn was already asleep—at least Buffy hoped so. She snatched up the phone so fast she nearly knocked it off the table. "Hello?"

"Buffy."

Same old voice, same old Angel. A thousand memories shot through her mind complete with images, like someone was standing at an old-fashioned wind-up movie camera and furiously turning the lever. Some bad, most good, all triggered by the sound of that single word. "Hi, Angel."

"I got your message."

She couldn't help grinning. "So I noticed."

"Listen, we need to talk about what you said on the machine."

He sounded way too serious and the smile faded from her lips. "All right. What's the news? Has something happened to Faith?"

"No, Faith is fine. She's still in prison and probably kicking butt every time someone looks crossways at her." He'd started off light-toned, but now Buffy could picture him leaning into the telephone receiver, intent on making his point. "This is someone else, Buffy. And if this woman you're looking for is who I think she is, then the news is all bad. They're even talking about her in the demon clubs here in L.A."

"Yeah, well, people in nightclubs talk about a lot of things. Especially when they get the alcohol in there to fuel the rumors." Feeling vaguely relieved that Faith was okay, Buffy scooted down the wall until she was sitting on the floor, then twirled the phone cord around her finger. "It's not like there's much else for the night crew to do besides drink and talk. Except kill, of course."

"Buffy, this is serious. You said you think her name is Catia? If it is, then I'm pretty sure I know this woman. I've crossed paths with her a couple of times, and if she's after you for some reason, she isn't someone to take lightly. Both times I barely got out of there alive."

Buffy sat up a little straighter, her attention caught. "You know her?"

"I don't *know* her, know her. Past her name, all I've got is remembering how it was to fight her. And it wasn't good."

"When was this?"

On the other end Angel was silent for a few moments. "Maybe 1960 or so—I don't recall the exact year. I ran across her twice, and the second time was because she was *hunting* me. I met her in a roadhouse in Nebraska. It wasn't a great time for me, things weren't going so well for a bunch of reasons, and all I was doing was biding my time until I could leave that miserable little town behind. Anyway, she tried to kill me just *because*."

"Because what?"

"Because *nothing*. That's my point—she didn't care whether I was vampire or human. I didn't realize she was a vampire until she caught me rummaging around behind the place. She came after me and I went into vampire form, but she didn't stop."

Buffy frowned, trying to figure this out. "So she turned into a vampire in front of you?"

"Yeah. I think she did it became it was obvious it was going to take more than a normal human could do to beat me."

"But you got the best of her," Buffy pointed out. "So she's not such a badass after all—"

"The only reason I got away was because a pickup truck full of the local good old boys showed up, looking for a good time. Back in those days the townies had racks on their back windows holding things like rifles and shotguns. We both took off—me as far away from her as I could get."

Buffy considered this. "And then you say she found you again?"

"It wasn't an accident that she found find me, she *hunted* me. When you're staying on the streets of a small town for a couple of months, you get to know people, and they get to know you. There weren't any other vampires around, so she interrogated the poor alley rats who were living like me." Angel's voice lowered. "What she left behind after questioning them wasn't a pretty sight."

Buffy tugged harder on the phone cord, then made

herself stop when she realized she was stretching it flat. "She killed them."

"Eight men, one women," Angel told her. "All just to get to me. If I remember right, the papers around there were calling her the 'Drifter Killer.' The last one she murdered gave her enough to find me before she finished him off."

"What happened?"

"A little bad luck for her, and a lot of better luck for me. They weren't much on bums, but the local sheriff had had enough of the townsfolk screaming about a murderer being loose. He'd deputized just about every man in the town."

Buffy's frowned deepened as she tried to understand. "So if you're saying what I think you're saying—"

"The only reason I'm still walking around today is that they shot her, Buffy. I was going *down.* She was *winning,* fighting like no one I've ever run across before, and I was an inch away from having a piece of wood—yes, she had a stake—buried in my chest. One of the town's patrol cars went by the alley, saw the fight, and turned in. I was down and she was raising the stake. I guess it looked like a club or something, because the deputy pulled his pistol and let loose, didn't even tell her to freeze. She got up and he shot her again, and then she went after *him.* He nailed her with everything he had, and she finally went down. He was so freaked out he didn't even notice me when I hightailed it."

Buffy inhaled. "But you don't think she's dead? I mean, they would have put her in prison, the sunlight—"

She could almost see him emphatically shaking his head. "No way. I was four towns away by the time I heard the news, but she got away. My guess is they thought she was dead and dropped her body in the town's morgue. She woke up and . . . well, you figure it out."

"Yeah." Buffy grimaced, remembering an experience or two of her own in the morgue at Sunnydale Hospital. Even her recollections of her mom weren't immune to that, and without someone capable of stopping her, the vampire babe would have been out of there in no time, probably leaving a bloody trail behind her. "Giles says he thinks he found a reference to a killer vampire in Poland fifty years ago or so. It might be the same woman. Does anyone have any idea what she wants?"

Angel made a noise that Buffy had come to recognize through years of being around him, a kind of half-impatient, half-questioning exhalation. "Buffy, she's after *you.*"

Buffy's expression hardened and she pulled herself back to a standing position. "Hey, she can bring it on. I'm always ready to dust one of these pains in my neck."

The phone rattled and she wondered if he were switching it to his other ear. "Buffy, this isn't a joking matter. This woman is *dangerous.* Her fighting skills are incredible—don't you get it? She nearly *killed* me. She—"

"At a time when your living conditions weren't the best," Buffy interrupted. "You said yourself you were living on the streets, eating . . . what? Rats, probably. No one can fight when they're malnourished, not even you."

"I wasn't malnourished!" His voice had gotten louder and now he sounded defensive. "And there was nothing wrong with my fighting!"

"Of course there wasn't." Oops—she probably sounded patronizing. "I mean, I get the point. Okay, she's tough."

"Look," he said, and Buffy could tell he was trying to calm down. "I just don't want you to get hurt, that's all."

Buffy smiled. "Thank you. But I'll be fine."

"If you really have to go through with this—facing her—then let me come to Sunnydale and help you."

For a few seconds, all Buffy could do was stand there with her mouth open, phone in hand. Then she tried to joke about it, a ploy to give her a little time to comprehend what he'd just suggested. "Two against one?" She laughed a little.

"Since when has that made a difference when we're talking about facing evil?" Angel demanded.

"Okay," Buffy said. "Stop—just stop." She took a deep breath. "I appreciate your concern, I really do. It's sweet and . . . noble—yeah, that's a good word for it— that you think you have to come swooping in here and rescue me. But I'm the *Slayer.* I can *handle* it, Angel. If I need help, I've got Giles and Willow and the rest of the bunch to count on. I'm doing fine."

"Great," Angel muttered. "Now I'm 'noble.' "

"Tell you what." Buffy found herself stretching the phone cord again and made herself let go of it. One of these days she might end up breaking the thing. "If it turns out this chickee is more than I think I can deal with, then I'll call. I promise."

He didn't say anything for a second. "All right," he finally said. "But really—be *careful* with this one, Buffy. *Extra* careful."

"I will," she assured him. "And I'll keep you posted on what happens." A few more pleasantries, a few more seconds of awkward silence, then he hung up. She put the telephone down and stared at it, as if doing so could make him appear in her living room. Had that conversation really been as stilted as it now seemed? How sad that their talks had come to be limited only to those occasions when safety demanded it. They used to talk about so many things, for hours nonstop, but now everything had changed. Or maybe it hadn't changed at all—at the base of their existence, she was still human, a Slayer, and he was still a vampire. What was it Willow had quoted? *Never the twain shall meet,* she remembered. She shook her head.

Never, indeed.

Anya could hear Xander's breathing in the dark.

The room wasn't really all that dark—she favored lighter-colored curtains that didn't block out the moonlight or the gentle shine from the streetlights below the building. In the world of Sunnydale and the Hellmouth, there were a lot of things that were way too terrifying about utter darkness, and she and Xander had long ago decided their lives were a lot more comfortable when they could see a bit of the room in the middle of the night. It also kept them from stubbing their toes on the way to the bathroom.

All right, she thought. *It's just a matter of pros and cons for each, so that's how I'll treat it. I'll just make a mental list, like any intelligent businesswoman would, and then it'll be easy to decide.* There were only two choices involved, so how hard could it be?

As D'Hoffryn had pointed out, life as a vengeance demon could be pretty good. Chief among the pro points was immortality; she would live a long—as in forever—life (provided she didn't supremely screw up like his last bubbleheaded vengeance girl had). That meant she could see the world evolve way beyond the ability of the oh-so-lifespan-limited mortals. One of the cartoons she liked to watch on Saturday morning television was *The Jetsons,* the somewhat outdated animated telling of family life in the far future. Dated cartoon or not, Anya was sure that someday there really would be flying cars and apartments on concrete-and-steel posts hundreds of feet in the air, just like in those cartoons. And she really, really wanted to drive one when they were finally invented.

The downside was that she wouldn't have any companionship, no one like Giles to work with, and certainly there would be no man like Xander with whom she could share her time and exchange affection in a humanlike manner. People found it difficult to forge a lasting friendship with a vengeance demon, much less a romantic situation. But now that she had tasted the rewards of human physical and emotional involvement, would she be satisfied without it?

As for Xander, the pros were obvious—unqualified love, a seemingly limitless amount of patience where her integration into society was concerned (although she really didn't see what she was doing that the others found so incorrect), a possibility of future commitment and procreation which awoke all sorts of inexplicable warm and fuzzy feelings inside her.

On the other hand, he might turn out to be unfaithful, or mean, or just fat and lazy—she'd seen it a thousand times in her life as Anyanka. So many men who started out promising later revealed their true natures, as if they'd had a naturally occurring invisible shell with which to blind the women who loved them. Did she, too, have that unseen blindfold? And did her very own Xander have that same deceptive cloaking device?

If he did, she should get out *now*, save herself the heartache that was headed her way.

But how could she know for sure that this was going to happen? In all honesty, there were plenty of woman in this dimension who'd found mates who were faithful and dependable and who suited them just fine. Some of them were even really in love.

But where was the guarantee that Xander was one of those perfect mates?

Then again, who said he *wasn't?*

He shifted beside her, as though he could sense her troubled thoughts. Anya felt the middle of the mattress dip and then Xander slid closer and slipped his arm around her waist, snuggling behind her and murmuring something in his sleep that she couldn't understand. It had sounded like "... *love you.*" but she couldn't be sure. She couldn't be sure of a lot of things.

It was going to be a very long night.

At five A.M. the house was as quiet as a grave and just as dark, and Buffy couldn't stand it any longer. She got up and dressed, experience making her move nearly soundlessly without having to turn on the lights. Since her Mom had died, she'd ventured out alone mostly out of necessity, the possibility of losing Dawn always in the back of her mind when she was out and Dawn was alone in the house. She had people watch her younger sister as much as possible, but it just couldn't be done all the time; not only were there limited baby-sitters available, the whole concept of 'baby-sitter' sent her 'baby' sister right through the roof. Maybe someday circumstances would change, but for now Buffy tried to keep Dawn in sight. But now, replaying the conversation she'd had with Angel, she need to get out, post-haste, and clear her head.

A quick peek into Dawn's room for assurance, then Buffy went back and slipped out the front door, making sure it was securely locked behind her—no leaving through the upstairs window anymore. She couldn't chance someone—or some*thing*—besides her using that for a handy entrance, and she wanted the security of a locked door between the world and her little box in it. The air outside was cold and damp, breezy, and Buffy shivered a little as she walked, thinking it was time to dredge out the heavier clothes. Pretty soon it would be Thanksgiving, then Christmas. How strange those holidays would be without their mother, how *sad*. Would they hear from their dad this year? Only time would tell.

Besides the wind and the leaves blowing around, there wasn't much going on this morning in Sunnydale. There was a half-moon, but it was already on its way to setting, not much help in the lighting department. Streetlights buzzed now and then, competing with the rustle of the bushes and the crunch of leaves under her feet. All in all it felt pretty darned lonely, and thinking about the talk she'd had with Angel earlier just made it worse.

The neighborhood was a wash, not a vamp in sight so still that even the alley cats had hidden themselves away. She knew the main shopping area wouldn't be much better, so she headed for that old standby, the cemetery. There were a bunch to choose from—Sunnydale was certainly rich with them—but the best choice was always the biggest. It was also the one she knew the best and, if it could be said for such a place for the living, she was as comfortable in it as anywhere else. Her mom was buried here, and every now and then, when she felt like could deal, Buffy would go by the grave and stand there in the moonlight, wondering about things like life and death and forces in the universe that kept a dead person walking and talking and feeling, but that took a terrible price for it. Those forces obviously existed—somehow souls were brought back and reinserted, and at times it seemed ludicrously easy, like no more than reshelving a borrowed library book. This meant that when a soul left the body, it went somewhere else, and if it didn't go to Hell, where was that other place? And why did they never see any evidence of *it?*

These were troubling questions indeed, and far too complex for Buffy to answer on her own. Pretty important, though; maybe she would ask Giles—

"Only one kind of woman walks a cemetery at night in a town like this," said a silky voice from behind her. "You must be Buffy the Vampire Slayer."

Buffy whirled and went into an instinctive fighting stance, but the woman who'd spoken was still a good thirty feet away. Funny how the moisture-heavy air of predawn could carry sound—Buffy could have sworn the words had come from only a yard off. "Who are you?" She didn't dare let it show, but the way this woman had snuck up on her had rattled her more than a bit, unwittingly giving a whole lot of credence to Angel's warnings.

"You wouldn't know me." Her visitor's answer came with a careless shrug. The stranger reached up and drew her fingers through reddish-blond hair that carried a pinkish tint in the glow from the half-moon, pulling it outward from scalp to ends to revive the spiky 'do. She was dressed in a hip-hop way that Buffy would have loved to try on for size, except she would have needed to add another foot to her height to make it work. This gal had no such problem carrying off the funky-sloppy outfit; she reminded Buffy of a T-shirt she'd once seen, Betty Boop wearing camouflage army pants and boots below a black sports bra.

"I know exactly who you are," Buffy retorted. "Catia, isn't it?"

The other woman smiled, showing beautiful white teeth against ivory, blemish-free skin. Her eyes were dark, but Buffy could see a hint of brown; in the daylight—never happen, of course—they would have been a warm chocolate brown. Whoever she was, Buffy had no trouble believing she'd once made a few male hearts—the human kind—go pitter-patter. " 'Catia'—I haven't heard that one in awhile. I'm going by 'Celina' now."

"Uh-huh. And the last name would be what?"

Celina shrugged. "It's been so long let's just say I forgot."

Buffy slipped good old Mr. Pointy out of the pocket of her jacket. "Too bad your memory's given out with time. It's a shame to die nameless. You tend to be forgotten that way."

Celina smile widened, then instantly transformed into a sneer. "Then I suppose you will be well remembered."

They leaped at the same time and crashed together in midair.

When they hit the ground, Buffy's downward swipe with the stake missed by a country mile—Celina simply wasn't *there* to be staked. Buffy, however, had apparently been exactly where she *shouldn't* have been; it happened so fast she didn't see it, but she sure felt the aftermath of a vicious knife-hand strike that caught her along the jawline on the left side. If she hadn't learned in training a long time ago to keep her chin tucked, that blow would have cracked her straight across the throat, and it had been hard enough to crush her windpipe and take her down.

She came up from her side roll to find Celina already on her feet and waiting, knees bent and ready to rock. Not wanting another airborne smash, Buffy lunged forward, going for the other's legs in a wrestling takedown. Celina stopped her short by slamming her hands down hard on Buffy's shoulders as she came in—a normal person's clavicle would have snapped like a toothpick. Buffy grunted at the shock but hooked her hands over

Celina's wrists, then yanked backward until the vampire tumbled over her. She tried to hold on, but the momentum pulled her grip loose, and by the time she swiveled around, Celina was already on her feet and smiling. Again.

"Ready for round two?" she asked pleasantly.

"A minor inconvenience," Buffy snapped.

Celina laughed and Buffy jumped at her and threw a cross punch at the same time. The vampire slipped to the side, and the blow only grazed the vampire's cheekbone; the left hook Buffy followed with landed on empty air, and the next thing she knew, she was on the ground and looking, wide-eyed, at the sky. There was a horrid, hammering ache in her stomach from Celina's knee, but Buffy knew she didn't have time to think about that. She rolled to the right and barely escape a repeat of the vampire's knee, although this one would have been across her ribs. Celina grabbed for her, and Buffy slammed an elbow into her face, then dragged herself upright again. She felt like everything inside her abdomen had been given a hard shake, but there was no stopping now.

The throbbing in her stomach, increasing as each second passed, slowed her reaction time just a hair too much, and when Celina threw a punch Buffy didn't get her hand up to block it quickly enough. She took the vampire's knuckles full in the mouth hard enough to snap her head backward and taste blood as her lip split. Before she could recover, Celina hit her again, this time with an uppercut that yanked the ground out from under Buffy's feet.

She hit the ground too fast to roll, taking the full brunt of the impact. A half second later Celina was standing over her, one booted foot on either side of Buffy's hips.

"Too easy," she sneered. "You're a Slayer. I thought you'd be *good*."

Buffy felt her cheeks flare red, and she started to push herself to one elbow, but Celina lifted one foot and slammed her back against the ground. "Huh-uh," she said. "Bad little Slayer. Down, girl. And stay."

Despite the pain, Buffy felt her humiliation level rise above everything else. Who did this chick think she was, talking to her like she was a dog? She swatted the vampire's booted foot aside and levered her body upward, aiming to take advantage of that split second that Celina was off balance—

—and, somehow, everything went from bad to worse.

Buffy thought things were going just peachy when Celina's legs buckled. Unfortunately, the fall turned out to be completely controlled; as the vampire went down she turned sideways and hooked one foot behind Buffy's neck. The other leg slid beneath one of Buffy's shoulders as Celina twisted her body. She dropped all her weight on top of Buffy's rib cage, bounced, used the momentum to twist her own body—

And suddenly Buffy was facedown against the ground, with both arms and legs pretzel-wrapped by Celina's body. She literally couldn't *move*.

"How're you doing down there, Buffy Summers?" Celina asked affably. "Not very comfortable, is it?"

Buffy tried to yank free rather than answer. It was a huge mistake; pain razored through the joints of her shoulders and hips, and her neck felt strained to the point of cracking. She was in serious trouble here. *Deadly* trouble.

"You see," the vampire continued in a conversational tone, "everybody badmouths it, but actually there's something to be said for age. Getting old isn't all bad if you use the time wisely. It's called experience." She loosened up one leg, but only enough to allow Buffy to turn her head so that she could just see Celina's face. If it was difficult to hold Buffy like this, her captor sure didn't show it. She didn't even look strained as she instantly reestablished the lock she'd had on Buffy's neck, and the only semi-hopeful thing that Buffy could see in any of this was that Celina only had one hand free. Still, that was all the vampire would need to kill her.

"If you're wondering how you ended up in this predicament, there's an incredible martial art I studied in Malaysia called Pencak Silat," Celina told her. "But again, it's that experience thing."

"Cut the crap," Buffy managed. Her teeth were grinding together in an effort not to cry out. "What do you want?"

Buffy couldn't see the vampire's face, but her answer sounded surprised. "I don't *want* anything—I'm going to kill you. Isn't it obvious? So if there's anything you wish to say before you die, now is really the most opportune time."

"I do, but I can't talk like this," Buffy ground out. "If you'd just loosen up on my neck a little—"

Celina's chuckle cut off her words. "Do you really think I'm that stupid?"

"Despite your high self-opinion, you are not the sharpest fang in the vampire's mouth," Buffy shot back.

The was an almost imperceptible tightening of her hold, yet it was enough to make the joints in Buffy's shoulders scream for release. "Excuse me?"

"It's sunrise."

Celina made a sound Buffy couldn't exactly label, something between a hiss and a growl. She tensed, waiting for the vampire's killing blow, trying to find some minuscule measure of comfort in the thought that at least Celina couldn't bite her while scrunching Buffy's neck up like this, and the woman was out of time anyway. Celina's hand and legs shifted and Buffy got a nauseatingly hard twist—

—then she was free.

Celina had fled.

Every muscle and tendon, every end of every bone, throbbed with pain and release. Buffy pushed herself over until she was lying flat on her back and staring up at the quickly lightening sky, gasping and thinking, again, how grateful she was that she could see the sun each morning . . . today in particular.

She'd sew her mouth shut before she'd call him and admit it, but Angel had been right. This woman was one of the most dangerous opponents Buffy had ever faced. Beyond the run-of-the-mill vampire stuff, she didn't even have any supernatural powers, but clearly she didn't need any. Celina hadn't even had any *weapons* other than her own two hands, yet she had still beaten Buffy right onto the ground. Almost *into* the ground.

Buffy dragged herself upright and headed home, thankful that no one was around to see how it took nearly half the way there to smooth the limping out of her step and get her arms to rotate again without her moaning out loud.

Chapter 7

THE SUN RISING OVER LOS ANGELES LOOKED LIKE A dirty circle of mustard.

Angel chanced a glimpse out the window, ready to dodge back behind the safety of the draperies. He needn't have bothered; this morning's murky cloud of pollution was bad enough to rival a thorough cloud cover. It didn't make for a very pleasant sight, but it gave enough shielding to let him look out the window; he didn't have to breathe it, but humans all over the city would spend the day gasping and wheezing. It also made the air stink.

That was something he definitely missed about Sunnydale—the clean, clear air, crisp and a little damp in the hour or so just before sunrise. In the spring and summer it had always smelled like freshly mown grass; in the fall and winter, the scents of burning leaves and California pine had floated on the breezes. Here the only thing the breeze carried was exhaust fumes and, a little too often, the smell of whatever demon he, Cordelia, and Wesley were chasing down.

What's Buffy doing right now, right this very moment?

Sleeping probably, or maybe just getting up and readying Dawn for school. How sad that Joyce had died, sadder still that Buffy had been robbed of yet another part of her life. So much of her chance to be a teenager had been stolen by the Slayer's calling, but she seemed to have gotten it together, rallied to find a balance between Slayerdom and college and a possible future. Now that was gone; by day she was Buffy the Caretaker of Dawn; by night, Buffy the Vampire Slayer. Where in her life was there room for Buffy the Young Woman? He'd heard Riley was gone into the jungles of who knew where, that the college boy had, because Buffy had refused to admit she needed him, realigned himself with some Initiative-clone outfit that secretly fought demons. Now Buffy fought, for the most part, alone.

A dangerous thing, that solo Slayerism, especially when facing someone like Catia. His memories of back in the sixties weren't good, fraught with being miserable and living in the snow-choked alleyways of that small town. Yeah, it had been in Nebraska, and to this day he wasn't even sure how he'd ended up there, some hole in the wall called Mullen with less than five hundred people in it. Even the alleys hadn't really been *alleys,* more like mini-roadways between the backs of the few businesses and the backs of the houses that surrounded them. Bless the American rat, though—to a down-and-out vampire they were like juice bags with legs, and one could find 'em no matter how clean people tried to keep their town.

Angel didn't know what had made Catia focus on him instead of someone else—at the time he certainly hadn't been anyone special, and if he had anything resembling potential now, it had been invisible back then. Maybe it was his soul, that blessing and curse thing all rolled into one. He'd been at the height of personal torment then, and the spirit within that had made Darla reject him and sent him tumbling into self-imposed hatred had made Angel a recluse among his own kind. Perhaps all that pain had been like a beacon to Catia—*something* had drawn her down the alley, made her chase after him and force a battle. Had it not been for the Mullen Sheriff's Department, Angel would have been nothing but ashes blowing into the crevices behind a greasy little restaurant called Sandy's Family Diner. The narcissistic side of himself wanted badly to think she'd recognized him as someone special, but the honest side of his brain just snickered and whispered that the woman was nothing but a true, stone-cold killer.

To bear that out, Angel found he couldn't *not* remember his second encounter with Catia. The way she'd fought, the pure joy she'd taken in pummeling him to his knees, the glint in her eyes as she'd raised the stake over his fallen form—he'd seldom seen such happiness in killing other than in Darla. For a while he'd thought Faith had it, but it had been nothing but a mask, a shield behind which the dark-haired rogue Slayer had hidden her emotional agony. The worst of the vampires he'd known in his overextended life—even Spike at the height of his butcherhood—hadn't come close. No, there was only one other person—vampire—he'd ever known who enjoyed killing so much.

The soulless version of himself.

Angelus.

Angel bunched his fists and scowled out at the daylight. He glanced back at the clock on the desk and realized it was at least the tenth time he'd done that since positioning himself by the window an hour ago. The minutes were passing like molasses on a winter morning—damn the sunlight that kept him trapped in this city until its passing.

Since fleeing Callaway the night Catia had been gunned down by the sheriff's deputies, he hadn't looked back—hell, he hadn't looked back on *any* of the places he'd wandered through until he'd found Buffy. He'd been like a pinball, bouncing off whatever was in his way to head somewhere else without direction or reason. He'd heard tales of Catia now and then, whispered rumors full of fear and retellings of fights that had always ended in blood and death for her opponent. The stories had her surfacing less and less over the years, driven to hide by her own reputation and the increasing ability of the humans to use their computers to track a person, even a vampire, from state to state. To the average town's law enforcement, Catia wasn't a vampire or anything out of the realm of the everyday . . . except that she *was* a murderess, and if they took notice of her in one place, nowadays it wasn't so hard to find out she'd been somewhere else. She was smart enough to know that facing that kind of combined manpower was a bad idea, so she'd finally gone into keeping a low profile.

But now Catia was back, threatening not him, but the woman he still loved.

Could Buffy survive an encounter with a vampire who fostered that same addiction to giving pain and death that he had once embraced? Was she strong enough to endure against one who gave herself freely to the evil he'd spent years resisting? He wished he could be more sure. Though she'd bested him when he summoned Acathala, he worried. The very idea of Buffy fighting Catia terrified him beyond words, left him pacing his room like a caged leopard while the sun-filled world beyond the glass laughed at his imprisonment. No, he couldn't just sit idly in Los Angeles while Buffy faced an opponent whom he knew from firsthand experience was more than she expected. The chance was too great that she would fall in combat, and he just couldn't let that happen.

As soon as twilight hit, he'd be on his way to Sunnydale.

"You're late," Anya snapped at Giles. "Do you expect me to do everything by myself around here? Open the shop and total the register, dust all the merchandise items and check the inventory, stock the shelves, *and* take care of any early-morning customers? I suppose now that I've proven my worthiness as an employee, you plan to make a habit of this behavior. They say it's typical of an employer to take advantage of his best employees."

Three steps inside the door, Giles stopped and his eyes widened. "Anya, you're my only employee. And no, of course I'm not going to be late every day. It's simply that this morning—"

"I don't want to hear your excuses. You'll only make me angrier." Anya slammed the cash register drawer shut hard enough to make the counter vibrate. "Tomorrow you might try getting here before *noon.*"

The older man squinted at her from behind his glasses, then held up an armful of books. "I was doing research—"

She held up a hand. "Stop. I thought you wanted to run a business where people come in with money and leave without it. *You* own the business, therefore you should also contribute something to it. I am just a worthless employee, remember?"

Giles frowned and set the books on the counter. "I never said you were worthless—"

"Don't put those there!"

He snatched them back up. "But why not?"

"Because I just *polished* there, that's why. And they're dirty." She jabbed a finger toward the table. "Keep them over there with the rest of the dusty things. And *don't* touch anything."

Giles started to say something, then closed his mouth and retreated to the safety of the table, where for the first time he realized a carefully quiet Xander was sitting. Lunch—a peanut butter sandwich, an apple, and two bags of barbeque chips—was spread in front of the young man, but it was mostly untouched. When Giles eased onto a chair next to him, Xander gave him a weak grin. "I thought about eating, but I'm afraid if I open anything and get a crumb on the table, Anya'll decapitate me." He made a concentrated effort to keep his voice low.

Giles nodded sympathetically. "She's quite out of sorts, isn't she? Is there something wrong?"

"Beats me. She's been like this since last night. I mean, I know she was acting a little weird yesterday during the day, but this is a hundred times worse."

Giles tapped his fingers on the table and tried to think. "Do you think something frightened her, or—"

"Giles, would you *please* stop that irritating noise?" Anya barked from the other side of the room.

Giles's fingers froze in midair, then he carefully placed his hands in his lap. "Right."

Xander reached for one of the bags of chips, then reconsidered when the bag crinkled a bit too loudly. "She didn't tell me about anything," he told Giles. "I went after a pizza last night because Julio's was delivery-deprived for the evening, but we figured she'd be okay by herself, it being highly unlikely that Anya would invite a vampire inside. When I got back she was kind of . . . " Xander looked puzzled. "I don't know. Distant, maybe."

Giles took off his glasses and inspected them. "It's been my experience that when a woman begins to act distant without explanation, the man in her life is usually in trouble. You're sure you didn't do anything untoward?"

Xander shrugged. "Hey, I was breathing in and out. Given Anya's history, she might decide that's wrong at a moment's notice."

"True."

The bell over the door tinkled, and they looked up to see a smiling Willow and Tara amble in. "Hi, guys. What's new?"

Xander smiled back, glad to see a couple of friendlier faces. "New Jersey, New Mexico, New York, New—"

"Delhi," Tara put in.

Xander blinked. "Excuse me?"

"New Delhi. That's new." Tara looked from him to Willow. "Isn't it?"

Willow patted her on the arm. "Think domestic."

Tara looked disappointed. "Oh, okay."

"But that's okay," Willow added hastily. "Sometimes it's good to branch out."

"Like a tree growing in the spring," Xander said mildly. He was still being careful to speak quietly. "Branch right on out there and have a seat here." Tara gave him a self-conscious smile after glancing at Willow for reassurance, then settled on one of the chairs.

"So what's up in the world of—" Willow began, then stopped when Xander pressed a finger to his lips. She looked over at Giles just as Anya slammed something

down at one end of the counter, and saw him jump at the
sound. "Huh?"

"Anya's having a bad day," Xander explained.

The glare that Willow sent him way was accusing.
"What did you do to her?"

"Nothing," he said indignantly. "I've been the best
of boyfriends. I go out and get her a pizza while she
takes a nap, I drive her wherever she wants to go, I
even come over here to eat lunch with her." A corner of
his mouth turned up. "Of course, I did the lunch thing
on the assumption that she was going to actually *talk*
to me, but given the present circumstances I see that
was taking way too much on faith. Her sociability level
has been on a definite downhill slide for a couple of
days now."

"Maybe she has PMS," Willow suggested.

Giles looked startled. "I believe that's what your gen-
eration refers to as 'way too much information.' " His
cheeks reddened a bit, and he picked up one of the
books on the table as a distraction.

"No, really. If that's it . . ." She nodded meaningfully
at Tara. "Whoa."

"Yeah, well let's hope it *is,*" Xander mumbled around
a half-hearted bite of his sandwich. "I'd hate to think
she's acting like this because of some fickle-woman-
whim-thingy."

"What fickle-woman-whim-thingy?"

Xander jumped at the sound of Buffy's voice, then
craned his head fearfully in Anya's direction. Thank-
fully she'd headed into the back room to check on the
inventory or get supplies or maybe just give his nerves a
break. "I think that would be Anya's mood today."

Close behind Buffy was Dawn. "Hi, guys."

"Bad-attitude day, huh?" But Buffy clearly wasn't

concerned with Anya. "Giles, what's up with the research?"

Instead of answering her, the Watcher frowned at Dawn. "Isn't today a school day, Dawn?"

"She had a free period after lunch," Buffy said quickly. "I suggested she spend it here with us."

Dawn rolled her eyes. "Yeah, she's afraid I'll hang out on the street corner with the bikers or something."

"I see." It didn't take a degree in rocket science to see that Buffy was still determined to keep a protective shield around her younger sister as much as she could. "In any event, I found some more references that I believe can be attributed to our mystery woman," he said, eager to get back into familiar territory and away from the whole overprotective Buffy and Anya-PMS-fickle realm.

"Buffy, did you get hurt?" Tara asked suddenly.

Giles stopped and they all stared at Buffy, registering for the first time the dark bruise beneath her chin and along the bottom of her lip, where the soft flesh was already trying to mend from a nasty split. It didn't stop there—they could tell by the way she was standing that she was favoring one side, hunching slightly to take the pressure off sore ribs. Giles pushed the book aside and rose. "Buffy, what happened? Did you find her? Are you all right?"

"She got her butt whipped," Dawn said flatly. "When I got up this morning, she was spitting blood into the bathroom sink and her clothes were full of dirt. She looks a whole lot better now."

Buffy glowered at her sister. "Would now be a good time to mention how happy I am that you're sharing this information?"

Dawn wasn't intimidated. "Always glad to help."

Giles reached for her wrist. "Buffy—"

Buffy pulled away from him. "I'm *fine*," she insisted. "Anyway I was going to tell you that I ran into her but then you got all eager to fill me in. It's just a few bumps and thumps, nothing not included in the Slayer Job Description. Just look under the subsection titled 'Surprise Attacks.' "

"I can give you a poultice for that cut on your lip," Willow offered. "And some Arnica for the bruise on your—"

"Stop," Buffy said. "Can we talk about finding out more about this woman? She says she's going by the name Celina now, not Catia."

"So," Xander exclaimed, "those aren't run-of-the-mill vampire whaps!"

Buffy sighed and pulled out a chair to sit down. "Could everyone just focus on what's important here rather than tunnel-visioning on a few minor bruises? The important thing being the rampaging vampire woman with the bad rep, remember?" Even so, she winced a little as she settled back.

Giles studied her. "We will, but first let's talk this out. Clearly the battle was more difficult than you anticipated. Can you put your finger on why?"

Buffy grimaced and took a long time to answer. "She knew stuff," she finally admitted. "Some kind of martial art or something, lockdowns that went way beyond the usual break-the-arm or choke-hold stuff."

Willow sat straighter. "Lockdowns? You mean like immobilizing?"

Buffy hesitated before answering, clearly reluctant to admit how far it had gone. "Yes."

More stares as they tried to comprehend what had happened, mentally inventing their own details when Buffy just wasn't going to fill them in. Xander cleared his throat. "So given this whole immobilization thing, how exactly did you—"

"Sunrise," Buffy said flatly.

"Ah." Xander pushed a shock of hair off his forehead. "We of the good-guy variety must never fail to appreciate that big bright ball of fire."

Willow looked from Xander to Buffy. "So no poof goes the vampire?"

"I'm thinking not," Xander said.

"Maybe she . . . caught on fire or something before she could get to her hiding place," Tara suggested hopefully.

"I don't think so." Buffy sounded tired. "She's just way too slick for something that stupid. Sunrise caught her by surprise, but not by much . . . and only because she was having way too much fun with me. She was gone so fast I didn't even see which way she went."

A door slammed in the rear of the shop, and Anya strode in carrying a few items to put on display. Her heels cracked smartly against the floor, and she solidly ignored them all as she passed. "Incoming," Xander muttered.

Dawn shrugged off her backpack, her gaze tracking Anya. "What's up with her? Wake up on the wrong side of the bed or something?"

Xander raised one eyebrow. "She didn't get up on the wrong side of the bed, she got up on the wrong side of the *universe*."

As if she'd heard, Anya looked back over her shoulder. "Can't you people take your vampire talk in the back room or something? This is supposed to be a *business*. Loosely translated, that means we should conduct matters only pertaining to the making of money and customer satisfaction." She emphasized her words by slamming something down—she'd been doing a lot of that this morning. "Those who aren't customers should therefore *leave*."

"That would be me." Xander stood abruptly. "Time to go charging . . . *happily* . . . back to work."

Dawn stared over at Anya. "Wow, who dipped *her* tongue in poison this morning?"

"No one knows," Willow said.

Xander stood and wadded his mostly uneaten lunch back into the paper sack. "I'll catch up with you guys later."

"And where are *you* going, Xander?" Anya demanded before he'd taken three steps.

Xander swallowed. "Uh . . . me?"

"I'm certainly not talking to those *others*."

Dawn's eyes widened. "Make us sound like we've got ebola or something."

"Never mind," Anya said with a withering glance. "Go on if you're going to leave. Typical—just like a man."

"But you just said—"

"Don't throw my words back at me!"

Xander's mouth worked, then he gave his girlfriend a strained smile. "I wouldn't dare. But really, I have to get back to work. I'm putting in a new fence in front of the hobby store on Walnut where one of the kids ran into it with a scooter, remember?"

Anya folded her arms across her chest. "Fine."

"Anya," Xander said patiently, "I'm doing the job-thing that helps pay the rent, remember again?"

"I said fine already. Go."

He looked like he wanted to say something more, but wisely decided not to. "Bye, guys."

"Anya, won't don't you go buy yourself a frozen mochaccino?" Giles suggested. He pulled out his wallet and offered her a ten-dollar bill. "I'll even treat. In fact, buy yourself the biggest one you can find."

"All right." Her fingers flashed forward and the money disappeared from Giles's hand, then she lifted her nose a bit. "I could use some time away from this place." They watched silently as she snatched up her purse and stomped out.

"Whew," Willow said when she was gone. "She sure has a bee up her butt."

"Yes, there's certainly something on her mind." Giles glanced after Anya, as though it would somehow help him figure it out. "No idea what, though."

"I'm not so sure paying to hype her up on a triple dose of sugar and caffeine was such a great idea," Buffy said. "Does she really need more zip in her lip?"

"Not unless it's zipped shut," Dawn said smartly.

"I'm sure she'll be fine," Giles put in. "Maybe she just needs a bit of time to clear her head and be away from us."

"Oh, by all means," Buffy said with a roll of her eyes. "After all, she's Queen Anya and we're the *others.*"

"We all need time to be alone sometimes," Tara said. "Just to get our thoughts straight, think out any problems we have."

Buffy felt her lip carefully. "Well, it's pretty clear Catia or Celina or whoever she is has me in her sights and won't be bothering her again. But I guess I can understand her being shaken up."

The rest of the gang considered this and nodded their heads in agreement, then went back to the problem of Celina.

The sunshine outside felt good on Anya's skin, the same skin that was now so fragile and human and had to be protected from the sun and cancer with things like moisturizers and sunblock. She'd never had to worry about stuff like that when she was a demon, and she hadn't had to worry about things like customers, cash registers, inventory, rent, or glasses that broke and sliced your finger in two, not to mention angry vampires who used her to try to get to the Slayer. She had to admit there were things that she did enjoy now that had never occurred to her in her demonhood—clothes, for one. She liked shopping and buying things and looking nice. She found her own reflected image quite pleasant and had discovered that certain colors were extremely complimentary against her human skin tone. Xander wouldn't say so around his friends, but in private he was always very appreciative of her appearance and hygiene.

Speaking of Xander, why *had* she been so mean to him? Actually, it wasn't just him she'd been cranky with; she'd been irritable with *all* her friends this morning. While it was true she had a big decision to make, it certainly wasn't their fault she found herself having to make it. She detested it when others spread their misery to her, so why had she done just that? They'd been quite patient with her, hadn't they? Had the situation been reversed, she would have been biting their heads off for being crabby with her.

The Espresso Pump was crowded with people of all ages, and she had to wait in line for a long time. The woman in front of her smelled good, like vanilla body spray, the man behind her was a little grubbier but not totally disgusting—more like he was wearing the efforts of an honest morning's work. Like Xander, and that was another thing she really liked about being human—Xander and all the things that came with him—love, and sex, and companionship, popcorn and movies on a chilly night, waking up on a Sunday morning to find he'd tried to cook her breakfast and burned the bacon like he always did because he always thought it looked too rare. A thousand other things, good memories and bad—come on, who was perfect?—and if she chose the deal that D'Hoffryn had offered her . . .

It would all come to an end.

But . . . could she even *be* Anyanka again? Could she give up all the things that she had so painstakingly learned since her amulet had been destroyed?

Anya paid for her giant frozen mochaccino and wished she could think, but the pros and cons just kept whirling around in her mind—

Xander versus eternal life.

Love versus the power of the wish.

Earthy comforts versus unearthly benefits.

—and she was no better than when she started. She could live forever, but she would be forever alone. She could love and live and die as a mortal, but she would never be alone, at least in the time allotted to her human body.

Or would she?

Again, she'd seen it enough times over the centuries, the promises made by a boy to a girl, or a man to a woman, those same promises broken so that the female was left bitter and devastated, her heart little but a charred scar of memory. Who was to say that Xander wouldn't do the same to her—was he not a very typical example of mortal man?

What would she be like as an old and lonely mortal woman? Would she be all dried-up and bitter, wrinkled beneath salon-styled gray hair, perhaps drinking and plucking badly at some musical instrument in smoke-filled bars like Giles occasionally did? The thought was horrifying.

Still . . . would Xander really do that to her? He'd told her enough times that he loved her, but not so many that he seemed to just be carelessly tossing off the phrase. She could feel his sincerity in his words, in the way he held her—darn it, she *believed* him. Then again, hadn't so many other women done the same over the thousands of years of human relationships—trusted the men they loved?

Outside now, Anya found a spot to sit and huddle over the oversize cup, warm in the sunshine but chilled by the drink. She just couldn't make this decision by herself, but at the same time, she *had* to do just that. It wasn't like she could turn to anyone else and say *"Hey, what was your experience when you had to choose between eternal life or death?"* The only people she knew anymore who were immortal were vampires, and they'd never had a choice. Her friends, of course, would be all rah-rah cheerleader for the human side of the coin, but they really had no experience with the flipside. So who—

Willow.

Anya sat up and clutched the cup tighter. Yes—Willow. Old rival but not really enemy, who could forget the damage that Oz had done to Willow's spirit when she'd caught him cheating on her with Veruca, the female werewolf? They'd all found out after the fact, but Willow had very nearly dropped a serious load of black mojo on Oz's spiky head, and even though she'd been at the beginning baseline of her Wiccan powers back then and not really in control of everything, she'd had plenty of punch to pack. In her grief she'd cast as ill-fated spell on her friends that had backfired alarmingly. All that dark energy hadn't gone unnoticed, either—D'Hoffryn himself had stepped in, sucking Willow down to his dimension for a little chat and offering her a job as a vengeance demon, exactly what Anya had once been.

And Willow had refused . . . but *why?* All the power she could have wanted, the ability to make Oz pay once and for all for what he'd done plus the chance to bring total pain into the lives of men just like him—and let's not forget the whole immortality thing either—yet the little redhead had turned away from it. Anya just couldn't understand her refusal. It wasn't as if Willow had had anything to hold her here back then. Oz had abandoned her and she wasn't involved with Tara yet. Beyond a few friends, parents who seldom realized she was alive, and a heavy load of college courses, what had held Willow Rosenberg rooted in the mortal dimension?

There was one way to find out. Anya finished the last of her coffee drink and shoved the empty cup in the trash bin, feeling overstuffed and a little zingy at the edges from all the sugar and caffeine. Yeah, it was definitely time to have a girl-to-girl with Willow, and maybe Tara, too. Willow's fair-haired companion had had her moments in the darkness, too. In fact, hers had gone in the other direction—she'd thought she was a demon and found out she was just another puny human. How had she felt? Tara didn't talk much, but Anya didn't have time to be deterred by things like reticence right now.

Not when her mortal—and perhaps immortal—future depended on it.

"Can we talk?"

Willow brushed her hair back and eyed Anya warily. "What, you're going Joan Rivers on me?"

Anya tilted her head. "Who's Joan Rivers?"

"Talk-show hostess," Giles said without looking up from the book he was reviewing, something in beat-up black leather with indecipherable Germanic writing stamped across the cover. "Before your time as a mortal."

"Oh." Anya looked from Willow to him, then back again. She looked like she was struggling to keep a cheerful face . . . and losing. "Then, yes, I would like to go Joan Rivers with you."

"On you." Willow said, then sighed. "Never mind. What do you want to talk about?"

"I would like to speak in private."

Willow's suspicions deepened, but she couldn't exactly refuse. "All right." She pushed away from the table and patted Tara on the shoulder. "I'll be back in a few minutes."

"Actually I would like to speak with Tara, too."

Tara's expression changed into something resembling a rabbit in the headlight of a motorcycle. "Me?"

"Yes, please." Standing very straight, Anya smiled, but it really looked more like a grimace. When Tara hesitated, some of her old impatience couldn't help but break through. "There's no reason to be afraid of me. When I was a demon, I only cast pain spells on men, you know. And of course I'm not a demon anymore anyway. I haven't been for quite some time. You know that. Everybody knows that. Well, not everybody, but everybody *I* know knows that." She stopped and glanced around, as if she suddenly realized she was nearly babbling.

Tara looked hesitantly at Willow, then stood and followed her and Anya to the back of the store, where Anya pushed open the door to the training room. They followed her inside and waited while the former demon paced around for a half minute or so, apparently trying to gather her thoughts and words. The room seemed very big and empty without Buffy and Giles, and Willow tried to think if she had ever been in here—this particular room—without them. She wasn't sure, but she didn't think so. Finally she just couldn't wait any longer. "Anya, what's going on?"

Anya stopped her fidgeting and took a deep breath. "I would like you to tell me exactly what it is that keeps you here on the mortal plane."

For a long moment—a *very* long moment—Willow didn't know what to say. "Uh . . . that would be the whole biology aspect. The flesh-and-blood anatomy concept. You know, oxygen in, carbon dioxide out—"

Anya shook her head vehemently. "But D'Hoffryn offered you a chance to become an immortal, to live forever. You chose not to. Why? How can you stand to stay mortal when you could live for eternity?"

Willow's first impulse was to be sarcastic, but she quelled it. There was something going on here, something deeper and a whole lot more insidious, and it couldn't be dealt with offhandedly. "Because there are things that I would have had to give up," she said, choosing her words carefully. "Tangible and intangible things. Eternity is a *long* time, *too* long to live—or unlive—without them."

Anya frowned slightly, trying to understand. "Which things?"

Willow's hand sought Tara's and their fingers entwined. "Love, for one. The feeling of goodness inside yourself when you know that you care for other people and they care for you. Friendship. Companionship."

Anya rubbed her arms and paced back and forth in front of the two of them. "But you and Tara weren't together when D'Hoffryn made you the proposal," she pointed out. "You barely knew each other, and Oz had just hurt you terribly. You could have so easily made him pay for the pain he inflicted. So much was offered, yet you still refused immortality and the chance for revenge."

Willow squinted at her. "Anya, are you mad at Xander about something? I mean, I know he can be a doofus, but he doesn't mean to—"

Anya waved her hand impatiently. "No, he has nothing to do with it. Answer my question, please."

Willow pulled in a breath. "I don't know if I can explain it. Yes, I was furious with Oz—I've never been so angry in my life. I even started to mojo him, *seriously* mojo, but in the end I chose not to go through with it. Why? Because deep down inside, I knew I wouldn't be like that—hurting—forever, no matter what I feeling at the time. I knew I would eventually *heal*. And when I did, I wanted the rest of my life to be okay—I didn't want to do anything that would make the good parts of it go bad. You know?"

"No, I don't know." Anya only looked even more confused. "But *how* did you know any of that?" she pressed. "Did you use a crystal ball to see the future, or a time-folding spell? It's a nasty mixture, but I've heard that reading black tea leaves soaked in a solution of lizard urine will—"

"No crystal ball," Willow interrupted. "And no tea leaves or potions or tarot cards. I just knew in *here*." She touched the center of her chest for emphasis. "See, immortality . . . it's more than just what happens to the physical body. It has to do with what touches the *spirit*, too, with the essence of yourself that lasts forever, whether or not you've got a bunch of blood and bones carrying it around. I kind of think that even if we don't have a body, we still go on forever. We're all part of the energy of the universe, but it's our choice whether we're going to be on the dark side of that energy, where everything is in the shadows and it all feels cold and angry and always full of pain, or on the light side, where it's just the opposite."

Anya was silent for a moment, then her gaze turned to Tara. "And you," she said, "how did you feel when you found out you *weren't* a demon, and you *weren't* going to live forever? I mean, the whole mean family thing aside, weren't you disappointed to discover that you were nothing but a mere mortal? No special powers, no extended lifespan—nothing."

Tara smiled, and as Willow often thought it did, the expression made the blond girl's whole face shine. "No. I never wanted to be cold and evil inside. That's like . . . living in a prison, I think. Trapped by what you are, and always wanting the warmth on the outside that you can never have."

"I suppose." Anya hugged herself again. "Well, thank you for answering my questions." Without another word, she turned and walked away.

"I hope we helped," Willow called after her.

She and Tara watched the door close, then Willow felt Tara's fingers tighten in hers. "Do you think we did?" she asked anxiously. "Help, I mean?"

Willow lifted one shoulder in a shrug, but it was anything but a careless move. "I don't know," she admitted. "I've got a feeling that Xander's biggest rival for Anya's heart is a lot higher on the competition level than he ever expected." Silence settled over the training room, giving Willow's next words an echoing quality that seemed out of place in the brightly lit afternoon.

"And I don't know if he can win."

"You're so lucky."

Coming out of the training room, Anya stopped at the sound of Dawn's voice. When she turned, she found the slender teenager leaning against the wall next to the door, a nearly resentful expression on her pretty face. That she'd been eavesdropping was a given, so there was no sense in griping at her about it. To some extent, that's what teenagers did—sneaked around and learned what went on in the world while the adults or their friends or whomever constantly tried to hide or protect them from it. In her time as Anyanka, Anya had known hundreds of girls who'd caught their cheating significant others by just such means.

"I'm lucky? Why is that?" Anya clasped her hands in front of her and waited.

"Well, look at what you have," Dawn said. "It's like you have *everything*—a guy, a job, you look pretty. You think you've got some big dilemma here about whether you should go back to being a demon or stay human?" Anya blinked and started to say something, but Dawn just kept going. "I mean, get *over* it. At least you've done it both, you've got the firsthand view. You have *choices*." Dawn flipped her hair back, as if she were impatient with the weight of it against her neck. "Look at me—I feel like I'm nothing," she said glumly. "I'm not immortal, but I'm not sure I'm really mortal, either. I just *am,* but it isn't even a good 'am.' I just sort of . . . I don't know. *Poofed* into being or something. And no matter how everyone tries to convince me—and themselves—that my 'being' is okay, I know I got cheated out of stuff big time along the way. I'm like a big fat lie." She kicked out at a spot on the floor, a bug or a shadow or something imaginary. "And I still have to do all the crappy stuff, like homework."

Despite the decision that was weighing on her, Anya felt a rush of sympathy for Dawn. It must, indeed, be difficult for the girl. One day she's going along like everything's just peachy, and the next—sorry, gal, it's all been one big fib and you've never really been *real*. In that respect, Dawn was definitely correct: Anya at least knew what awaited her on both sides. The only problem was that *this* side had a limited shelf life.

From somewhere inside, she found a smile and put it on, then reached out and smoothed the silken hair falling over Dawn's shoulder. "You could have appeared as an ogre, you know. Or a toad. If a person has to poof into existence," she said, "at least you poofed into being something beautiful and an existence where everyone loves you, no matter what you are. Or aren't."

It was the best thing she could think of to say, so she patted Dawn on the arm and headed back into the main part of the Magic Shop.

With Dawn headed back to school and everyone else cleared out, Anya spent the rest of the afternoon trying to imagine herself as a demon again, wrecking vengeance and havoc hither and yon without Xander and the rest of her friends to worry about. Xander wasn't there to try and start a fight with, and she really didn't want to anyway. Part of the whole getting used to being human again was learning to be honest with herself, as well as learning to understand how her mind functioned as a mortal woman's. It wasn't that hard to put two and two together and get five—subconsciously, that was exactly what she'd been trying to do, goad Xander into an argument, get him to say something he'd regret and that she could hold against him. There was a part of her that wanted the effortless way out of this, and if she could push Xander far enough, maybe even make him angry enough to break up with her, it would make it easy to choose to become a demon again, even justify it. Then she wouldn't have to make this horrible decision about whether to live forever as an evil demon or have a pathetically shortened life as a mortal . . . with all its benefits.

But Xander and the others had shown her something that was rare indeed in the dark dimensions of the universe: *tolerance.* It seemed that no matter what she did or said, no matter how nasty or blunt her words, they were determined to shrug it off and wait for the best part of her to reemerge. Knowing that Xander and her friends believed that part was there, and that it would always come back, made everything more difficult.

Time ticked onward, her thoughts swirled madly, and before she knew it, Anya was looking at early evening. A few customers had come and gone, but nothing notable; night had fallen and any minute the gang would start trailing in. Giles had opted to stay out of her range for most of the afternoon, retreating to the safety of the loft to pour over his tomes in the hopes of finding out more about the woman who was hunting Buffy. By now Xander was off work and he would be here any minute—

Anya smiled.

It came without her thinking about it, without her wanting it. An involuntary reaction.

Kind of like a heartbeat.

Just thinking about him made her warm—his dark hair, laughing eyes, that lopsided grin. Part of it was sexual, yes, but a big part—the *bigger* part—wasn't. The feeling was more like something soft and plush had come down and enveloped her, made her feel comforted and needed and whole all in the same sweet rush. It was . . .

It was *love.*

For a long few minutes, the longest she'd ever spent in

her short mortal life, she really put effort into imagining herself as Anyanka again. No more Xander, no more Giles or Magic Shop or Willow, Tara, Buffy, Dawn, even Spike. Just her and her restored powers tooling along through the ages, dropping vicious little vengeance-bombs on the heads of unfaithful men as she went. Thousands of years would pass and she'd be doing the same thing, century in, century out. She'd get to watch others in love and in pain, but she'd be safely out of range and never have to experience it herself. Why, in time she'd probably even forget Xander and how she felt now, just skip along her black little way unconcerned about that mortal man with the excellent kissing technique and a never-ending addiction to junk food. The thought was all so . . .

Dreary.

No love, no friends, no *Xander*. Was it really so hard to see that the "intangible" thing that tied her to this mortal world wasn't really intangible at all? Xander and his love for her, her friends and this little shop, they were the essence in her life and her entire existence, her *future*. In her changeover from demon to human, she'd come to grudgingly treasure them all, just as they accepted her and all of her sometimes shocking little quirks. They all faced and conquered so many obstacles on a daily basis, but they struggled with bigger issues, too. Even Willow, in her relationship with Tara, had had to face huge and unknown territory from all angles; if Willow and Tara had been able to stand strong, shouldn't she also be able to?

Anya found herself pacing back and forth in front of the counter, impatient for Xander's arrival, looking forward to the rest of the gang and the noise and energy they always brought in with them. Her crankiness had gotten her nothing but isolation today. Certainly no peace of mind, just solitude, and in that was a good lesson. D'Hoffryn had originally been drawn to her because of her anger, just as he'd been drawn to Willow because of her pain. Willow's words in that respect were true—she'd known she wouldn't always hurt that much and had refused to give up her humanness because of one immense incident, however agonizing.

As for herself, Anya knew she was no longer the same angry and scorned little peasant girl who had first caught D'Hoffryn's demonic attention. While she might still have a few suggestions for zinging a wayward boyfriend or unfaithful lover, she really couldn't be much bothered with other people's love lives, be they bad or good. She wouldn't admit it aloud in a million years, of course, but half of those airheaded girls deserved what they got for fooling around with boys they knew were trouble to begin with. And the ones who'd been wronged and were now seeking rightful vengeance? They were just going to have to find it somewhere else.

Because Anyanka wouldn't be coming back.

Chapter 8

"PLACE SURE DOESN'T CHANGE MUCH," ANGEL MURmured as he stood at the corner of the block down the street from the Bronze. People milled in and out of the familiar structure, mostly younger men and women, all looking for a good time and thinking they were safe enough if they hung around here. The truth was exactly the opposite. The Bronze was like a vampire magnet—they were drawn to it like a mosquito to the bare and enticing shoulder on a hot summer night. Even from here he could pick out at least two of them, and besides Buffy the only thing that probably kept Sunnydale from being completely bloodsucker-swamped was the low-level instinct folks around here had. It showed in the way most—but not all—of the kids wouldn't leave with strangers or wouldn't walk the streets by themselves, in the odd but frequent addition of garlic bulbs to the artsy-craftsy wreaths hung on the doors of houses, in the way kids were called in way before twilight even when it was still warm and early in the season.

He stood there, blending quietly with the shadows and playing with the toothpick in his fingers for a few minutes, content to just stand and watch the crowd. The two vampires he'd seen left alone, the only reason he let them go; tonight, he had bigger fish to find. The air had a definite chill in it, though in his time on this earth he'd been to a few places that would give chill a whole new meaning—these southern Californians had no idea how really good they had it in the weather department. He might be undead, but he still preferred being warm to being cold; cold was just way too much like the grave.

Enough of this waiting around. Nothing much was happening out here anyway, so Angel tossed the toothpick aside and decided to go on inside. He passed the two vampires, and they looked at him warily and side-stepped to what they thought was a safer distance. Did he still have a nightside reputation here in Buffy's stomping grounds? It would seem so.

The Bronze hadn't changed much inside, either, a little redecorating, some new tables and chairs—no doubt the result of the latest smash-and-bang creature fight. They had a band tonight with a female singer who reminded him a lot of Suzanne Vega, that same great combination of sweet voice and good guitar work, interesting lyrics. The tunes had pulled about half the crowd onto the dance floor while the other half did the usual drink and gab in the shadowed alcoves around the rest of the place.

He didn't really have a plan, just a vague idea that he could keep eyes open and ears tuned to the ebb and flow of conversation, find out the lowdown on Catia's sudden appearance here. The female vampire was pure trouble, and her presence would not go unnoticed—it didn't matter if she was trying to lay low. She was like a glass of black oil poured onto the surface of a clear pond; even if the water was calm, her evil would slowly spread and spoil everything.

Angel bought himself a beer he didn't really want and was still thinking about this, contemplating which of the Bronze's patrons looked the most likely to have information, when he turned and nearly ran face-first right into her.

For a long, shocked moment they both froze. Then, before her expression on her face could go fully into hate-mode, Angel tipped his bottle toward her. "Hey, Catia. Long time no see. Buy you a beer?"

Her eyes narrowed but her features smoothed out, the skilled acting that had kept her alive for so many centuries kicking in. "The name is Celina now. And yes, a beer would be fine, Angelus."

"It's Angel now. Like you, I've had to adapt with the times." Angel signaled at the bartender, who had another bottle in front of them within seconds. He handed it to her and pushed a couple of bucks onto the bar. "So what brings you to little Sunnydale?" he asked. "Still chewing up the less fortunate and spitting out the pieces, or have you finally learned to live in harmony with the rest of the world?"

Celina took a swig from the bottle and ran her fingers up the side of the label. "Is that your idea of a pickup line? From the way you're dressed, I would've thought the last fifty years taught you a little better."

Angel chuckled. "You're not my type."

"So I've heard."

He rolled the beer bottle between his palms, feeling the cool moisture from the glass trickle down his wrist. "So what the hell are you doing here, Ca—Celina?"

She arched an eyebrow. "Since you're so concerned, I've come to do a little housecleaning. And it looks like I'm going to get a two-for-one—the one what I came for *and* the chance to finally take care of some old and unfinished business."

"Meaning me."

She smirked. "Are you always so blunt?"

"I don't have time to waste on niceties." He set the bottle down on the bar hard enough to make the bartender look over at him and frown.

Now Celina laughed outright. "Time? You have all the time in the world, Angel. Or at least you did, until I got here."

He folded his arms and stared at her. "What is it with you, anyway? What, you've got a grudge against the whole human race? Or vampires? Maybe the Powers in general?"

She shrugged and tilted her bottle up, nearly finishing the liquid. "You could put it that way. Since there's too many of both sides to wipe out, I'm just going for the most kill-worthy. Around here, I believe that's your ex-girlfriend." She snickered at his surprised look. "Oh, don't look so freaked, L.A. Boy. Your Bad-Self prominence has spread far and wide."

Angel felt his fingers digging into the fabric of his coat. "Then why aren't you in Los Angeles?" he asked. "Why even bother with Sunnydale?"

"Oh, I was on my way," Celina said carelessly. "Sunnydale today, L.A. tomorrow." She grinned nastily. "But now I see I don't have to make that long trip."

"Why don't you do everyone a favor and just put Sunnydale on your been-there-done-that list and move on?"

"Oh, I intend to." Her eyes glittered in the multicolored lights shining from the stage. "Right after I can put the truth in the 'been-there-done-that' statement. Just like I have in a hundred other places."

Angel's hand snaked out and wrapped around her wrist. "Stay away from Buffy, Catia. You—"

"I *told* you it's Celina now." She did something with her other hand, slapped it across her body against the inside of his arm, and she was free almost instantly. Angel was left holding on to empty air, with a stinging sensation that went all the way up to his elbow. "If we were outside, Angel, I would kill you for touching me. That there are too many witnesses around us is the only reason you're still among the ranks of the walking undead. Or did you forget how you escaped both times before?"

He wanted to rub his wrist, but he'd be damned if he'd do anything to show how much that had hurt. Instead, Angel shoved his hands in his pockets. "You'll find I'm a changed man."

"You're not a *man* at all," she sneered. "You're a vampire, remember? And one who's obnoxious on top of it."

Angel regarded her thoughtfully. "You don't care much for your own kind, do you?"

Her mouth turned down at the edges, and this time there was no masking her disgust. "I never said I did."

"But you don't like humans, either."

"Why should I?" she demanded. "Look how *stupid* they are—no wonder they end up slaughtered like dumb cattle. For these fools I . . . never mind."

"You what?" Angel asked.

"And you," she snarled instead of answering. "You think you're the best of both worlds? You're not—you're the *worst*. Nothing but a half-breed who doesn't fit in either place. A monster with a human soul that makes him too soft to feed on the same brainless herd that cursed him to begin with. You should be a killing machine, the Angelus of the Council's history books, but you can't do that, can you? And you'll never be human, either. You're nothing but a *misfit*."

Angel grimaced. "Quite the pleasant drinking companion, aren't you? Had I known, I would have saved my money."

Celina eyed him coldly. "I'm not interested in you right now, Angel. But make no mistake about it, your time is coming. You escaped me twice, but three times isn't going to be any kind of charm for you." She turned to walk away.

"How can you exist when you're so full of hate?" Angel called after her. "If you can't enjoy anything about your existence, why bother to go on?"

Celina whirled. "Because it's my *job*," she growled. "I'm a vampire—I kill humans, and the vampires they become. As far as I'm concerned, you *all* deserve to die."

"But that doesn't make any sense," Angel persisted. "Why both sides?"

For the briefest moment she morphed—then she snapped back into human form. "Because of *that*. Because I *hate* being a vampire, and I hate humans in all their helplessness. If the world were annihilated tomorrow and I lived through it, I'd have a party to celebrate it the day after. And I'll start with you and your little human girlfriend."

Despite his best intentions, Angel felt his temper start cooking. His hand slipped beneath his coat and folded around the cool wood of a stake; it would be blatant, staking her in a crowd like this, but it wouldn't be the first time the folks of Sunnydale had seen weirdness. "You just hold on—"

But she was gone, slipping into the crowd of dancers and drinkers with a smoothness that rivaled his own.

* * *

"Looky, looky," Spike said softly.

Sitting in a shadowed alcove, he sipped his beer and watched Angel's gaze search the crowd and try to find the woman after she'd zipped away, so fast that even Spike hadn't seen where she went, despite being sure he hadn't let her out of his sight. When he finally gave up, Spike could tell by the way Angel moved that he was frustrated and angry, maybe even embarrassed that she'd pulled the cape over his eyes instead of him doing it to her. The whole thing gave Spike a nice warm fuzzy.

Spike was too far away to have heard the conversation over the noise of the music and the crowd, but he *had* seen Angel buy a beer for the woman with the strawberry-blond hair, then have a little heart-to-heart with her. By the expressions on both their faces, especially hers, it hadn't gone well. From all the info floating around and the description, this was definitely the killer babe . . . and *that* she was. Good-looking woman, she was, tall and lean, with a punky hairstyle that in his eyes always got a woman big bonus points.

Maybe she was an old girlfriend of Angel's? They certainly knew each other—the surprise on her face when she'd seen Angel had been unmistakable. If one took Drusilla and Darla into account, Angel didn't have a history of having his ex's come back as girlfriendlies. It was a mystery to Spike as to why, but Angel's past flings always seemed to show up wanting the bloke back. No indication of that here, though, and while Spike liked to think it was because the sexy-looking woman had more brains than most, it likely meant they'd parted as anything but lovey-dovies.

Still, what he'd tell Buffy was on a need-to-know basis only, so while the animosity between Angel and the visiting vampire doll was clear, Buffy just didn't need to know that. With a tad of careful wording—not an outright lie, mind you—he might be able to make this little meeting in the Bronze into something that would put a tarnish on that coat-of-arms Buffy seemed to think Angel wore.

"A funny thing happened on the way to the cemetery tonight," Spike announced gleefully as he strode into the Magic Shop. "It seems your ex-boyfriend is in town and chatting it up with our friend Celina." At the startled looks on everyone's faces, Spike arranged his expression into one of feigned amazement and turned to Buffy. "You mean he didn't mention it? From the way they were all whispery, I'd guess they've known each other for quite some time." He shrugged. "I mean, a man buys a beautiful woman a drink . . . well, you get my drift."

Buffy's face smoothed out and she waved him away. "Spare me the gory and very imaginary details, Spike. Angel already told me he's run across her before, a couple of times, and that she's bad news. I just didn't expect him to come to Sunnydale, that's all."

Sitting next to Willow, Tara smiled. "Oh, I think that's sweet," she said. "It's like he's coming here to rescue you or something."

"I don't need rescuing," Buffy said. She sounded on the grumpy side, but there was the slightest softening in her eyes that inferred she didn't mind him showing up nearly as much as she let on.

"Well," Spike began, "I just think—"

"Must you? Think?" Xander leaned back and lifted his feet, then crossed his ankles on the library table.

Next to him Anya reached forward and swatted them down. "Hey! This is a table, not a footstool," she said, but her tone of voice was a lot milder than it had been earlier in the day. It didn't seem to matter that there was a killer vampire slinking around Sunnydale—they were all in a good mood.

Blah, Spike thought. *What happened here? Everyone get a dose of happy-radiation or something?*

"What Xander said." Buffy glanced at Giles, then stood. "Can I leave Dawn here with you for a couple of hours? I think it's time I went on a little search-and-destroy mission."

"I could go with you," Dawn began. "I—"

"That would be in what universe?" Buffy retorted, but she gentled her comment with a quick hug along her sister's shoulders. "No way—this chick is vicious. You stay here and be safe."

"As a matter of fact, that's exactly true," Giles said with a frown. "I'm not so sure that it's a wise move to go out there by yourself."

"Let's all go," Willow said, standing. She grinned. "Strength in numbers and Wicca."

Buffy started to object, but Xander, Anya, and Tara were already on their feet. "Looks like you got out-voted," Dawn said.

A corner of Buffy's mouth turned up, and she gave Dawn a little poke in the ribs. "Down siteth thee, kiddo. I didn't get overruled on the *you* part."

Dawn glanced to Giles for help, but he only nodded. "Dawn and I will hold down the magic fort. I'd wager Dawn has studies to be completed for tomorrow's classes."

In response, Dawn flounced back onto her chair and sulked, then grudgingly began pulling schoolbooks from her backpack. "What *ever.* You guys get all the fun, and I have to stay here with Mr. Bookworm."

Giles was unperturbed. "Not the worst fate in the world," he said mildly.

"I think that depends on your point of view," Spike said.

"Are you coming with us, or are you going to stay here and take potshots at the old guy?" Xander demanded.

This time Giles did look up. "I beg your pardon!"

"Old as in, uh—"

"Well-seasoned," Anya said brightly.

Spike gave Giles an evil grin. "Sounds like dinner to me."

"You can leave anytime," Giles told him stiffly. "I rather think you'd be doing me a favor."

"Just remember who got you the information on Celina to begin with," Spike reminded him. "I'm a valuable part of this team, you know. You just won't admit it."

"Not in this lifetime." Giles slammed his book shut.

"Enough," Buffy cut in. "While you guys are having fun sniping at each other, Celina could be playing shop-and-chop all over Sunnydale. Let's go." Sometimes being brusque was the only way to get through, so she headed for the door. As she expected, her friends snatched up their stuff and followed.

Outside it was chillier than it had been all week. Although darkness had fallen several hours earlier, it wasn't that late yet; last-minute shoppers hurried along the streets, almost always traveling in twos—funny how a lot of people in Sunnydale instinctively did that once the sun's protective rays were gone. People huddled inside their jackets and peered suspiciously at the shadows cast by trees and bushes along the sidewalk, the darker spaces between parked cars, the long stretches between the pseudo-safe pools of soft light cast by the street-lights. Buffy wondered if they knew that someone new was among them, someone more than just a notch or two darker than the usual horrors that crept along the sidewalks of Sunnydale. If they didn't know, they sure acted like it—maybe it was that subconscious thing again, the primitive sixth sense that kicked in to help mankind survive.

For all the bantering that had taken place at the Magic Shop, the gang fell quiet as they wandered. They hit all the usual hangouts—the Bronze, the late-evening quiet of the high school grounds, a half dozen of the most common cemeteries. They checked Weatherly Park, found the Sunnydale Natural History Museum appropriately dark and peaceful, scouted out the rapidly emptying mall, even checked out by the Armory. But they found nothing out of the ordinary, much less supernatural.

"Maybe she's gone away," Tara suggested after they'd been walking for nearly an hour and a half and most of the spring had sprung out of their steps. "Maybe she's afraid of you."

"I doubt it," Buffy said as she peered around them. "The woman I fought with the other night wasn't afraid of anything."

"It looks like she's a no-show for tonight," Xander said. Anya was holding his hand tightly, acting like a jumpy cat every time a leaf crunched underfoot.

"There's a whole bunch of night left," Buffy reminded him. "Part of the problem could be that 'strength in numbers' thing Willow brought up. Even for Super Vampire, six against one might be a bit overbearing. I'm thinking I'd stand a better chance of drawing her out if I was alone."

"And when was it that you became human bait?" Willow protested.

"I think when they added the words *the Vampire Slayer* to the end of my name," Buffy answered wryly.

"Well, we're not getting anywhere here," Anya said. "What are we supposed to do, walk around the cemeteries all night? Xander, I want to go home and have sex." She paused, then added, "Twice."

Willow rolled her eyes as Tara's cheeks turned pink, but Buffy waved them all off before the slightly flustered Xander could reply. "You guys head on home," she insisted. "Really—I'll be fine." She cocked her head to one side. "I've got this feeling I won't be alone."

"I'll be right by your side," Spike said. "All bloody night, if you like."

Buffy made a face at him. "You weren't the 'not alone' I was talking about."

"Oh." The vampire pulled back. "*Oh*—you think La-La-Land Boy is around here somewhere, do you?" He gave a short laugh that had a distinctly bitter edge to it. "Reaching a bit, aren't we? Last I saw him he was following the tail of someone more his type—a strawberry-blond baby with legs out to here." He made a long gesture with his hands. "You know, the kind who can stick around with him for a few centuries . . . and with whom he can do the rockabye all night to boot."

"Only because he wouldn't be happy with her," Willow spoke up in defense of her friend.

Spike lifted his chin. "What's the difference, Red? It still means he can't cradle with the Slayer here."

"If you don't shut up, I'm going to impale you on a low tree branch," Buffy said blandly.

For a moment no one said anything. Then Spike shrugged. "Have it your way. But if you wake up dead tomorrow night, don't say I didn't offer to stay here and be your champion." He spun and stalked away.

Buffy and the others watched him go, then Xander

shook his head. "I just can't understand why we don't kill him."

"Well, he does prove useful now and then," Willow noted. "And with that chip in his noggin, he's pretty harmless to humans, but he can be hard on the demon populace."

"Harmless to humans?" Xander's mouth drew down. "So's bleach and ammonia, until you mix them together."

Anya tugged on his arm. "Xander, let's go. Buffy says she's fine."

"Anya, sometimes people say stuff just to make you feel good," Xander began.

Anya's eyes widened in distress. "They do?"

"Not this time," Buffy said and gave him a little push. "*Go*. All of you. I'd like some quiet time before I have to zip back and pick up Dawn." Her friends looked less than pleased, but finally they waved goodbye and headed on home.

And Buffy was left alone at the outskirts of Sunnydale Cemetery.

Chapter 9

"WHAT THE HELL DOES SHE SEE IN THAT GUY, ANY-way?" Spike picked up his shot glass and stared at it. "It's not like he ever says anything, you know. Just stalks around being all tall and dark and broody—not very interesting. Not very interesting at all."

He swirled the shot of whiskey in the glass, but he really didn't want it. He'd only come in here for a drink or two because he was peeved at this latest of a thousand rejections by Buffy. And, of course, there was always the chance that he might pick up another hint or two about Celina's whereabouts, always the hope that if he got some really good lowdown, it would make him look a little brighter in Buffy's eyes.

Spike glanced around warily. He didn't much like this place—the Fish Tank—because it seemed like every time he set foot in the place, he ended up in a fight, some bloke would show up and pop off at the mouth, and Spike would just have to rearrange his face. It got old after a while. But he hadn't been in here in, what, six or seven weeks, so maybe the clientele had rotated out, brought in a fresh new crop of no-gooders to replace the stale old scum. If so, the rumors and comments and yes, even the insults, would all be new, or at least as close to "new" as these types of ground-crawlers could get. That new might include word of Celina, so Spike figured he'd sit here quietly and wait awhile, keep his attention on the bar's customers without being obnoxiously obvious about it, and try to learn a few tidbits without having someone throw a punch at his nose.

"Are you going to drink that or play with it?"

The husky female voice came from behind him, and when he turned—

Spike found himself face-to-face with Celina.

If he had a heart—a *beating* one, anyway—it would have skipped a beat, but he wasn't entirely sure it would have been out of fear. Well, maybe a little . . . okay, a *lot,* but there was the other thing, too.

Damn, but this was a *beautiful* woman.

For an embarrassingly juvenile moment he couldn't say anything. Watching her from across the crowd at the Bronze had not only *not* done her justice, but it had made him miss out on a vital bit of old info. The sight of her now, this close to him, filled his mind and dug in deep, wriggling down to a few memories years forgotten—

Madame Rilétte's.

It is . . . what? 1900? 1890? Spike doesn't really recall, and it doesn't matter anyway. From the outside, the building is just another wind-beaten structure on a street filled with dust, fancy horse-drawn carriages and horse droppings, crowds of people, beggars, and streams of sludge where shopkeepers have dumped dirty water and buckets filled with infinitely more nasty liquids off the sides of the wooden plank sidewalks. He hasn't seen sunlight in what seems like forever, but he remembers it; he has a hard time believing that the light of day does anything but illuminate even more filth in this small and grubby turn-of-the-century city.

Still, he's heard about this place. He could use a bit of fun—Drusilla's gone off on her own for the evening and God knows what she's getting into. Every now and then her temper rises and she needs her space for whatever spooky goings-on whirl around in that dark and beautiful head of hers; rather than face her wrath, Spike gladly steps back and lets her go. Of course, while the cat's away, the mice will play and all that—so tonight, Spike's gone out to play a bit.

There is an ornately painted sign on a heavy mahogany door that says Entrez, *so he pushes through without bothering to knock. What he sees is so different from the world outside that he stands still for a moment, just to drink it in and enjoy. Wood, dark and richly polished, seems to be everywhere; the heavy Victorian furniture matches the woodwork and is upholstered in lots and lots of red brocade—how he loves red. There are no blank and boring expanses of wall in here, no empty corners or bare tables—marble and brass statues are everywhere along with Fabergé eggs and elaborately carved boxes; paintings abound, all reproductions of French and Italian masters in wide, gilded frames and centered between thick folds of draperies tied back with silken tassels. The oil lamps are turned low, and the room is accented by strategically placed candles that make the crystal pieces around the room sparkle like diamonds, while soft music—someone lightly fingering a piano in the farthest corner of the room—filters through the murmured voices of the patrons.*

Spike loves everything—the whole place has an atmosphere of wealth and decadence that is so far overboard he just wants to wallow in it. People—mostly women—drift by, filling the air with muted laughter and the scents of a dozen different perfumes. The ladies of the evening here are no doubt expensive—perhaps beyond anything he's ever encountered before—but Spike has plenty of currency, and it isn't long before he spies exactly what he wants.

She is half-reclining on the chaise lounge a few feet away from the baby grand piano. Next to Drusilla—for him, then, it would always be Drusilla—she is the loveliest creature upon which he has ever set his sights. Swirled hair nearly the color of snow frames translucent ivory skin that seems to glow above the edge of the black lace trim of her low-cut crimson gown. Her dark eyes entice him nearly as much as her full lips, painted to match her dress; nothing—no necklace of pearls or chain of gold—breaks the expanse of fragile flesh between her chin and chest. She is like the oddly negative image of some exquisite China doll, and the sight of her is enough to take his breath away . . . well, if he had breath to take.

He makes his way across the room and stops in front of her, wearing his most engaging smile. "Good evening." Her response is classic—a glance, an uplifted eyebrow . . .

Dismissal.

So. He will have to work at this a little.

He has always loved a challenge.

Spike gestures at the space available at the end of the chaise lounge. "May I join you?"

She sighs. "Must you?"

He lowers himself to the cushion without waiting for further permission. "I must, I'm afraid. You're far too lovely for me to simply walk away."

The ghost of a smile then, the prelude to a conversation that will, as Spike would later realize, be far too short for him to fathom just exactly with whom—or what—he was getting involved. He cajoled and flattered and finally enticed this intoxicating she-vampire, who told him her name was Callia, into one of the unoccupied bedrooms—

Where, amidst forest-green satin and silver crocheted bed curtains, Spike got the nastiest surprise of his not-nearly overlong life.

Was Angel around? Buffy could have sworn she sensed his presence. Or was it only wishful thinking on her part, her wanting him to be there so badly she was having a psychosomatic moment? She'd told him not to come, but of course she'd really wished he would . . . and according to Spike, Angel had responded just as she'd hoped. She didn't need any help—she thought— but if given the chance, she'd jump at the chance to see Angel again. Anytime, anywhere.

It was such a quiet, cold night suddenly, with all her friends gone and no one else around, not even a vampire to challenge her to a fight. Dark, quiet, and empty—suddenly Buffy felt depressed when she realized just how much like this the rest of her life could actually turn out to be. No matter what was going on with Her Keyness, Dawn wouldn't be around forever; a few more years and she'd be heading off to college, and what if she wanted to go somewhere other than Sunnydale? As badly as Buffy had once wanted to leave the Hellmouth behind, she certainly wouldn't be able to protest if Dawn felt the same. She could do it now, but she wouldn't always be able to protect little sister twenty-four/seven.

Anya and Xander might be around in the years to come, but face it—they had their own life to build and they had each other. It seemed pretty clear where they were headed, little spats and altercations in the meantime notwithstanding. On the surface was constant surprise and challenge, but there was also a growing sweetness underlying the way those two looked at each other that even Buffy could recognize.

Willow and Tara . . . well, Buffy thought that Willow might be meant for greater things than little old Sunnydale, and it was a good bet that if things stayed on an even keel, Tara would go wherever Willow went. Then again, both of them were smart and powerful, and together they made an incredible Wiccan combination. Maybe they *would* end up staying in Sunnydale and helping in that never-ending-battle-thing. Funny, it sounded all romantic and exciting in the sword-and-sorcery books, but when you had to swing that sword and get covered in the oogey stuff on a daily basis, all the high fantasy fun went right out of it.

Still, Willow and Tara had each other—who did she have? Giles was her friend and her Watcher and almost like her father. He was just sort of an always-there entity . . . but then her mother had also always been there. Now she was gone and Buffy had stepped into the shoes of Mom-person in addition to Slayer, giving up the dream of college and whatever things would have followed on the heels of that elusive college degree. Those new shoes were bigger and they came with bigger responsibilities—besides Dawn, there were things to deal with like bills and the mortgage and Dawn's future. Right now they still had Mom's savings, but someday Buffy was also going to have to step into the boots of career woman. And without that expensive piece of parchment . . . the thought made her shudder.

An owl hooted somewhere, the sound lonely and

echoing. No other sound, not even enough of a breeze to make the leaves rustle. She'd never liked the sound, never cared for the Halloween images—it was hard to keep that childhood love of Halloween when you knew what kind of beasties the night *really* held.

Scanning the still-leafy trees made her think of Riley. Where was he now? Still in some South or Central American jungle? Or had he and his team moved on to some other hidden location? Was he even *alive?* She had no way of knowing, and the notion that he might be dead, that he might have died months ago without her finding out, depressed her even more. Such a mistake she'd made, letting him go without telling him that she really had needed him, sending him out of her life thinking that all the love he'd given her was unreturned. The pain she must have caused him made her feel guilty and ashamed of herself, and she hoped that wherever he ended up, he found the happiness he deserved, someone who would adore him like he had adored her.

First Angel, then Riley . . . is that what the future held for her—more heartbreak? *New* heartbreak with someone she hadn't yet met? She'd let Riley go out of indecision and foolishness, but Angel was here in Sunnydale now, and she had never, *ever* lost that place in her heart for him. It would be so nice, sweet and *familiar,* to be with Angel again, even if nothing much had changed and they could only go so far with their love. She knew Angel, he knew her—she knew in her heart that he still *loved* her. If he didn't, he wouldn't be shadowing her as he had been since the rest of the gang took off a half hour ago, guarding her safety from just out of sight.

"Angel," she said softly.

She waited for a long, breathless moment, but he didn't come out. He was close, she had felt it all evening.

She had loved Riley, yes, but not with the strength and the . . . *foreverness* that she felt for Angel. Her future seemed so bleak and cold, so *empty,* without the idea of her family and her friends and no one to love. Unlike the others, Angel could be there for her, literally for eternity. But could she . . . *would* she . . . try to convince Angel to return to her and Sunnydale?

Such a tempting, tempting idea . . .

Oh, yeah.

Angel wasn't the only one who'd met Celina before.

She smiled at Spike, but now, in the Fish Tank, there was no hint of the anger he'd seen in her expression when she'd talked to Angel. "You know, I never did catch your name back in Marseilles."

Spike cleared his throat. "Spike," he said, and decided to try to play it nonchalant. "You're Callia, if my memory isn't too far off track. That was when, eighteen . . . ?"

Celina shrugged. "Now the name is Celina. After so many centuries, the dates all blur together. I don't care enough about them to keep track."

"Celina, then." Spike's eyes narrowed. "You know, I was only trying to get to know you a bit . . . *closer.* Do you often try to kill your suitors?"

She grinned wickedly and settled on the stool next to him. "As often as possible."

Spike signaled the bartender. "Buy you a drink?"

"Sure, as long as you don't try to lure me into a dark room and bite me on the neck again."

Now it was Spike's turn to smile. "I'm not stupid, luv. I knew you were a vampire the instant I touched your hand. A meal was the last thing on my mind—I was hoping for a roll on those satin sheets. If I remember correctly, they were green."

Celina laughed outright. "My mistake! And here I thought you were trying to make me the night's main course."

The bartender set down another shot glass of whiskey, and she reached across him and grasped it. The perfumed scent of her crawled up his nose and tickled his senses, different from her choice of a hundred or more years previous, but no less enticing. "The offer's still open."

Her smile widened. "Is it, now? You know, I've always loved the Brit accent."

Spike swiveled around on the barstool until he could face her. "I like yours, too. What is it—Russian? Hungarian?"

"Greek," she said, then suddenly frowned as if she hadn't meant to reveal that.

"My tomb or yours?" Spike asked before she could think too long about doing something to cure her information leak. "I've got pretty nice digs going, and you're new in town." He toasted her with the shot glass. "It's not often I bring a lady home, so you might find the place a bit dusty."

Celina's features smoothed out, and Spike relaxed a bit. He'd been afraid she'd stake him outright when she realized he'd gleaned a bit of her history. "Don't give up very easily, do you?"

He gave her a slow, inviting smile. "Not when it comes to an extraordinarily beautiful woman."

She looked at him thoughtfully, then finally returned his smile. "You know, Spike, I can't remember the last time I let someone show me a good time. I believe I'll take you up on your offer and see what I've been missing."

"Then why are we still here?" He downed the rest of the whiskey in the glass and barely suppressed a grimace—nasty stuff the way they watered it down here, why on earth did he drink it?—then offered his arm as formally as any gallant knight. "Let me escort you, m'lady."

Celina chuckled as she slipped a hand into his arm, and they walked out. "Such manners. You've become quite the gentlemen since the last time we crossed paths. Not at all how you acted in Marseilles."

"That probably had a bit to do with the stake you kept trying to poke into my heart," Spike said with a sidelong glance. "My behavior back then was strictly based on survival. I say we let bygones be just that—gone."

"Excellent suggestion."

It didn't take long to get to his tomb in the cemetery, and Spike actually regretted that. Oddly enough, this woman made him feel like he was on an honest-to-God date—how long had it been since he'd taken a woman out, alive or dead, and shown her the town? In a sense, that was exactly what he was doing for Celina, though while he made everything sound as scintillating as possible, he was also *very* careful to keep the information he gave her deliberately innocuous. She seemed interested in everything, whether it was the story of Mayor Wilkins or how the swim team at the high school had once turned into mutated fish men. He felt like it'd been years since Drusilla or anyone else had truly paid *attention* to his stories, and now he had this exquisitely lovely creature on his arm, and she seemed so, well . . . *normal.*

Okay, Spike found himself thinking, *I have to keep my focus here. It wouldn't do to get sucked in by a snake in mink's clothing.*

But it was *hard.* The Celina who strolled beside him now simply didn't equate with the killer named Callia with whom he'd squared off on a moonless night in Europe a hundred or more years ago. The Callia of back then had been vicious and nearly deadly; the Celina of the here-and-now was charming and flirtatious, and, he had to admit, incredibly appealing—she had the seductive dark side of Drusilla combined with the brightness and personality of Buffy. How could he *not* respond?

"Well, this is it," he announced as he led her into his tomb. "Home, dark home."

"Not bad," she said and sounded like she meant it. She walked around the main area, touching this, lifting that for closer inspection. There was nothing at all ferocious about her—well, beyond that crack she'd made about killing men as often as possible, but that had probably just been a smartass remark. He was good at those himself, as were most of the people he knew. If there was a reason to substantiate all the rumors and innuendo floating around town about Celina, he certainly hadn't seen any of it tonight.

She asked him a few questions, and Spike answered as best he could while he dragged out a bottle of old French Merlot, something he'd been saving for some unnamed special occasion. Tonight seemed to fit the bill, and he decided he needed the wine anyway, to try and calm the whirlwind that his thoughts had become. The longer he watched her moving gracefully around his place, *filling* his space, the more enamored of her he became, the more he was unable to connect this woman to the one who the others claimed had tried to attack Anya, kill Buffy, and who murdered everything in her wake for no sane reason. If she was going the acting route, she was doing a rousing good job of it.

Spike brought Celina a glass, and they toasted and sipped, spent a little time savoring the flavors of oak and berry that permeated the forty-year-old vino. The wine and small talk gave him time to think through the things that had happened over the past couple of days, to take it person-by-person and try to make sense of it all. He'd never been much on sugar-coating stuff or trying to soften the grit of a fact-based story, but now, with Celina standing so close to him and smelling vaguely like tropical flowers and incense, his mind was more than happy to muddle up the statistics a bit. Part of him knew that was exactly what he was doing; the other part, instead of resisting, happily let him formulate the same excuses and smokescreen that he would've sneered at on any normal night.

In short, Spike wanted to believe this was all nothing but a huge misunderstanding.

They had Celina mixed up with some other night slasher wanna-be. Hell, Buffy was always fighting in the darkest hours and in places where there weren't any street-lights—how could she be sure *who* she'd seen? Angel had always been prone to run off at the mouth about some bloke or demon or whatever that was running amok in the town. If you asked Spike, they all blew everything sky-ward anyway, turning the smallest sighting of the most in-significant of pests into Mondo Problem Number X.

That stuffy old ex-librarian didn't help matters, but his brain was probably so full of dust mites he couldn't think straight, so maybe he couldn't be blamed. Wait, sure he could—he was supposed to be the oldest and wisest and they all looked to him for guidance. The man ought to be able to separate reality from the drivel he gleaned from those rotting history books. And Anya—well, if she wasn't the biggest airspace-case around next to scardy lit-tle Tara, Spike didn't know who was. The woman had been a demon so long she couldn't even integrate into human society now—Celina had tried to hold a civil con-versation with her and Anya had freaked. Typical woman.

Still, the annoying rational part of his brain reminded him that he could be playing with something a lot worse than fire here—he could be playing with *death*. This woman certainly wanted to see Buffy dead. But . . . Buffy was more than happy to let Angel watch out for her. Of course, what if she just wanted to get his guard down? He didn't much fancy the inglorious idea of going out as something that could be cleaned up with a Handy Vac fitted with a few batteries.

He was still thinking about this when Celina took the wineglass out of his hand and set it on the table. "So I believe back at the bar you mentioned something about a roll in the dirt?" she asked. She stepped close and slid her arms around his waist, her dark eyes glittering in the light of the candles he had lit here and there around the big room.

His logic had been pretty much headed out the mausoleum door already, and when she pressed her lips to his, anything remotely resembling coherent thought just vanished. It'd been a long time since he'd had a willing woman with whom he'd *wanted* to be—Harmony had tried hard, you had to give her that, but his little unbeating chunk o'heart just hadn't been in it. She might be a pretty little thing and she took care of herself, but . . . well, he could do the love motion but not the love potion, so to speak.

But Celina was a different story altogether.

"I was thinking we could leave the dirt on the floor and use the bed instead." He pulled her tightly against his chest in one move, and she laughed, low in her throat, then tackled him like a football player. He went backward but held her weight, then lifted her and carried her over to the rumpled spread covering his mattress.

She might not have been warm in the flesh, but whatever shadowy spirit drove her was *hot*. And hungry, too, but not in a *Gimme a burger, fries, and a bloodshake* way—from the way Celina responded, Spike had to assume she hadn't done the lateral tomb dance with anyone in a long time, indeed. Vertical, sideways, and eleven ways to Friday—it became real clear, real fast that this lady was going to make up for lost time.

And hey, ol' Spike was definitely the man to bring her up to date.

Later, a *long* time later, Celina lit a cigarette from one of the candles now burning low in a red wax puddle on the crate Spike used for a nightstand. He liked that she smoked—everyone around here was all Goody Two-shoes and unhealthy-this, cancer-that about the cigs. Hell, they didn't hurt him—his stamina was fine (just ask Celina), and he certainly wasn't going to die of emphysema or anything else. If you asked him, the whole nicotine-cancer thing was just another downside of being alive.

Celina blew a lazy, thick-rimmed smoke ring toward the faraway ceiling. "So tell me some more about this quaint little town," she said with that marvelous Mediterranean accent of hers. "It's so pretty, with all these little painted houses and shops. All these attractive, well-fed young people. Like walking, talking snack bags just waiting for a straw."

Spike lifted his arms over his head and stretched, enjoying the fatigue that inched along the muscles, the tingling that still crawled across the surface of his skin. He felt *fine,* he did, hadn't felt this good since the lovely Drusilla had graced him with her perpetually twisted presence. "It'll do," he said. "For easy pickings, it's hard to beat. I've been here awhile, left and came back—I suppose it's as close to home as I'll likely ever get." He decided it would be better to leave out the part about how he figured staying around would give him a better chance of getting the Initiative's bloody chip out of his head someday.

Celina's expression was amused, as if she knew damned well he was holding out on her. "You make it sound so very bland, Spike. The word in the world is that there is a Hellmouth here. And the Slayer."

He shrugged, suddenly uneasy. "It is where it is," he said. "I don't tune in much to what the humans are babbling about. I figure they don't live long enough to where it matters much anyway."

Celina ran a hand down his chest, her cool fingers making him shiver, though certainly not from the cold. "Don't worry, baby. I know you hang around with Buffy Summers and her groupies. Hey, a guy's gotta do what he's gotta do to stay alive in a Slayer-infested situation, you know? I understand."

Spike ground his teeth to stop himself from spilling the whole sordid story of the blasted electronic zinger that had been planted inside his skull. It wasn't his fault, but would she think less of him if she knew? Would she think he wasn't as much of a man? He'd just proven all to the contrary, but he'd never been able to figure out the working of the female mind. It was all so *unfair*—

"So tell me about the Slayer," Celina said, nicely derailing his entire string of self-centered thoughts. "What she's like. Her strengths, weaknesses."

"Why would you care?" he asked warily. "Don't tell me you're daft enough to go looking for her again."

"Of course not. I'm just curious, that's all." But even as she continued, Celina's voice sounded just a little too smooth, as though every line was carefully rehearsed. "She's quite the fuel for the story mill—long-lived, something about a vampire boyfriend. They say she once even came back from the dead."

"That was just a fluke," Spike muttered. He'd been doing pretty nicely, except for occasional cautious info-seeking questions on his past, he'd had no thoughts of the Slayerdom type at all, thank you very much. He'd never expected the tomb romp, but why not. Here he was, putting his unlife on the line for the Slayer and all she did was moon over Angel. Now all his good tingly feeelings were gone, and he wished they'd come back. Couldn't they just turn the clock back to where they'd been ten minutes ago? They'd been having a damned sight more fun then, that's for sure.

"Really." The beautiful vampire glanced sideways at him. "Say, all that boyfriend talk—the lucky guy wouldn't be you, would it?"

"Not in this lifetime," Spike answered. How was his acting holding up here? The words were more than a little true, and he hoped they didn't sound as bitter as he felt inside. "And I've been dead just a few years longer than the Slayer's been doing the daily inhale-exhale."

"Well," Celina said, "I'd always heard it was a tall-dark-and-handsome, but you know what happens when the legends pass from person to person. It could just as easily have been a tall-blond-and-handsome." She slid her fingers into his hair, and he felt her nails lightly scrape his scalp. More shivers, this time all the way down to his toes and back. It made him want to purr like a contented cat.

Spike grinned. "Let's not talk about boring things like slayers," he said, rolling on his side until he was facing her. "I can think of a whole sight more interesting things to do."

She smiled, showing fine white teeth against pale lips. "I bet you can." She laughed, flicking the cigarette into the dirt and reaching for him. "I just *bet!*"

And eventually the candles fizzled out in spent pools of wax, and the two of them rested, entwined, in the safe darkness of Spike's tomb.

Celina was already dressed and waiting when Spike woke from his post-hanky-panky nap.

It was still dark, a good hour or so before sunrise. Being older gave her that edge, a sense of timing that came in oh-so-handy at certain times, like now, when she needed to have a bit of an advantage over someone of her own kind. Besides, when she did stuff like this, well . . . it was really fun to stand back and watch the fireworks.

The blond vampire smiled a little before opening his eyes, that familiar sort of lazy, satisfied grin that she'd had herself this morning when she'd first slipped out of sleep's embrace. He really was a handsome devil—she just loved tall, lean blonds, and he was definitely built right. Nice eyes, too. The problem was going to happen when he decided to stretch, which he did right now—

—and found himself tied spread-eagle to his own bed.

His would-be luxurious stretch found itself severely curtailed, and Spike's slow and easy awakening went to Instant On mode. His eyes snapped open at the same time the muscles in his biceps and chest strained forward, all to no avail, of course. The centuries—and a few months masquerading as a night-shift crewman on a massive whaling vessel—had also taught Celina how to tie really good knots.

"What the bloody hell is *this?*" Spike's gaze found her standing calmly at the side of the bed, and he relaxed. "Love, if you wanted to play this game, you could've at least warned me. I've got silk scarves somewhere around here that would feel a whole lot better than these rough things." He lifted his head and glanced irritably at the ropes wound securely around his wrists and ankles. "Rope's a bit on the tight side, wouldn't you say?"

Celina only looked at him. "Let's see. You're not dressed, Spike. You're tied up. I'm dressed. I'm not tied up. Do I really need to give you a crib sheet for Logic 101?"

This time his thrashing was a little more enthusiastic and punctuated by growls of aggravation. Celina couldn't help but grin when Spike morphed to vampire-face, found the increase in strength didn't do any good, and morphed back. Too sad.

"Your sense of humor needs an injection of reality," he spat. "This isn't exactly *Saturday Night Live* funny, you know."

"Oh, I think it's very humorous." She dragged a chair over and sat where she could face him. "I mean, think about it. For thousands of years, men have been using women and discarding them, thinking they're the weaker sex. Turned the tables a bit on you tonight, didn't I?"

"You sound like that ex-demon who hangs with the Slayer's grand little bunch," Spike said. "Anya. Had I known you were on a crusade, I would've kept my distance. As in stayed in another bloody *county.*"

"Anya is a former demon? I *knew* there was something off about her." She grinned at him, dismissing the notion. "We all have our crusades, Spike. Some of us are fortunate enough to live long and keep on fighting them."

On the bed Spike became very still. "I know I'm going to regret asking this, but what's that supposed to mean?"

Celina shrugged. "I thought it was obvious—I'm going to kill you, of course."

Spike's eyes widened. "Hey, now don't go all Black Widowy on me—"

"Little late for you to figure that out, dear." She looked at her nails. "Hmmmm. Conscious . . . or unconscious?" Then she answered her own question. "Definitely conscious. That's so much more fun. I just can't decide whether to do it now or later."

"Later," he said hastily. "Definitely later."

"I'm not so sure." She studied him. "The bigger question is whether the benefits of letting you live a few hours longer outweigh the risks. There's that whole might-escape thing, but on the other hand I might need more information about your Slayer and her friends. Your usefulness might still be in the unused realm. Hmmmm . . . decisions, decisions."

"I have a lot of potential," Spike said.

"So you claim." She looked doubtful.

"And I did show you a damned fine time last night," he reminded her. "You can't say otherwise. That ought to at least be worth a couple extra hours of existence."

Celina didn't say anything for a long moment, just scraped the tips of her fingernails along the sheets. The *scritch, scritch, scritch* sound made Spike wince, but of course he was powerless to stop her and he didn't dare complain. "All right," she finally agreed. "I'll let you live . . . for now. But you're staying right there on the bed." She stood.

"You can't just leave me like this," Spike protested.

She shook her head. "Yes I can. You'll just have to wait."

"Well, at least have the bloody decency to cover me up! What if someone walks in and sees me like this?"

She gave him a wide wicked grin and flicked a finger under his chin. "Ever heard the expression 'boytoy,' Spikey?"

And, laughing outright, Celina left Spike tied securely to his own bed while she went out into the last of the Sunnydale night hours to start the wheels turning and take care of this slayer problem.

Chapter 10

Xander had already gotten up, showered, and left for work by the time Anya finally paid attention to the annoyingly insistent snooze button on her alarm clock. Even so, it was dark outside, with still a good half hour to go before sunrise. Usually she'd get up with him, but this morning he'd wanted to get a particularly early start, was determined to finish the fence in front of the hobby store and start on his next job. What was that again? Oh, that's right—something that Xander was calling Mrs. Wedgeman's Emergency Greenhouse Effect, the latest efforts of the rich but eccentric elderly lady on Argyle Street. This time it seemed she wanted Xander to make her a small building with lots of windows and shelves for her plants, which she'd suddenly decided were putting too much oxygen into her seventeen-room house and therefore making her dizzy.

While this one was a funny job, Anya had to admit that Xander, once he'd discovered his skills with wood and carpenter's tools, had never lacked for work. She felt secure with him, well-cared for, but not just in the material world. Her emotional world was pretty darned good, too—she even understood Xander's little comment about how people sometimes said things just to make you feel good. That didn't mean she was going to make any huge changes in her own vocal announcements, thank you very much, but life was considerably shorter for mortals, and so it made sense that some of them, the more pleasant ones, might try to make the day-to-day passings of someone else a bit more enjoyable.

Like Xander did for her.

Actually, he made things very enjoyable for her . . . her existence was considerably brighter and fuller than it had been when she had been Anyanka. She even had sex, and let's face it, that was something that had been in short supply as a vengeance demon—for some reason, guys had lost their inclination to Hokey Poke long about the time she'd started turning ex-boyfriends and unfaithful lovers into legless frogs and sacrificial straw scarecrows for burning. She didn't understand what the problem had been—after all, she'd never done anything to a man who didn't deserve it—but men were typical and pack-ratty and they liked to stick together.

Having seen D'Hoffryn so recently, this time Anya was a little more in tune with his aura of darkness, and she felt the buildup when he was materializing on this plane. She had the briefest of seconds to wonder why he didn't simply pull her down to his level, then he was there, his big old smelly self in her bright, clean kitchen, and poking around in her cabinets. And there was her answer—he'd come to her because he was nosey about the way she lived, pure and simple. Demon, human—

wasn't it just so typical of a male to go digging through stuff that he had no business messing with?

"Stop that," she said sharply when he opened a cabinet and reached for a jar of pine nuts inside. "Those are expensive."

He ignored her and folded his dark fingers around the jar. "What does it matter anyway?" He sounded conceited, overconfident. Man, Anya still hated that tone of voice, the one that implied *I'm so sure of what you're thinking I'll just save you the trouble of saying it yourself.* Had D'Hoffryn once been a human male? He certainly acted like it. "You'll have no need of any of these earthly items when you return to your demonhood."

Anya reached forward and snatched the jar out of his fingers before he could get a good grip on it. She set it out of his reach on the counter, then folded her arms and faced him. "My answer is no."

For a second D'Hoffryn stood there and smiled at her, as if things didn't quite compute. Then his smiled faded when what she had said finally made it through his thick and pointy demon skull. "What?"

"No. I've decided that I'm going to remain mortal."

The pine nuts forgotten, D'Hoffryn drew himself up to his full height and glowered at her. "What are you talking about, Anyanka?"

"My name isn't Anyanka anymore," she said firmly. "It's *Anya.* And I know there's nothing wrong with your ears, except that maybe you haven't washed them in five or six hundred years."

Now D'Hoffryn's expression melted into incredulity. "You would choose life as a mere mortal over what I've offered? Eternal life, power—"

"Yes."

D'Hoffryn shook his horned head. "I don't understand you. First you're a human, then a demon, then a human who wanted nothing more than to regain demonic status. What is it that holds you fast within the mortal dimension?"

Anya decided to keep it simple. "I like it here." She had no desire to get into a heart-to-heart with her ex-boss.

D'Hoffryn's eyes glowed momentarily. "You will die like a bug," he said darkly. "Crushed beneath the inevitable boot heel of time."

"I can deal."

And—

Poof!

The demon from the alley was skulking around outside the back entrance to the Catbox, having apparently been barred from the place again. Who knew what he was hoping to score—maybe someone to bring him out a drink, though Celina had heard about that noxious mess from Spike and doubted the bartender would make them anymore. His back was to her while he scanned the alleyway in the other direction and looked for targets; the fool's inattentiveness to watching his own back made it easy to become just what he hoping to find.

Celina hit him so hard he slammed into the wall, leaving a nasty nose print of greasy greenish blood on the brickwork. He gasped and went down, then tried to turn and see who had attacked him. He got his face sideways but no farther; the side of it was the perfect place for Celina to grind the heel of her boot. "I hear you've got a case of runny mouth," she said and pressed harder with her foot. "Give me one good reason why I shouldn't put a permanent end to your overly noisy and foul fish-breath right now."

Whatever he said in response was lost in a mumble

because most of his mouth and nose was pressed against the dirty ground. She let up slightly, and he tried again; a loose translation of the garbled words could have been "Because I can be useful."

"I don't see how," Celina retorted, but actually she did—in fact, she already had grand plans for this little piece of dead sea-sucker.

"But I can d-do stuff!" he managed to choke out. "Run errands—I can take your dry cleaning in, walk your dog, even get roadkill for the mutt—"

"Like I would let you so much as touch my clothes. And I don't have a dog."

"Your fish, then! I could feed them for you!"

"What, you think I've got seaweed on the brain?" she demanded. "Even if I *had* fish, you'd probably eat them."

"No—"

"Shut up." She punctuated the order by again pressing her weight on the foot holding him down. "I *am* going to let your smelly little self continue to share space on this planet, but only because you might, *might,* be able to accomplish something for me. I'm going to give you a job to do, and you're going to have it completed by twilight tonight. If you don't, I'm going to give you a firsthand demonstration of how they make sushi . . . though in your case, it's more like spoiled meat and fish tartare. Got it?" Celina pulled her foot back and allowed the stumpy little creature to haul himself upright.

He looked at her resentfully as he wobbled upward and brushed at his pants. "I just washed these clothes, you know. If you'd wanted to talk business, we could have done it in a civilized manner."

"You are not civilized," she said flatly. "You're a fish demon."

He glared at her. "I'm intelligent, I got a brain! And I

don't work for free, no matter what you think—I got a right to be paid for my efforts!"

"You're right, of course." Celina gave him an understanding smile. "Your payment for services rendered will be the absence of death." Before the words could register, she had reached forward with one hand and dug her fingers around the lumpy parts in the center of his throat—two windpipes, one for each modified gill—and was tugging none too gently. "Did you know that it only takes five pounds of pressure to rip off the human ear?" she asked. "I'm thinking it's a lot less to rip out the windpipes of a slimy sea-scum demon."

He gagged and she let him go with a hard shove backward. He hit the wall and slid down to a squat, rubbing his throat and looking at her with frightened eyes. "Jeez, you're serious!"

"As a stake." She frowned at him. "I'm starting to think I'll have to break something of yours to show you just how much I mean what I'm saying. Can you breathe with only one gill, or will it kill you if I mangle it?"

"No, no!" He scrambled to his feet. "I get the message, really! Just tell me what you want me to do."

Celina smiled widely. "Cooperation—now, that's what I like to see. You must really want that extension on your miserable little earthly existence."

He shrugged but eyed her warily. "This place has its moments."

"So I keep getting told," she said. "But mostly by these pathetic humans who only value the ability to inhale because it's so easily stopped. Personally, I think life is what you make of it. Now, listen real close while I tell you what you'll need to do to make some more of yours." For effect, she pushed herself into morph mode, and the stupid little demon shuddered at the sight—all dressed up, she *was* a fearsome thing to see after all this time and experience. "And by the way," she growled around her mouthful of teeth, "let me stress the fact that you are *not* going to tell the entire underworld that you ever even talked to me. . . ."

D'Hoffryn was gone. No questions about reconsidering or an offer of a few more days for her to think it over. No second chances. Just a clot of nasty smoke that smelled like sulphur—D'Hoffryn always left that crap when he was angry—that would take hours to fade out of the air.

For a long moment Anya stood there, unmoving and silent, thinking about how terrified of the future and mortality she was, of all the things that awaited her as a mortal woman, like love and loss and perhaps even the human pain of childbirth and the possibility that some-day she might lose Xander and her own life. Still, when she inhaled it felt good—sulphur notwithstanding—human and . . . *right*. Facing her fear and doing these things . . . it would be worth it because without them, her existence would be empty and meaningless. She couldn't imagine giving up the joy and love and the *possibilities* that had come to her as a mortal woman, and for what? A life of immortality that would be geared only toward dark misery. What had D'Hoffryn told her?

"You will die like a bug."

Maybe she would, but by God, she'd be a *happy* bug. And they just didn't have those in D'Hoffryn's dimension.

Anya waved futilely at the sulphur smell, then put the jar of pine nuts back where it belonged. After that she took a shower, relishing the heat of the water and the cleansing steam, reveling in the just-washed scent of the clean clothes she donned afterward. All dressed, she couldn't resist the urge to walk through the apartment and stop at each doorway for a look around. Maybe it was a little materialistic—okay, a *lot* materialistic—but she loved this place, its bright openness, the way she and Xander had decorated it to suit their own unique combination of tastes. She liked to keep things as orderly here as she kept them at the Magic Shop, and so everything was in its place, right down to all the comic book action figures Xander had lined up across the headboard above the bed. Only one thing caught her attention as needing doing, and that was the garbage in the kitchen; she had just enough time to bundle it up before going off to work.

Anya locked the apartment and headed toward the Dumpsters in the back of the building. She struggled a bit with the lid on one, trying to lift it and heft the trash bag at the same time. It was heavy, but it finally came up—

And she nearly screamed when a demon grinned at her from inside the garbage container.

"Hey, pretty lady," the creature said. He plucked the garbage bag from her and tossed it behind him, then scrambled out of the mound of dirty plastic bags. He smelled like fish and used cat litter and a hundred other rotting things Anya couldn't bear to think about. "My name's Dunphy. What's yours?"

"None of your business," Anya snapped back. She wrinkled her nose and backed away. What kind of demon was he—some mixed-up genetic mistake between a fish demon and *der Kindestod,* or maybe *The Ugly Man?* In fact, the other part of him could even be a wet zombie—he certainly had the necessary body aroma. She wasn't as up-to-date on her demonic genealogy as she had been a few years ago. She really should pay more attention to the new breeds flowing in. "Are you insane?" she demanded. "What are you doing, crawling around in there like a . . . a *cockroach*, for Pete's sake?"

"Hey, there's some good eats in here," he protested. He held up a slab of something gray-looking that might have been a piece of someone's leftover steak . . . from four days ago. "And don't knock the roaches—they're very tasty."

"You're just disgusting. Get out of our garbage and go back to whatever abyss you crawled out of. If you don't live in the building, you can't eat in there." Anya turned to leave.

"Okay," the demon said agreeably. "I'll go. But you're going *with* me!"

And before Anya could run or protest, he had her arms twisted behind her and was dragging her quickly into the shadows between the apartment buildings.

Chapter 11

"I'VE CHECKED AT THE APARTMENT EIGHT TIMES SINCE twelve-thirty, I've left notes in every room, and when I'm not actually *there,* I've called ten times an hour since you phoned and told me she didn't show up for work," Xander told Giles. His eyes were wide with anxiety and rimmed with shadows as he paced the length of the Magic Shop from the door to the other end of the long room, his steps making frantic *clop-clop-clop* sounds. "Damn it, Giles, it's almost five o'clock. Where *is* she? My bad feeling about this is running into the super extra-large size."

Giles took off his glasses and rubbed his eyes, making an effort to at least look calm for Xander's benefit. There was good reason to be concerned, though—Anya was a stickler for detail and punctuality in work matters. Had she not roundly chewed him out for being late only yesterday? He'd never quite understood how a former demon could find such joy in money and material things, but not only had the young woman done just that, she didn't comprehend why everyone else around her couldn't, or wouldn't, exhibit the same, wholehearted devotion to those things as she did. She would *never* simply not show up for work, yet when he'd tried the door to the Magic Shop at half past nine this morning, he'd found the place still locked and dark from the previous night.

He'd made about every suggestion he could think of to Xander, called a few people on his own and asked them to keep a look-see out. At this point Giles couldn't even think of another *useless* recommendation to make, much less something that actually made sense. He was saved from the horror of having to try when Buffy and Dawn hurried through the door to the Magic Shop, followed immediately by Willow and Tara. His hopeful look, however, melted to dismay.

"Nothing," Buffy told him and Xander. "After I picked up Dawn, we checked every place I could think of and a few extras besides those. No one's seen her, no one's heard anything, no one's even speculating." She peered at Xander. "You didn't find *anything* at the apartment? Nothing messed up or broken—"

"No," Xander said. "Place is as neat as the proverbial pin. She even took out the garbage."

Willow and Tara looked at each other surreptitiously, but their exchange of glances wasn't quite quick enough to be totally private. "Hey, I recognize that look," Xander said. "It's the I-know-something-you-don't-know look that has been the bane of a million schoolyard kids." He seemed ready to explode.

Willow gave a little shrug, but it was obvious there was something going on. "It's probably nothing."

"Anya was just . . . asking some questions, is all," Tara added. "She didn't say anything specific."

"Questions?" Xander's pacing ground to a halt. "What questions?"

Willow made a hesitant face. "Well—"

"I think she was looking into demonhood again," Dawn said with complete impassiveness. "Getting her powers back and stuff."

Xander's face went white, and he was suddenly very, very still. "Anyanka?" he whispered.

"Nice going, Dawn," Buffy said reproachfully. "Remind me to sign you up for Practical Tact in Daily Life."

"What'd I say wrong?" Dawn sounded confused.

Buffy sighed. "Never mind. Xander—"

But he was slowly sinking onto one of the chairs. "But I thought that whole D'Hoffryn thing was over," he said. He looked like someone had suddenly set a four-hundred-pound weight on his shoulders. "I mean, I didn't even think she had that *option* anymore."

"I think D'Hoffryn might have come for a visit and offered Anya her powers back," Willow admitted hesitantly. "She was asking Tara and me a bunch of questions."

"What kind of questions?" Giles sat up straighter. "Did she say specifically?"

Willow shook her head. "No, and she never specifically said that she'd talked to D'Hoffryn. But she was asking stuff about why I would have turned him down and stayed a mortal when he was offering me immortality, what kept me tied to the mortal plane. Stuff like that."

"Immortality." Xander dug his hands into his hair until it stood up in tufts, then he dropped them and rested his face on his palms. *"Immortality? How the hell can I compete with that?"*

"I don't think it's a matter of competition," Giles said as he came around the counter and sat next to Xander.

Xander raised his head and glared at him. "You don't

think so? Then explain to me how it *isn't* exactly that! What can I give Anya that could be better than eternal life—one where she does *not* have to skulk around in the dark like a vampire, mind you—and she can do stuff like turn people into trolls or make them never exist to begin with?" He slammed his hands on the table. "What am I compared to *that*—just some weak little mortal who plays with wood and a hammer every day." He looked utterly miserable.

Buffy came over and put her hand on his shoulder. "Xander, don't sell yourself so short. You've done a world of things for Anya, made a huge difference for her. You need to have faith that she knows that, that she loves you enough to choose you over the darkness. You have to have faith in yourself, and in her."

"Really?" Xander asked bitterly. "If that's true, then tell me this: given that there's a really high possibility she got the job offer—with benefits—from her ex-boss . . .

"Where is she?"

Spike rolled into the Magic Shop about two hours after dark, looking like a hearse had rolled over *him*.

His hair was in fourteen different directions and his clothes were wrinkled and disheveled, as though he'd grabbed whatever was handy and hadn't thought about whether it needed washing or not. There were wide red, blue, and yellow bruises circling his wrists where they poked out of his jacket, and his eyes were wild and wary, his movements jerky.

"What the heck happened to you?" Buffy asked. "And where have you been. Anya's missing—"

"I know," the vampire interrupted. At the table Xander looked up from where he'd been staring glumly at the polished wood. Spike's next words made him literally jerk. "And I know what happened to her."

Xander was on Spike before he had time to so much as blink, much less put up his hands in self-defense. "Where is she?" Xander demanded. "Is she all right?" He had a death grip on the lapels of Spike's jacket, and he started shaking the vampire. Clearly already worked-over, Spike bounced back and forth in Xander's hold like a life-size rag doll. "You tell me where she is, or I'll shake every vampire bone out of your body and re-assemble them into an ugly piece of abstract sculpture!"

"Xander, get a grip on yourself!" Giles pushed himself between the two men, knocking Xander's hands aside. "Give him a chance to speak!"

Spike staggered against the counter and gave a shake of his head, as if he were trying to clear his thoughts. "I don't rightly know where she is—all I said was that I knew what *happened* to her."

Xander and the others stared at him, unable to keep from thinking the worst. Vampire attack? Or had she accepted D'Hoffryn's offer and was already channeling the frustrated rage of being mortal for the last couple of years into nasty spells of retribution against foolish and unfortunate men?

"Is she . . . is she alive?" Xander finally managed. He figured that ought to tell him everything he needed to know.

Spike's expression was mildly shocked. "Of course she's alive, you blithering fool."

Xander slumped onto his chair, relieved. "Great," he sighed.

Spike tilted his head, clearly not following. "Demon girl might not think it's so great, being kidnapped by the catch of the day."

"What?" Xander leaped out of his chair like he'd taken a shot of electricity right in the butt.

"Whoa—down, boy." Spike backpedaled just as Giles stepped between Xander and the vampire for the second time. "I'll be happy to tell all of you everything I know if you'll just stop shaking my brains out every time I try to open my mouth!"

"You have brains?" Buffy asked innocently.

Spike scowled at her. "Enough to save your little blonde head a number of times, love."

"Now isn't the time to argue," Giles reminded them. "Spike, you'd be well advised to tell us where Anya is before Xander keeps his promise about taking you apart."

"I keep *telling* you, I don't *know* where she is. Only what happened."

Buffy reached over and propelled the vampire none too gently toward a chair. "Then that would be a excellent place to start."

Spike rearranged himself on the chair until he was in his customary slouch, then crossed his feet. "Okay, here's what went down. Our little once-upon-a-demon is currently in the possession of that babe you've been trying so hard to find. It seems she's gotten it into her head that there'll be some kind of trade."

Buffy lifted one eyebrow. "Trade?"

"You for Anya."

"Why did I know *that* was coming?" The Slayer folded her arms. "All right, where exactly is Celina?"

"I don't rightly know that," Spike said honestly. "She said be at the main graveyard at midnight." He shot Xander a pointed glance. "I'm sure I don't have to go into detail about what she said she would do to Xander's much-better half if you don't show."

"Oh, I'll show, all right." Buffy looked grim. "This

woman has gone over her annoyance allotment. It's way past time for her to be disassembled."

"Buffy, she's extremely dangerous," Giles reminded her. "We still don't know very much about her—"

"I'd wager she's Greek," Spike suddenly said.

They all turned to stare at him. "And you based this theory on what, exactly?" Giles asked.

"It's her accent," Spike explained. "We were talking, and I asked her about it. I think she answered without thinking—she looked a bit perturbed about that bit of info slipping out, mind you."

"Wait," Willow said. She leaned toward Spike and studied him. "You were *talking?* And you know she took Anya, and you even know what she wants to give Anya back." She frowned and made a little wrinkling movement with her nose. "Does anyone besides me smell a rat here?"

"Yeah," Xander said. "A *dead* one." He lunged for Spike, but this time it was Buffy who slipped in and saved the vampire's hide. "What were you doing, Spike?" Xander demanded over Buffy's shoulder. "Playing it a little too far under the covers? If Anya gets hurt because of you, I'll—"

"Oh, you've made it quite clear what you *think* you're going to do," Spike sneered.

"This isn't *funny,* Spike!" The vampire yelped when Buffy let go of Xander, then cracked Spike across the top of his head.

"Ow—*hey!*"

"I think you'd better fill in a few blank spots," Giles said. His voice was quiet, but there was a rigid undercurrent to it. "How you know all this to begin with might be crucial to your well-being."

When Spike hesitated, Buffy took a menacing step toward him. "All right, all right!" He glared at her. "So I met up with her in a bar, all right? Wasn't any big deal, just kind of a . . . a . . ."

"Pickup?" Tara asked. When they all looked surprised that she'd suggested that, her cheeks reddened.

"Yeah, so what," Spike said resentfully. "You think because I'm a vampire I don't like a bit of comfort now and again?"

"Please let's not go into your sex life," Buffy said. "I don't think we need *that* much detail."

"But then you'll miss the best part," Spike said archly. He looked rather proud of himself, a tad too eager to share the details.

"I can do without a play-by-play of 'Night of the Dead Boys,' " Xander said.

"I second that," Willow added.

Spike made a *hmphing* noise in his throat. "Fine, then."

"I'm sure we can all intelligently guess what happened right after you and Celina met in the bar," Giles told him. "But I rather think you should pick back up on the story when you woke up the night after. An explanation of how Anya got into this picture seems well advised."

Spike's expression slid into reluctance. "She, uh, told me to tell you," he said.

"But that doesn't make sense," Willow said. "The timing doesn't fly—"

"All right!" Spike exploded. "If you *must* know, I woke up an hour before dawn and the bloody bitch had me trussed up like a pot roast!"

For a moment they were all silent.

"Uh . . ." Xander began.

"She left me like that," Spike continued crankily. "All *day*. I was so stiff by the time she came back this evening, I could barely move my legs."

"Where did she go in the meantime?" Buffy asked.

Spike rolled his eyes. "I'm sorry, am I on replay here? I don't *know*. What I do know is that when she came back, she untied me and told me to tell *you* to be at the graveyard if you ever wanted to see Anya alive again."

Xander made a small unhappy sound. "Oh, *man*."

"Don't worry, Xander," Buffy said firmly. "We'll get her back."

"That's assuming the woman hasn't already whacked her," Spike said with all the tactfulness of a garbage truck. "She's pretty bloody vicious."

"Shut up," Buffy snapped.

"Fine," Spike said again. "That's all right, use me and then shove me off. I'm used to it."

"I'll bet." Buffy ignored his angry glance, then looked thoughtful. "You said you think she's Greek?"

"First you want me to shut up, now you want me to talk," Spike complained. "Which is it?"

Buffy gave him a sugary smile. "How about if I pull your vocal cords out and see if the answer I want is written on them?"

"Definitely Greek," Spike replied. "Plus I've seen her before—"

Giles's eyes widened. "You have?"

"Boy," Willow said. "She sure gets around, doesn't she?"

"Yeah," Spike said. "Her name was Callia then."

"When?" Giles asked eagerly. "When was this? Recently? Or—"

"I can't rightly recall the exact date," Spike told the former librarian. "Late eighteen-hundreds, I think. It was in a saloon."

"There's that bar thing again," Willow noted.

Spike made a face at her. "As I was *saying*, we met in a saloon. I knew she was a vampire the second I saw her, but I thought she was a right beautiful lady. Thought I might get myself a bit of company, but she was in quite a temper that night. Ended up running for my damned life."

"So why didn't she kill you this time?" Buffy's eyes narrowed. "Could it be because you were a good information source?"

The vampire sat up straight. "Absolutely *not!* Besides, what would I tell her that she doesn't already know?" He waved a hand at the Magic Shop. "Obviously she already knows about this place—it's where she first put the boogey-boogey into Anya. She—"

"And she knew about the connection between Anya and Buffy how?" Xander's face was dark. "It couldn't be because you've got that whole leakiness of the mouth going, could it?"

Spike managed to look insulted and puzzled at the same time. "Well, I don't *think* I mentioned anything. If I did, I swear it wasn't on purpose—"

"Never mind," Buffy interrupted. "How she made a connection between Anya and me isn't the issue anymore. What counts is that now she has Anya and we need to get her back."

"True," Giles agreed. "As much as I dislike agreeing with Spike, Celina did already know about the shop and Anya. One of the first things she did was ask Anya how to find Buffy."

"If she's been hanging out at the same skanky bars as Spike, she probably heard news of it in the rumor mill," Willow said.

Spike lifted his chin. "Well, it's not like we vampires have a lot of choices to socialize in, you know. Now, if they had a members-only club, maybe there would be a little more class involved—"

"The only members-only club you're going to get into is the one headed by Mr. Pointy," Buffy told him.

"What did I do?" Spike demanded. "A guy comes here with information, trying to help out, and all he gets is grief!"

"You get out of life what you put into it," Tara said gently. "Maybe that applies to unlife, too."

"I can do without philosophy from the butterfly gallery, thank you very much," Spike grumbled.

"Enough sniping at each other," Buffy said. "Celina wants something, and I want something. She'll get her fight, and I'll get Anya back. We're both going to get satisfaction. And it ends tonight."

"We still have a bit of time to prepare," Giles said. "Let me dig a little into the records. At least now we've got a reference point; if this woman is indeed Greek, that certainly narrows the focal point of the search."

"Just a little," Willow commented with a grin.

"Actually, I've just realized something." Giles hurried over to the counter and began pulling out older volumes of Watcher history from behind it, opening each and quickly flipping through until he found pages he'd marked over the last couple of days. "There are references throughout the centuries to female vampires with names that are all similar to Celina's," he told them. "All of whom escaped, and I believe if we research the extraction, all those names appeared to be based in the Grecian language."

Willow rose and went to study the books with him. "You think it's the same one?"

"Perhaps. Look here." Giles shuffled books until the oldest and most battered of the volumes was on top. "The stories run for centuries, but if you trace them backward, they make quite the history." He pushed up his glasses. "A vicious vampire named Calida in Salem, another named Caterina in Italy, Catalina in Spain, Christine in medieval London, the United States, several times where both Angel and Spike could have crossed paths with her."

"But where did she *come* from?" Tara asked. Her eyes were wide. "If she's that old, and they've been watching her all this time, don't they know where she started?"

Giles frowned, concentrating on the lineage he was scrawling down on a piece of lined yellow paper. "None of these references indicates that they do. We have to bear in mind, however, that these entries were made by different Watchers from a hodgepodge of countries around the world, with decades of time passing between each. No one may have ever made a connection before. If this *is* the same vampire, it appears that she felt it was necessary to hide her identity."

"But why?" Xander sat forward. "I mean, she's dead already, so it's not like she needs to worry about someone trying to kill her. As long as she stays out of the range of the current Slayer, she would have felt snug as a bedbug, wouldn't she?"

Giles nodded. "You would think so, but no matter where she's been—again assuming it's the same vampire—she's always chosen a Greek-based name. There are stories of her being everywhere from Portugal to Brazil to North America, but Greek seems to be what she likes best."

Willow came around and flicked the mouse on the computer, then began typing rapidly enough to make the keyboard shake. "Let's see what an Internet search comes up with given all this new info," she said. "Maybe we can work a little faster than going through page by page and trying to read faded handwriting in foreign languages."

"These books are very valuable," Giles said indignantly.

"Of course they are." Willow's voice was soothing. "But they don't have Web-range. That's what we're aiming for here." She kept typing as the rest of the gang, Spike included, crowded around the monitor. "Let's start by working backward. Buffy, you said Angel ran into her in the sixties, right?

"Yeah. He said she killed so many people in that town that they thought she was a serial killer." She looked thoughtful. "He didn't say what town it was, though."

"Hmmmmm." She concentrated on her work for a few seconds, then added a series of double clicks with the mouse. "Wait—here. It was in Mullen, Nebraska."

Xander squinted at the screen. "There can't possibly be a town named Mullen."

"There sure is," Willow told him. "Although population-wise, it's doing a fairly fast fade."

"Why do you say that?" Giles asked.

"According to the census statistics, the whole Hooker County population was 1,130 in 1960—"

Xander shook his head in disgust. "Hooker? Don't those people out there have any stretch to their imagination?"

"—*and,*" Willow continued after giving Xander an annoyed look, "it had dropped to 793 in 1990. But check this out." She pointed at the computer monitor. "The 1999 figures on the *National Geographic* site give the population of Mullen alone as 479."

"So the town itself is likely dying." Giles looked pained.

"One can only hope so," Buffy said darkly. No one had to wonder at the meaning behind her words.

"Here," Willow said. "There are newspaper references to that 'Drifter Killer' thing Angel was talking about, says the person was never caught—that might be the best they came up with if she disappeared after they'd thought they killed her. Let's see what happens if I cross-index that with a search for murders in one location, say . . . more than six, over the next forty years—here. A list of cases, almost all unsolved." Her eyes widened. "Say, look at this—there are a whole bunch of entries about a female suspect who was caught and arrested, but who subsequently escaped and was never reapprehended."

Tara frowned. "And they never noticed the connection?"

Willow shrugged. "Different dates, different towns, a few bigger cities all spread out across the Midwest. Computers have been around, but figure it's really not until the early nineties that the Internet truly exploded onto the scene and everything finally went all information-sharing."

"What are the dates?" Buffy asked.

Willow scanned the screen. "Pretty recognizable, actually . . . if you know you're looking for it. If this is our girl, she'd go on a spree somewhere, take out anywhere from six to maybe fourteen people, then drop out of sight—or escape, depending—for a couple of years."

"Any pictures?" Spike asked. He'd pulled a chair away from the others and was lounging in his customary slouched position. "According to my books, this elusive vampire did *not* like having her photo taken. So you're assuming a lot without visual evidence. It could be a totally different lady of the night."

"Well, let's find out." Willow's fingers zipped over the keyboard. "Bull's-eye—she might not like it, but occsionally she didn't have a choice. Here's a couple, in your basic police-mug quality."

Spike pulled himself up. "Okay. Let's see if we're

talking one and the same." He leaned over Willow's shoulder, then gave a sly grin when he saw the on-screen photo of a smirking but pretty young woman with coal black hair cut in a dated, chin-length pageboy style. "Oh, yeah, different hair but that's her." He gave them a sweeping, overly smug glance. "She looks better now."

Willow double-clicked on the mouse. "How about this one?"

"Yep, her again."

"And this one?"

"Ditto."

Willow took her hands off the keyboard. "I think it's pretty clear how she's been living. Or unliving."

"But who *is* she, really?" asked Buffy. "See if you can go back a lot farther."

"That's the next step." Willow bent to work again. "Let's see—I'll broaden the search to a global, although I don't know how well it'll work. It depends a lot on the record keeping of the local cop shops in the individual countries. Still, a lot of them are making up for lost time and inputting the older stuff in their files. It's just a matter of whether or not they look at it and think it's worth including."

Giles made a *hmphing* noise in his throat. "If you ask me, there's no need to 'input' what's in a good book. I say—"

"Jackpot," Willow interrupted. "Giles, here's that reference you found to Poland in the 1950s, when she was using the name Catia."

"Don't forget that she went by the name Callia in the eighteen hundreds," Spike put in.

"I haven't forgotten anything," Willow said, a bit sharply. "Before that . . . let me see." More clicking and mouse work, and Willow's frowned deepened as she stared at the screen. It was obvious the hunt wasn't an easy one. "Here's something that might hook in. It's a reference to a demon woman who appeared in a Malaysian village in the early eighteenth century. Apparently it's become a legend now—that's why they recorded it. They say at first she was normal. She befriended the local martial arts masters and studied under them until she became as proficient as the men in the village." Willow raised her gaze to Buffy's. "Then she killed them all."

Buffy rubbed her knuckles thoughtfully. "Does it say what she studied? Celina mentioned something, but I don't remember what it was."

Willow frowned at the screen again, dragging the scroll bar in a blur. "Pen . . . cat see-lat," she said, trying to sound it out. "I know I'm mangling that."

"You're close enough." Buffy looked a bit pained at the memory. "That's it."

"Sorry to break into your bad recall time, Buf, but time's a-wasting, and Anya's still unaccounted for." Xander's face was strained.

"Right," Willow agreed. "Let see, what else." She was silent for a time as the rest of them waited, but her expression just turned more grim as the minutes passed. "There really isn't much—the farther back you go, the skimpier the info. A couple of other things in the legendary realm, references to a female demon or vampire who slaughtered dozens before disappearing, but the descriptions are all different."

"Does she have to hit you on top the head with a bottle of hair dye to clear up that one?" Spike asked smartly. "If she took a notion to shave it all off and hide under a burlap robe, she could probably blend in with the best of the Buddhist monks."

"True," Willow said, too focused on what she was doing to bother retorting. She hesitated, then began typing faster. "I can trace her, I *think,* all the way back to about the middle fifteen hundreds. Maybe the Council files have something useful around that time period—"

Alarmed, Giles straightened. "What? Wait—you can't be puttering about in there any old time, you know. How did you get the password in the first place?"

Willow shot him a patient look out of the corner of her eye. "Relax, Giles. I swear I'm not going to sell the home addresses of all the Council members on eBay."

"Probably get it bid up to a pretty penny, if you do," Spike said with a sneer.

"Willow," Giles began. "I don't think—"

"Here we go," Willow said, cutting him off. "It says right here—*oh!*"

"What?" His complaint derailed, Giles moved up to stand next to her. "What did you find? Something more interesting?"

"A little more than that, I think." Willow sounded like she was trying to talk around something big and nasty that had gotten into her throat. "I got in there and searched the Council archives, then I cross-indexed it with Greek history files because you said all the names were based in Greek." Her eyes were huge as her gaze found first Giles, then stopped on Buffy. "I don't think Celina is just a vampire who's lived a long and happily murderous life. I think she's a *lot* more than that."

"What else could she be?" asked the Watcher. "A demon, perhaps? Some sort of cross between that and a vampire?"

Willow swallowed, then stood and gave the chair to Giles so he could get in close enough to take over. He slid onto the seat and skimmed what he saw on the screen, then gasped. Finally he read it out loud, his voice becoming deeper and more horror-filled as he continued and his mind made the logic leap from history to the present.

"According to the Council's microfilm files, 'The Watcher in Greece, 1527 A.D. reported that her charge, the Vampire Slayer Cassia Marsilka, left her quarters without reporting to her Watcher. She never returned and a new slayer was called; hence Cassia Marsilka was assumed to have died a mortal's death. The records were marked to record it as such.' "

For a long moment no one in the room said anything. Xander's voice was the first to break the shocked soundlock. "Please rewind and tell me you're not saying that my girlfriend's been abducted by a vampire slayer . . . *vampire*." He looked from Giles to Buffy and then to Spike. "You spent time with her—you boffed her, for crying out loud. She wasn't like that. Was she?" He sounded totally desperate.

Spike's expression was anything but comforting. In fact, the blond vampire looking immensely pleased with himself. "I knew she wasn't your normal bloodsucker floozy," he said haughtily. "I always pick them better than that."

"Spike, *shut up*," Willow said. Her mouth was a thin slash across her face. "Do you think she really *was* that—the undead version of a vampire slayer?"

Spike glared at her. "I thought you just told me to shut up."

"Spike, I'm warning you—"

"Don't bother interrogating him," Giles said wearily. "I think we all know the answer. The young woman who's wreaking havoc in our lives was once known as Cassia the Vampire Slayer."

Chapter 12

The coast of Greece—1527 A.D.

THE SUMMER BREEZE OFF THE SARONIKÓS GULF WAS WARM and sultry, heavy with the scent of salty water. Moonlight streamed from between the sporadic clumps of moisture-heavy clouds high above the water, making the waves sparkle for as far as Cassia Marsilka could see. The vista before her seemed endless, full of possibilities far beyond the scents of the fishing vessels carried on the winds that swirled up from the village. It could be so cleansing, that wind, washing away the smells that man always seemed to bring with him—cooking, waste, the need to bathe, even the more welcome scents of perfumed oils and sugar-coated figs. But there were other things that the ocean drafts couldn't mask, like the stench of death and decay, of an evil still unburied from centuries ago.

She knew the beast was behind her even before he spoke.

"You are even more beautiful than they say."

She turned slowly, standing straight and without fear. She knew that she was tall for a woman, built slender and strong by good lineage and a wealthy family that never wanted for food or medicines. She knew what the creature looking at her from a few meters away saw, could see his desire flame in his golden-flecked hazel eyes as his gaze touched on her brown eyes and flawless, ivory skin, the raven curls that spilled midway down her back. The breeze gusted again, molding her simple linen tunic against her figure; despite the distance separating the two of them, Cassia saw his nostrils flare like a wolf's. The sight of the short sword at her waist didn't appear to bother him at all, and despite herself, she admired that simple acceptance of her strength and her womanhood.

She was curious. "They?"

One never knew when the sea might bring a heavier cloud cover to obscure the starshine and moonlight, and to ensure she didn't face tonight's foe in near darkness, Cassia had built a small fire at dusk. Still in his human form, the vampire stepped a bit closer to the rocks surrounding the fire, and if a woman cared for Romans, she supposed he might be considered quite handsome. Above a soldier's strong build he had thick dark hair and a comely appearance; his slightly off-color eyes were large and wide-set in a rugged face. He was even bathed and wore clean, expensive garments in the style of the English Court.

To Cassia he still smelled dead.

"People in my circles speak of you with awe," he said. "Cassia the Vampire Slayer is indeed a woman to be feared."

"Your circles?" Cassia made no effort to hide her sneer. "More of the undead, no doubt."

He shrugged. "You were expecting what? Christian priests, perhaps?" When she said nothing, he continued. "I am Cyrus the Gladiator. I fought under the command of the Emperor Trajan nearly fourteen hundred years ago, and I have continued to fight over the centuries since." His gaze locked with hers. "No matter how tall the tales about you may reach, you have neither the experience nor skill to defeat me, Slayer."

Cassia laughed. "Is that why you seek me, then? Because you believe you can best me? A coward's play."

Cyrus smiled faintly. "I have been many things in my life, Cassia, but I have never been a coward."

"No?" she demanded. "Why else would a mighty gladiator challenge an unworthy opponent except that he might live to see the dawn—or dusk—of another day?"

The dark-haired vampire took a long step closer, drawing in a false breath so that he could speak. "To ask you to join me, Cassia. I seek a companion, someone worthy to be at my side."

For a moment his words didn't register, then Cassia laughed outright. "You must be mad—a vampire and a slayer? Such a thing could never be."

Cyrus shook his head. "No, not simply that. A vampire and a slayer . . . vampire."

She stared at him, suddenly nearly too enraged to speak. "I will kill you for even suggesting that," she finally managed. "How dare you even think I would agree to such a thing?"

His mouth twisted into a sly smile. "You answer in haste, Cassia. Perhaps you should look inside yourself first, examine the darkness that lies within."

"There is no darkness within me," she snapped. "You talk of things you wish for, but which will never exist in the real world."

"If you are so sure of that, then why do you even listen to my words?"

Below the pleats of her tunic, Cassia's fingers closed confidently around her stake, and she gave Cyrus the Gladiator a slow smile. "Because while it may have been so many centuries ago, at one time you were once a man. It has always been my habit to allow a dying man to speak his final words."

She leaped.

He was not surprised, but he was also not quite fast enough to completely avoid her. Her stake met empty air as he turned and tried to backfist her, but like him, Cassia was not where he expected. His blow caught her on the back of the shoulder blade, resulting in little besides a harmless if slightly painful thump. She drew her sword with her left hand and blocked a downside swing of Cyrus's heavy blade, one that might have taken her arm off at the elbow. She tried to hook his wrist with the pommel of her sword and snake her arm around his, but the gladiator was too quick— he bent his elbow and dropped back before she could disarm him.

Their blades met again and again, metal against metal throwing up sparks in the darkness, the sounds of the battle sending the night-birds screaming from their roosts in the trees and bushes at the edge of the cliff overlooking the shore. For every step he would gain, Cassia made him retreat two; for every bone-shuddering punch or kick she took to dodge the cutting edge of his sword, she gave three. For all his age and strength, Cassia could feel him tiring, could catch the growing sluggishness of his blade strokes and take advantage of them. Fourteen hundred years old and experienced he might be, but he was, after all, still just a vampire.

And she was Cassia the Vampire Slayer.

A double sword-strike in an X pattern took Cyrus to one knee. Cassia struck downward with the flat of her blade from the left, then leaned to the right, intent on pounding home the wooden stake below the arm he raised as he tried to block. Her distance was off by the slightest bit so she took the tiniest of steps forward—

—and the toe of her right foot landed on a round stone and turned inward.

Her stake missed as her ankle twisted beneath her weight. The stake's tip scraped sideways along the fabric of his shirt and she lost her balance; Cyrus saw his opportunity and took it, transferring his sword to his left hand over her head and pulling her right wrist hard. Cassia fell sideways as he twisted her arm and jerked, felt the moment stretch in time as her fingers gave up their grip on the precious wood and it went rolling somewhere unseen in the pitch-dark shadows of the tall grasses.

She still had the sword, but Cyrus threw his weight forward, pinning her facedown against the ground; an instant later his left knee was crushing her wrist and the blade was useless. She started to struggle, then something cold and sharp slid between her throat and the ground—

Cyrus's sword.

The gladiator had won the day.

"A most excellent battle, Cassia," the vampire said against her ear. The air he had drawn in to speak washed back out and smelled of the grave, dry and cool, fetidly sweet. But Cassia would not let this creature feel her shudder of revulsion, would not so much as chance that he might mistake that minute movement for fear. She did not fear. She did not. "You fought well."

"You won only by chance," she ground out. The words cost her, the movement of her throat making the sword's edge slice a bit into her flesh. The sting made her breath catch and she felt blood seep from the wound to trickle down to her collarbone.

Cyrus tensed against her, then smiled. "How sweet your blood smells," he murmured. He rubbed his cheek along hers affectionately, like a dog wanting to be petted. Against her back, his weight felt oppressive, and she had never wanted anything so much in this life as to be able to shake it away. "We've had little chance to become acquainted, Slayer. You have so much to offer, so much that I've sought in a companion, in a woman, for centuries. Beauty, skill, passion—a lust for life that should not be snuffed out. This world would be a sadder place for the losing of it."

"What do you know of life?" she hissed. "If you would kill me, gladiator, then be done with it!"

Cyrus chuckled. "I know more of life than you do, child—how quickly you would throw yours away! I have seen much through the ages, lived and died, felt the pain of injury and isolation, of loneliness the span of which you can never imagine." He said nothing for a long moment, then she felt his flesh move against her face, the skin twisting as he slipped into his vampire form. The tone of his voice lowered and became more like a soft growl. "Join me, Cassia. Stay with me through eternity, and I will show you the beauty of the dark side of existence. What you have seen in your short seventeen years on this earth has been through eyes narrowed by righteousness, and who is to say that sight has been justly imposed upon you? There are things in the underworlds of which you have never dreamed, pleasures you cannot even imagine. I offer all these to you."

"No—"

Cyrus sank his teeth into the soft meat of her neck.

The searing pain of the punctures was instantly replaced by pleasure, intense enough to make Cassia's body go rigid. Her fingers spasmed at the air as the gladiator nursed at her throat, working carefully and not spilling a drop. Blackness swirled at the edges of her vision, and she would have cried out—"Not this—kill me instead, I beg of you!"—but her voice would not work, had become as useless as the rest of her. Numbness spread insidiously through her body as he slowly bled her, and she weakened as though he'd given her a poison in her food. She could hear her own heartbeat, at first panicked and fear-filled, then

Slowing . . .

Slowing . . .

Sloooowwwwing . . .

The edge of eternity beckoned, but Cassia wasn't quite there, not dead yet. She was floating, no, falling, into an abyss, dark but soft, impossibly never-ending, still somehow filled with the whispered, echoing invitation of the creature that had once been Cyrus the Gladiator as he pulled his mouth from her neck.

"We all have a dark side, Cassia Marsilka." The animalistic timbre of his voice was so soothing and inviting, the last link to which she could cling before death would claim her forever. She suddenly felt loath to hear it stop. "Some, unlike the Christian Jesus in the desert, fall under temptation. I offer you myself, and immortality, but it is you who must choose to take these gifts. I will not force you. Think of it, my lovely. Who can truly say that what awaits you on the other side is anything but black oblivion?"

She felt him lift her helpless form from the ground, as limp as a child's doll made of rope and cloth. Face up then and her eyes were slits through which she could see *only a shadow of Cyrus's face; more than anything, the star-swept sky above him beckoned, endless and, to her, utterly terrifying. Then something else blocked that vision—his wrist, dripping from a self-inflicted gash. It brushed her lips, and she could smell his blood, coppery but old like Cyrus. What had once been repulsive smelled suddenly like very finely aged wine. She had only to open her mouth and draw it in—*

"You must make your own choice, Cassia. Take a mortal's uninspired death, or join me in glorious immortality."

And Cassia the Vampire Slayer drank.

"You smell disgusting. When was the last time you bathed?"

On the other side of the small dank room, the nasty little demon named Dunphy that had grabbed Anya out by the garbage area this morning looked up from where he'd been digging industriously into a dwindling bag of potato chips. "What?" he asked with an utterly stupid look.

"I know there's nothing wrong with your hearing," Anya said testily. "Don't you know personal hygiene is a key element to being integrated into modern society? I read all about it in *Cosmopolitan.* You'll never be accepted in public circles if you don't learn the value of soap and water."

The demon stared at her. "I can't use soap," he finally said. "It gives me asthma attacks."

"Then plain water," Anya said. "You must like water. You're a fish . . . thing."

The creature shrugged. "I like seawater, not the stuff that comes out of the faucet here. It's chlorinated, like standing under a bucket of bleach. It does bad things to my skin."

"You could stand to use some of that bleach," Anya told him. "Especially around here."

Dunphy put down the now-empty bag of chips and shook his head in amazement. "Wow, you're a piece of work," he said, getting up and ambling over to her. "You sure do have a mouth on you for someone in a less-than-favorable position." He tugged sharply on the ropes wrapped around her.

"Ow—hey, cut that out!" Anya glared at him. "You know, I also read that there are guidelines for prisoner treatment. I don't think you're abiding by the rules."

"Do a lot of reading, don't you?" the demon said, then laughed. "Rules? There are no rules, missy. And you aren't a prisoner, you're a hostage. There's a difference."

Anya rolled her eyes. "Have you looked in *Webster's* lately?"

Dunphy just looked blank. "Huh?"

"It's a dictionary, you putrid beast. It contains many everyday human references. If you're going to reside on the mortal plane, you should at least be familiar with the source of their culture. I've read—"

"You're giving me a headache," he interrupted. "I tend to act a little disagreeable when that happens." Suddenly he moved in close to Anya, way *too* close. "I guess I never actually told you what it is I *do* when I get a headache. . . ."

Buffy was listening to Spike say that he might have an idea about where Anya was being held when Angel walked in.

Buffy's eyes brightened, then she quickly tried to slip a mask over her face. "Angel, what are you doing here?"

His answer was typically short, completely uninformative. "I was in the neighborhood."

Giles eyed him. "Do tell."

Angel ignored the former librarian. "So have you found any more information about Celina? Who she is or why she would want to tangle with you?"

"Yeah," Buffy answered. "We have. We think she's a turned vampire slayer."

Even Angel looked surprised. "A slayer?"

"From the sixteenth century," Giles added. "That would make her quite a bit older than you."

Angel's head swiveled toward Buffy, and his dark eyes glittered. "Then you'll need all the help you can get."

"Actually that's not our biggest problem right now," she told him and gestured toward Spike. The vampire still slouched on one of the chairs, but now he looked distinctly displeased at the sight of Angel. His words had faded in mid-syllable and he'd gotten instantly irritated when the attention of almost all of the others had focused elsewhere. He might not have bothered finishing now had Xander not reached forward and rapped his knuckle, hard, into the muscle right above Spike's right knee.

Spike yanked his knee away with a yelp. "Hands off!"

"You were talking before Blood Boy's grand entrance?" Xander reminded him grimly. "Strangely enough, it was about something I really wanted to hear. Keep going or I'll wrap my hands around your throat and squeeze the rest of it out of you."

"I thought patience was a virtue and all that." Spike massaged the sore spot and shot Xander a resentful look.

"Patience is for people who have time. You're quickly running out."

Spike acted like he wanted to make a smart retort, then changed his mind. "I'm not sure exactly," he admitted. "But I'd wager my next fresh meal that fish-breathed demon Dunphy has something to do with it.

He's just a bit too much in the know about Celina and her whereabouts, a bit too available for dirty little jobs like snatching up human women."

Angel glanced at Buffy and his eyes darkened as the inference behind their words sank home. "Wait—someone's missing? Who?"

"Anya."

Angel looked at her blankly.

"That would be my girlfriend," Xander snapped. "Former demon now turned helpless human woman."

Buffy stepped in front of Spike. "And where do we find Dunphy?"

"I'm not sure of that, either," Spike said. Xander made a growling noise in his throat and reached for him, but Spike swatted the dark-haired man's hands away. "But I'm quite willing to put a little research into the matter."

"Very considerate of you, seeing as how Celina left you trussed like a hog on your own bed," Giles noted gently.

This time Angel laughed outright. "I see you still know how to pick the ladies, Spike."

"I don't recall anyone inviting you to join in on this little happy hunt," Spike ground out. "Shouldn't you be cheerfully rotting away in the Land of Fruits and Nuts?"

Angel's mouth turned up slightly. "Those nuts fall far and wide. Just look at you."

Xander stood abruptly, then reached over and yanked Spike to his feet. "Time for you to play Dog Boy."

Spike looked appalled. *"What?"*

"Sorry," Xander said. "I guess that came out wrong. I must have meant to say bloodhound."

"Okay," Buffy cut in before Xander and Spike's repartee could blossom into full verbal combat. "Xander, you and Giles go with Spike to find Anya. Odds are you'll have to fight to get to her, and if she's in a private residence Spike won't be able to get inside it."

"Buffy, we should talk about this," Giles said. His face was the color of ashes. "The implications behind this battle—"

"There isn't time, Giles." She met his eyes and knew he was thinking not only about her, but about his own worst fears—that she would be turned into a vampire—as he had once seen them in a dark and terrible dream they had shared. "I'll be fine, I swear it."

"I don't think Dunphy will be at anyone's house," Spike tossed in. "Those nasty little demon types are far more partial to places like smelly basements in big buildings. I remember one time—"

Giles grimaced, then reluctantly pulled on his jacket. "All right, then. Let's go down Spike's memory lane some other time, shall we? Right now we need to find Anya before something unfortunate happens to her."

"Yeah," Spike put in. "You know I've heard rumors of humans getting eaten and—"

"I thought I told you to shut up," Willow said in a high voice as Xander made a choking sound. Something dark flashed in her eyes, a glint that looked like onyx and polished steel.

Spike flinched. "Well, that was awhile ago. I wish you'd make up your mind, love."

Willow only stared back at him. "I don't think you want me to do that right now," she said.

"Willow," Buffy said quickly, "can you and Tara stay with Dawn?" She had a sudden vision of Spike with his mouth fused shut, and while it was appealing on one hand, it would be probably be easier if he had the ability to verbalize for the next couple of hours. Willow's protective surface had risen higher with each shot that Xander had taken due to Spike's insensitivity, and it was probably best to keep Willow separated from the vampire for a little while. "I'd like to have extra protection à la Wiccan should our bad girl come calling."

"Of course," Willow said.

"I don't need a baby-sitter," Dawn said. "How many times do I have to say this?"

"Sadly, you do seem to be stuck on repeat," Buffy said with an affectionate rub on her sister's shoulder.

"I want to go with you and Angel." The younger girl eyed Angel with intense interest. "He's like private detective to the stars, a California Kolchak or something. He could tell us about life in Hollywood and stuff. Plus he's your ex-boyfriend."

"Actually, Kolchak was a reporter," Angel said, looking uncomfortable. "And he operated out of Chicago—"

"I think you can stay here and just keep working on that homework," Buffy said. "Trig, wasn't it?"

"Come on, Buffy. I won't get in the way, I promise—"

"It's not like we're baby-sitting at all," Willow put in hastily. "More like a girl party. But . . ." Willow sent a dark grin toward her partner, then looked back at Buffy. "Give us ten minutes before you leave. I think Tara and I will have a meeting of the minds and send you off with a little extra ammunition."

Behind her, Tara smiled in agreement, her face looking deceptively angelic as she stood and picked up her backpack. "It won't take long."

"All right," Buffy said. "I'm not supposed to meet her until midnight anyway. We've got plenty of time, but I do want to get there early."

"Let's go, Spike," Xander said. His mouth was a hard line. "Here's your big chance to play leader."

"Of what?" the vampire retorted. "Morons?" Nevertheless, he stood and headed toward the exit. "Come on, then. Let's see what we can find out and about this wretched little town."

"For your sake, let's hope that's Anya," Xander retorted, and Giles fell into step alongside them.

"Oh, we'll find her." Spike's voice faded as they filed out the door. "Let's just hope her pieces are all still attached to each other. There's a rather ugly story going around about a group of—"

The door shut, leaving Buffy, Angel, and Dawn to stare after them and think for a few seconds too long on what Spike had been saying.

"Still attached?" Dawn repeated weakly.

"It's not going to come to that." Buffy's voice made arguing about the matter out of the question. "We'll find her and she'll be just fine. You'll see."

The three of them stood there without talking while the moments ticked past, each of them wondering privately about the possibility that the three men who'd just left might *not* find Anya in time. "Or maybe she'll escape on her own," Dawn said suddenly. "I mean, she was a demon for all those hundreds of years and stuff, she must know all kinds of things to help her, tricks or magic or something." Dawn looked at her sister hopefully, then at Angel. "Don't you think?"

"Oh, definitely," Angel said, but somehow his expression didn't go along with the falsely comforting phrase and Buffy's pseudo-enthusiastic nod.

It felt like forever but it was probably only another few minutes before Willow and Tara returned from where they'd retreated into the back room. A few well-chosen Wiccan items were cradled in their palms and Willow smiled craftily and held out the largest, swinging it enticingly back and forth. Buffy reached forward and closed her fingers around a small bag made of purple velvet and loosely tied shut with a black and gold cord. It didn't weigh much, but it tingled immediately in her hand, as though something warm and energetic inside couldn't wait to be released.

"Wow, what's in here?" Buffy asked and started to open it.

Willow's hand folded over hers. "No, don't open it until you're going to use it. And be sure not to get any in your own eyes. It's got pennyroyal root in it, galangal root, some other stuff that has to do with certain animal body parts that you'd rather not have the details about." She leaned forward and whispered a few more instructions in Buffy's ear, and the Slayer's smile grew wider with each word.

"Got it," Buffy said. She tucked the bag carefully into the front pocket of her pants, where she could easily reach it. "Very handy."

"Also," Willow said, handing her another tiny item, "stick this little packet into your other pocket, nice and deep where it won't fall out. It's a protective charm and blessed to you. You don't need to do anything with it."

"Everything's always a big mystery," Dawn said crankily. "Why can't we all just talk about stuff in the open, like normal adults?"

"Normal adults don't talk about stuff in the open," Buffy said absently as she slid Willow's charm all the way down into the front pocket of her jeans. "They do everything behind your back and call it politics."

"I think Giles would beg to differ on that," Willow commented.

"Sounds pretty accurate to me," Tara said under her breath. Willow glanced at her sympathetically, knowing she was again remembering the twisted and totally false story her family had told her to try to get her to return and be barely more than a housekeeping slave to the male members of the family.

"What's that in your hand?" Buffy asked, deciding it was best to redirect. "More stuff to take with me?"

Tara's eyes brightened. "We're going to burn a couple of candles and make an extra blessing to give you extra strength and speed, another to keep your eyes free of deception in case she uses any magick of her own. We figured it couldn't hurt. You don't have to be here for that, though."

"Sounds righteous to me." Buffy pulled out her stake and inspected it for cracks, then tucked it back into the waistband of her pants, making sure her shirt covered it. "I'm ready. I'll see you guys back here after it's all over." She made a special effort to sound confident and poised; Dawn wouldn't show it in front of anyone else—maybe not even to Buffy—but she needed the reassuring sight of Buffy the Fearless Sister.

He'd been silent most of the time, but now Angel stepped forward. "I'm going with you."

But Buffy only looked at him. "Not."

"How about I just walk you part of the way?"

Buffy couldn't help grinning. "Like walking me to school?"

"Something like that."

"Want to carry my books?"

Angel chuckled, but the sound was strained. "Sure."

Buffy gave Dawn a peck on the cheek and waved to Willow and Tara, then she and Angel made their way to the door and out into the evening. It was a beautiful night, breezy but not too cold . . . or perhaps it was just Angel's presence that took away the chill Buffy had felt earlier. Clouds scuttled across the sky, combining with the waving tree branches to make moonbeams dance in and out of view on the sidewalks and lawns, the celestial version of a gigantic shadow-puppet show. Still, every time a cloud concealed the moon's glow, Buffy felt like the temperature dropped several degrees—ridiculous, of course, since the moon gave off no heat. Then again, the moon reflected light, and light lifted the soul and provided comfort; in a roundabout way that probably accounted for the imagined temperature decrease.

Such a deceptively lovely evening to take a walk with an ex-lover, one who was still so very much in her heart. Why, then, could she not shake the fear that she was going to her death?

She awoke in a new world with the taste of blood and death in her mouth.

It was dusk and she was in a cave, some small hole hidden in the rocks off the forested shoreline beyond the village. Cassia stood and explored the small space restlessly, shaking the dirt of last night's battle from her tunic. The surrounding darkness was almost . . . not there, as if her eyes provided a private source of never-dimming torchlight. She could sense that somewhere outside the sun was just disappearing over the horizon, knew instinctively that she must avoid it at all costs even as she crept closer to the outside. Cyrus, her murderer and would-be eternal lover, must have brought her here to keep her safe. Yes, he was here—she could hear him stirring in the deeper section of the cave; soon he would join her at its entrance and expect to begin their existence together. The years that might be stretched in front of her, but she couldn't yet comprehend them.

With the last of its rays muted, twilight slipped over the Grecian shoreline, and Cassia stepped outside, not bothering to wait for Cyrus. The shoreline and the ocean that spread before her looked different, brighter and sharper despite the impending night, tinged slightly at the edges with red. Cassia thought she could smell everything and hear everything—the carrion smell of a predatory owl roosting in a tree a few meters away, the grass rustling as an oversize beetle struggled along the ground directly in front of her. Her senses were magnified a hundred times, and she bent and picked up a sturdy stick, prodded idly at the luminescent shell of the insect before letting it continue on its way.

The wood in her hand felt the same, the cloth of her tunic set itself against the curves of her body in the same manner, her hair, though dirty and tangled, still curled. Why, then, did she feel so different?

I am a vampire, Cassia thought, and on the heels of those words she was filled with self-loathing.

Her cowardice had made her become what she most hated, one of the same creatures which had killed and feasted on her parents and brother on the same night that she had first learned of their existence. Her knowledge had come too late to save them though—how was her father, such a man of hospitality, to know he should never invite a pair of weary strangers into his house in the middle of the night? By the time she had heard the screams and come running, her family and two servants lay with torn throats, and that night she had discovered her hidden strength and skills and fought the first of many battles. The woman who had come to her a week later and called herself a Watcher had found Cassia filled with little but scorn. A vampire slayer she might have become, but she despised the so-called "Watcher" and blamed her, and those of her ilk, for the deaths of her parents and younger brother. What

manner of person knew of such things as these creatures, and of vampire slayers, yet had done nothing to
help keep her family safe? Could they not have given
her some warning, armed her with knowledge before
the night of their terrible deaths? Even now, her
Watcher would be searching in vain for Cassia, who
had slipped from the village to hunt for vampires on
her own and had actively avoided having anything to
do with the woman anyway.

I am a vampire, *Cassia thought again. That was un-
deniable, and she could feel the hunger of the beast
within, how it built with each passing minute like a
yearning that could never be filled. But somewhere inside her, she was also still a slayer, could feel the extraordinary slayer's strength now increased by a vampire's
otherworldly abilities. She loathed the vampires who
had killed her and made her one of them, the one who
had killed her, the creature she had become. Worse than
that, she loathed humans—how easily and instantly they
had become little more than cattle in her mind, weak
vessels to be emptied so that her own strength might be
maintained. After less than two years, she had given her
mortal life for these pathetic beings, and why? So that
they might live to the ripe old age of forty or fifty?*

No, *Cassia thought.* I am not just a vampire, or just a
vampire slayer. I am Cassia the Vampire Slayer Vampire.

*As she had known he was there prior to the battle the
previous night, Cassia knew when Cyrus was behind her
now. No doubt the handsome gladiator had grand plans
for murder and feasting and passion in the eons to
come, of power and wealth and pleasure, perhaps even
of travel to foreign lands and places Cassia had never
before dreamed of seeing. But she had plans of her own,
and she did not need the heavy hand of a Roman to*

*guide her. Such a great warrior Cyrus had been, but
also such a fool. He truly did not know that last night he
had won the battle, but today he would lose the war.*

*She heard him pull in air to speak, but before he could,
Cassia turned and drove the wooden stick deeply into the
center of Cyrus's chest. She didn't bother to say goodbye
as her sire's eyes bulged in surprise, then disintegrated
with the rest of his body. She was on her own now.*

*And there, beyond the gentle swells of the Saronikós
Gulf and the Mediterranean Sea, the world beckoned. . . .*

Angel walked beside Buffy without speaking for several blocks, then finally broke his silence. "You need help with this one, Buffy. Catia is—"

"Celina," Buffy corrected automatically. "That's what she goes by now."

"I don't care if she goes by Queen of Darkness," he snapped. "She's damned dangerous, and this isn't something to brush off lightly."

"I'm not brushing it off, Angel," she said tiredly. "Did you know that my worst nightmare is that I become a vampire? There was a boy named Billy and he was in a coma. He was having nightmares, and they started coming true, and in turn everyone else started having nightmares that were also coming true." Buffy squeezed her eyes shut briefly as she brought back the memory. "I was a *vampire,* Angel. Not for long, but it felt like forever at the time."

"Nightmares don't come true," he said, but his voice sounded too rigid.

"Don't they?" They kept walking and the vampire dropped back into silence again. She wished he'd talk—about Celina, about Los Angeles, about how Cordelia and Wesley were doing and what was up at the agency, ramble on about *anything* so she could keep herself from dwelling on the coming confrontation.

Was she afraid?

Yes.

Walking side by side with the man—the *dead* man—she loved despite all the time and events that had conspired to keep them apart, Buffy's fears wrestled with the facts in her mind, and in this one the fear always came out on top. Why? Because tonight she was facing what she had always secretly feared would be the worst of her own challenges and nightmares, a vampire slayer *vampire.* Celina was everything that Buffy had ever wanted *not* to be and was terrified of becoming. Gifted with extraordinary power and speed, this reportedly beautiful young Grecian girl had been turned to the darkside centuries ago, forced to turn her back on the fight for good and embrace everything that there was about evil.

And had not the First Slayer told Buffy that her powers were born in darkness? Faith, too, had insisted that Buffy had a dark side that she kept under rigid control. If these claims were true, then what would happen to her during this fight? Would the dark side of her soul, the flip side of herself, emerge and try to weaken her resolve to destroy this woman? There was no denying there was darkness within her: what else would prompt her, whose very presence upon this earth seemed to be to battle the existence of evil, to love beyond all hope one of the very creatures she was sworn to kill?

When Dracula approached her, Buffy had had felt the seductive pull of that Bloody King, had seemed about to tumble over the edge into the arms of his wickedness. She had defeated him—for now—but what would she do if she found a shadowy opposite within herself who ached to experience, to *welcome* the swell of power and immortality that might be only the absence of a heartbeat away? Perhaps with Angel by her side she would be better prepared to resist temptation. He could step in and help where needed, and she would be stronger—

But no. It was not Angel's job to fight her battles for her. He had done it before—they had made an undefeatable team, but this fight was different. This foe was her shadow self, even more than Faith had been. If he did it this time, if she found her strength lacking and he had to step in, she should not have the title of Buffy the Vampire Slayer at all, she would not *deserve* it. Just as Celina—or Catia, or Cassia—had lost the right to bear that title so many centuries before. Angel's presence would be most helpful, yes, but not in the way he thought, whether because she had been forced to drink the blood of her killer or had, God forbid, fallen to temptation on her own.

A concept which darkened Buffy's thoughts even more.

"What do you think made her turn?" she asked abruptly. "Whoever killed her *made* her drink, right? A slayer wouldn't . . . wouldn't do that on her own. Would she?" Her voice had gotten smaller, as though it was being smothered by the fear building inside her.

Angel didn't answer for a long time, and that didn't make her feel any better. When he did, his one-word reply just left too many doubts to comfort her. "Probably."

"Man of many words." She sighed and stared into the darkness.

"Some people are stronger than others," Angel offered then. "They aren't as easy to pull off the straight and narrow path. A slayer isn't any different—she's as human as the next person, just physically stronger. Emotionally she wrestles with the same questions and . . . demons."

"That she does," Buffy said softly.

"Buffy," he began, as if he knew the direction in which her thoughts were headed. "Let me—"

She held up a hand and his words broke off. "I have to do this myself, Angel. Argue all you want, but you *know* that. As easy as it would be to say 'Yeah, let's be a team,' there are a thousand reasons why this time, *especially,* I can't let you do that. Because Celina is a slayer, I have to know . . . I have to prove—to you, to Giles, and to myself—that I can beat her."

He stopped and faced her, and she thought he was going to protest anyway. Instead, he put his arms around her and pulled her to him, held her close. "I wish our lives had been different," he said softly.

She relaxed against his chest, enjoying the nearness of him but aware, always aware, that the heart within his chest did not beat and the only true physical warmth between them came from her. *If wishes were stardust,* she thought, *we would sparkle together forever.* "But they aren't," she said. "So we'll deal with it."

"I won't leave you," he said, and she could tell by the tone of his voice that no amount of bickering would change his mind on that. "I'll be close. Always."

She pushed back but still gripped his arms. "All right," she finally said. "Close is good. But *don't* interfere, no matter what happens." Her fingers gripped his cool forearms, feeling the strength in the muscles. "How did they do it in the old days? If I fall, you can be my . . . second."

He smiled tightly. "Your champion?"

"Always," she said, and meant it. She smiled back and marveled silently at how different the word *champion* felt to her when it came from Angel instead of Spike. "You'll always be in my heart, you know. If she beats me, then you can step in and take her down where I didn't. And if . . ." Her voice broke for a second, then smoothed out as she found the courage to say the words.

"If worse comes to worse and I fall, Angel, make sure I don't . . . come back. I don't *ever* want to come back."

Anya swallowed and tried to lean away from the demon, but it was difficult in her tied-up state. She really shouldn't ask, of course she shouldn't, she should just sit here and be quiet, but . . . "What exactly is it you do when you get a headache?"

"I tend to *bite.*"

Dunphy pulled his lips back in a wide grimace, and Anya couldn't stop herself from cringing at from the sight. "And I tend to get really *bad* headaches when I get nagged. Get it?" He had a mouthful of crooked teeth that showed an amazing array of unappealing colors. It reminded her of a television show she'd seen about Komodo dragons, and how the dragon's bite itself didn't kill you, but the infection that resulted from it did. The dragon gave a little chompy-chompy, then simply followed its prey around and waited for it to die from blood poisoning or whatever. Who could imagine what kind of bacteria was happily playing house in Dunphy's diseased-looking maw?

"I think I'll be quiet right now," Anya said brightly. "I've heard aspirin is an excellent form of treatment for head-related pain."

"It upsets my stomach," Dunphy said crankily, then promptly headed back to the couch, where he found another nearly empty snack bag—cheese doodles or some such—and started rummaging into it.

Upset stomach? Anya sat there and tried to be quiet, watching Dunphy chow into the chips, then get up and retrieve a bowl of something white, wet and lumpy from the filthy refrigerator in the kitchen area of the one room apartment—*or maybe* lair *is a more appropriate term for this little hellhole.* There wasn't much that was human going on here outside of the fridge and the equally disgusting-looking stove; apparently the demon didn't sleep on a real bed, but there was a pallet of smelly, dark bedding in the other corner. Anya was extremely grateful he'd chosen to tie her to this chair rather than toss her down over there—she didn't want to think about what kind of creepy crawlies might be lurking within the folds of gritty-looking fabric that had probably never seen the inside of a washing machine.

There was an old TV across from where Dunphy sprawled on a vinyl beanbag chair, but she couldn't see the screen from her spot. Too bad; she could have used the diversion. As it was, she had way too much time to think about her predicament and wonder if Xander and the others would even have any idea where she was. Sure, Spike had talked to this half-brained monster before, but did he have any clue where the creature lived? Probably not—they'd just done the bar thing, yakking it up over a couple of beers or whatever chud-breathed beasties like Dunphy drank. She was pretty sure no one had seen him grab her, and while she'd gotten off a pretty hearty yell or two before he'd threatened to take off one of his dirty socks and stuff it in her mouth—that had shut her up quite rapidly—apparently nobody had heard her screams either.

So she was stuck here, and while she was trying to think positively—she'd heard repeatedly that people who were optimistic lived longer and as a human she figured she needed all the help she could get—the truth was Anya wasn't really positive she was going to get out of here alive.

She'd managed to pry it out of Dunphy that she was the insurance that Buffy would show up in the cemetery tonight to have the knockdown drag-out with Celina. If Buffy didn't show, Anya was history. That wasn't so bad—Anya had quite a bit of confidence in Buffy. As a slayer and as a human, Buffy was extremely dependable—Anya knew a lot of people who ought to be taking life lessons from that. But really, when Buffy met up with that Celina woman and even if Buffy beat the vampire in a fight, was this motley piece of sea-soaked demon flesh actually going to let her go? Just untie her and allow her to waltz on out of here like it was the end of any normal neighborly visit, and by the way, hey, no hard feelings?

Fat freaking chance.

If he was smart, Dunphy would probably be way too afraid that Anya would do turnabout on him when she got back to Xander and Buffy and the rest of her friends. He had to know she'd finger him as her kidnapper and that if any of her acquaintances ever crossed his path, he'd end up the equivalent of pureed cat food, fish-demon flavor. So it didn't matter—either way, Anya figured she was doomed.

The hours dragged past, and she squirmed uncomfortably on the chair, wishing she could get up and go to the bathroom, stretch her legs, walk right the heck out of this rathole. The whole time she had that hindsight thing going on—if she'd known she'd end up trussed up like a rib roast, she might have gone for D'Hoffryn's offer and not ended up in this stupid situation. *But no, I had to go and turn him down, and now it looks like his* die like a bug *prediction would actually be a much better choice.*

In the meantime, Dunphy ignored her, quite absorbed in his consumption of just about everything edible in the place—she couldn't begin to eat that much, and she didn't understand why the demon didn't weigh five hundred pounds like that blobby-looking demon the gang had gone up against, Balthazar. She'd seen a drawing of it in one of Giles's books—disgusting. In fact, his whole eating obsession bothered her. Did he have some kind of demonic tapeworm or something? *It was getting close to midnight—isn't he full by now?* If the creature didn't lose his appetite and he ran out of food . . .

What would be next?

"Okay," Dunphy said unexpectedly. She jumped when he hauled himself to his feet and dusted the latest layer of crumbs off his hands, sending smashed bits of hot-sauce-soaked pork rinds in every direction. "Well, the appetizers are done, so I guess it's time to get the show on the road. Or"—he sent her a dark, food-flecked grin—"the main meal on the tray, as it were."

"The main meal?" Anya repeated faintly.

The glance he aimed at her was incredulous. "Man, for a former demon gone human you sure are stupid. You didn't really think you were gonna be wrapped up and delivered back to your nice, cozy house, did you? And all this time you've been acting like you were so smart." He shook his head. "See, Celina told me that unless she came back for the merchandise—that would be you, by the way—herself, I could do what I wanted with it after twelve o'clock. It's a quarter to. I figure that's close enough."

Anya swallowed. "I'd hoped you'd do the honorable thing and let me go. I have friends who will reward you."

Dunphy laughed wetly. "What, did I suddenly become a stunt double for Lancelot?"

"Listen—"

He held up a dirty-fingered hand to stop her. "No

sense arguing, cutie. You *are* my reward. You can't give me enough cash to match what I got waiting, I guarantee it. See, I know who you are, and who you used to be. I got good ties, and there's a ring of flesh-eating demons that'll pay good money for you. They love that ex-demon meat." He shrugged. "I guess the only reason I'm safe is because they usually won't eat a current demon—too much like eating their own kind. They prefer the has-beens, and that would be you, the infamous *Anyanka.* Oh, yeah, you'll pay my rent for a year, plus they said they'd give me a couple of butt steaks."

Anya's mouth formed a horrified *O.* "You're going to carve *steaks* from my . . . from my . . ."

"Butt," Dunphy said with absolutely no emotion.

What did she care if he got a headache? Anya opened her mouth and screamed.

Chapter 13

"LINE THEM UP THIS WAY," WILLOW TOLD DAWN. THE younger girl was holding five candles ranging from white to bloodred. "At each point of the pentagram, with the white one on the top."

"Okay." Dawn set each candle in place, carefully positioning them as she'd been instructed. Her heart was pounding and she was trying to concentrate, but she couldn't help being afraid that Buffy would suddenly come through the door of the Magic Shop and catch her doing this. Willow and Tara knew Buffy had told her never to mess with this kind of stuff . . . didn't they? She was way too excited to remember, and even though she knew she shouldn't, she didn't want to remind them of that in case they'd forgotten. But this wasn't supposed to be a big deal, like a spell or a curse or anything. Just a charm. A blessing. Yeah, that was all. "Now what?"

"Now we make sure everything that's supposed to be on our altar is in place," Tara said. She inspected the array of items they'd meticulously spread out on a piece of crimson velvet on the table, then began ticking off each one as she explained its purpose. "The white candle on the pentagram stands for purity of thought and intention—you should always include one in your spells or blessings because it helps to block evil energy. Although most people think black represents evil, it doesn't. It's a universal color that symbolizes the night. We include a black candle for the same purpose as a white one—to protect and send away darkness, not draw it in."

"The red candle is for protection," Willow added. "It will also help Buffy maintain her strength and her courage, even though she's facing a really scary opponent. We added the orange one to give her an energy boost."

"Okay." Dawn studied the layout. "And what's the yellow one for?"

"Yellow usually represents intellect. In this case, we're using it as a symbol for the sun, a request to attract illumination to Buffy, so that she can always see what she's getting into, no matter how disguised something might be."

"What's all the rest of this stuff?" Dawn asked.

"Sea salt, a wand, a bell, a bowl of purified and blessed water. A little cauldron to burn some incense and herbs—especially sage to keep the mind clean—and, of course, the ritual knife."

"Speaking of," Dawn said a little nervously. "We need that for what, exactly?"

Willow smiled. "Tonight? Nothing. It's just here as part of the altar, in its usual place."

Dawn looked relieved. "Good. I really hate the whole letting of blood thing. It's very painful."

Tara gave her a gentle smile. "I think the whole point

of our blessing tonight is to try to avoid any bloodshed at all. Buffy's, in particular."

Dawn pointed at the table. "What are these rocks?"

"Stones," Willow corrected. "Rocks are kind of . . . well, what you'd find in a parking lot, little chunks of concrete. These are specific pieces of the earth, very special. Like the candles, each one has a certain strength and meaning, and can pass on its power."

"The golden one is a piece of beryl," Tara said. "It should be a big help for Buffy because it can help protect her from anything mental that Celina might try. We included a tiny bit of crushed beryl in the packet we made for her."

"And this?" Dawn reached for a purple- and green-hued stone.

Willow's hand stopped hers before it could make contact. "Don't touch the stones or you'll interrupt their energy flow. That's fluorite—it will help keep Buffy's eyes and thoughts clear, make sure she don't get confused, or if she does, keep her from staying that way." She scanned the altar. "The third stone is a cat's-eye. It's another protective one. There are spells you can do to it to make the person wearing it invisible."

"Really?" Dawn was wide-eyed. "Is that what you're going to do to Buffy—make her invisible? That would be so *awesome*—"

"Awesome, yes," Tara said with a small grin. "But I'm afraid not tonight. That's way more complicated than we have time for."

"Oh." Dawn was disappointed for a moment, then she brightened. "But if you had time, could you do it? I mean, could you turn *me* invisible?" Her eyes sparkled mischievously. "Wow, just think of the things I could do at school. Instead of *The Invisible*

Man, I'd be the 'Invisible Dawn,' rising up over my buds—"

"There isn't going to be any Dawn Rising," Willow said firmly. "You have to remember that in Wicca, you can't abuse power. Your intent has to be pure because what you do to others, you get threefold in return."

Dawn brushed her hair back, looking completely unconvinced, almost rebellious. "Yeah? Then what about all the people who use it for evil?" she demanded. "Maybe I've got 'naive' tattooed on my cheek, but I sure don't see *them* getting any retribution."

"Their . . . *reward* will come," Tara said softly. "If not here, then in the afterlife. Sometimes they are too blinded by greed and power to realize that until it's too late."

There was something quietly ominous in the blond woman's voice that raised the hair on the back of Dawn's neck. "Oh."

Willow cleared her throat. "So let's do the blessing, okay?" She gave Dawn a reassuring smile. "You know, it's good that you're here—it'll be much more powerful with three people instead of just two."

Dawn was pleased. "Really?"

"Absolutely. Three is the number of power. Come on." She knelt at the top of the pentagram and Tara knelt to her right. "You kneel here, and then we'll join hands." When the three of them were in place, Willow continued. "Now close your eyes and imagine a white ball of light in the center of our circle. Picture it in your mind. It shimmers and glows, and keeps growing until it encases us in a protective bubble."

Kneeling there and holding the hands of her two older companions, Dawn really expected to feel nothing. After all, not only was she *not* a witch, she wasn't even supposed to be doing this stuff. Instead, she had to force her eyes to stay shut when she began to feel a warm tingling and an image—exactly what Willow had suggested—began forming behind her eyelids. Heat started on her cheeks and her nose, then slowly spread to the outer edges of her face and neck and the rest of the front of her body, as if there were a campfire in center of the pentacle. If she opened her eyes, she wondered if she would actually *see* the ball of white light that Willow had talked about, a physical rendition of the image in her mind at this very instant. Tempting, but she didn't dare—she was too afraid she'd ruin the blessing, and then Willow and Tara would think she was a dork.

The seconds ticked past and Dawn waited, basking in the sunlight-like warmth. Finally Willow said quietly, "You can open your eyes now, Dawn."

Dawn did, then barely suppressed her gasp. She'd been right—the three of them were surrounded by a shimmering, barely visible "veil" of light, like a smooth, domed curtain of glitter. It was shocking . . . and utterly beautiful enough to leave her breathless. She wanted to say something, *anything,* about how totally cool this was, but again she was afraid—she might spoil the blessing, break the mood, whatever. Better to just keep her silence and enjoy the fact that Willow and Tara had brought her in to be a part of this incredible experience. It was harmless, and Buffy just didn't to know about it. After all, they were doing it for her.

"Focus on the candles and the stones," Tara instructed Dawn in a barely audible voice. "Concentrate on the words and their intent, *see* the result in your mind."

Dawn nodded. This was her big chance to actually *do* something to help her sister, instead of just standing around all the time like an extra thumb—something useless and annoying. She wasn't sure how much she was contributing to this—maybe not much at all—but she was still scared to death of flubbing it.

"Thank you, God and Goddess, for hearing our words tonight, and we ask you to protect us from any evil influences," Willow intoned. "We come before you to beseech your assistance to our treasured friend Buffy the Vampire Slayer in her struggles against evil."

Dawn risked the slightest of peeks toward Willow and thought she saw fire dancing in the redhead's eyes. Maybe it was just a reflection of the candles or the sparkling shroud that still encompassed the trio. Then again, maybe it wasn't—as the last syllable left Willow's mouth, the flames on both the white and black candles suddenly surged upward into three-inch columns. Each burned fiercely for about five seconds, then eased back down to the height of a normal candle flame.

Willow looked toward Tara, and her companion leaned forward slightly without loosening her grip. "By your will, we ask that, should she need it, you give Buffy energy and light with which to see the unseen in both the physical and hidden realms. Let nothing be obscured in shadows, those too either seen or unseen." This time the yellow and orange candles flared to life, and Dawn watched, fascinated, as for a few seconds twin fires burned so brightly above each that it seemed like miniature suns were sitting atop the colored tapers.

When the candle flames had settled back down, Willow squeezed her hand. "Your turn, Dawn."

"You mustn't lose hope, Xander."

"Oh, I'm not," Xander said to Giles. "Just call me 'Hopes R Us.' " But despite his blithe words, Xander's face was grim beneath hair rumpled from repeatedly running his hands through it. He couldn't seem to stop his gaze from darting anxiously from side to side, even when there was nothing new to be checked out, no unexamined shadow or alcove along their path.

"Buck up, Grumpy." Spike stuck a cigarette in his mouth and lit it as they walked rapidly down the block. "We haven't checked all the down and dirty spots yet. There's at least a half dozen more."

Xander inhaled as he saw Giles try to glance at his watch without being obvious about it. "Maybe not," he said. "But we *have* checked all the best ones . . . with zilch luck. And we're not exactly running fat on time."

"That we haven't gotten anything yet just means she hasn't been nabbed by one of the classier scumbags," Spike said matter-of-factly. "We haven't gotten a bead on Dunphy yet, but there's a whole passel of slimy nutjobs who could've grabbed her up—"

Giles made a sharp noise. "Spike, you're not helping matters."

The vampire looked at him blankly, then tried to look contrite. "Oh. Sorry 'bout that, mate."

"You have to believe we'll find her," Giles told Xander after glaring at Spike for a moment.

Xander couldn't help smiling a little sadly. "You sound like Anya. She read some New Age self-help book a couple of weeks ago, and for days afterward all I heard was how optimistic people live longer, think positive, believe in yourself. Blah blah blah."

"Well," Giles said as Spike paused before a darkened side street thoughtfully, then decided to turn into it. "I suppose I could see a correlation. People who maintain an optimistic attitude are generally happy. Happy people are generally healthier, with less tendency toward stress-related illnesses such as heart disease and such."

"Right," Xander said. His voice sounded caustic even to his own ears. "Happy on the Hellmouth. That's us."

"Heads up, laddies," Spike said in a quiet voice. He jerked his chin toward a couple of shadowy figures lounging around the mouth of an alleyway about a half a block away. They were trying to look nonchalant and stay in the darkness at the same time, and managing quite nicely to do neither. "I believe we've found us a couple of blokes worth giving a talking to."

Giles peered into the darkness. "What is that they're wearing? Feathers? Masks?"

"Both," Spike told him. "Don't you recognize the getup? These guys were originally Iroquois warriors in the seventeen-hundreds. They ascended to demonhood because they tortured their war captives to death, then ate their flesh."

"If that's ascension, I'd hate to see what happens when you *descend*," Xander muttered.

"Cannibalism?" Giles frowned. "Why don't I know about these demons?"

Spike gave him a wry glance. "Your Brit is showing, Watcher. Guess you need to bone up on your American history."

"Why the masks?" Xander asked.

"They were used in rituals or whatever. Rumor has it that they got stuck wearing the masks because they're possessed—they can't get them off. In real life, people were always afraid of them. I guess they had good reason."

"I know a bit about Native American history," Giles said huffily. "There are differing reports about cannibalism and whether or not it existed in certain tribes, especially in the Northeast—"

"A, this is not the Northeast, and B, now is not the time for a history lesson, Giles." Xander ran his hand through his hair again, unconsciously tugging on it. Worry had made his face drawn and put purple circles beneath his eyes, while the constant hair pulling made his dark hair stand straight up in places, as though he'd walked through a wall of static electricity.

"You want to watch your backs with these guys," Spike told Xander and Giles as they approached the loitering duo. "They're sneaky and majorly nasty—can't trust 'em for nothing."

"Like you can trust other demons and beasties of the night." Xander rolled his eyes. "Can we just get this over with? Trusting them is not high on my list of need right now. Obtaining Anya-related information is."

Spike lowered his voice even more as they closed the last of the distance. "They don't usually hang about in the open—I'd wager they're waiting for something. Or someone."

"If they're cannibals, that might well be their next meal," Giles said in a sour semi-whisper. "Let's make sure it's not us."

"Me?" Dawn whispered. Panic blossomed in her chest and her heart hammered in sudden alarm. "I'm supposed to do something? Say something? What?"

"First of all, relax." On her other side, Tara's voice was calm, like a soothing summer breeze. "Just say a few words to go with the red candle. Remember that's the one that will give Buffy strength and courage. Don't worry—we'll help."

"O-Okay." Dawn tried to keep her voice even, but the trembles kept worming their way in. All she could do was give it her best. "Please help Buffy to be strong and not to be frightened no matter what happens." She paused, then added, "And to believe in herself."

For a long, painful moment, nothing happened. Then Dawn felt . . . *something.* A zap of power, like a little electrical jolt, zipped into each hand. The flame on the red candle flared high, and she exhaled in relief, hadn't realized she'd been holding her breath until then. *Was that me?* After all, she had done a spell after her mom had died, performed a shot of dark magic that had nearly brought her mother—or what had become of her when touched by that bit of darkness—back. Thank goodness she'd come to her senses before Buffy had gotten the front door open, because there was no telling what the consequences might have been, what twisted creature had shuffled out of her mom's grave and was using her form.

But right now, tonight? Dawn figured it probably hadn't had much to do with her—more than likely Willow and Tara had worked the magic here, channeled their more than sufficient energies through her to complete the blessing for Buffy. But that was okay—Dawn still felt like she'd helped, and it was the end result that counted. The worst thing about feeling like she wasn't real, a nonperson, was just sort of *being* there, doing nothing. This time she'd *contributed.*

Didn't I?

"Relax," Tara whispered. "You did fine."

The rest of the blessing—a small closing thank-you and then the opening of a "door" in the protective shell they'd erected around themselves—flew past, and in no time at all Willow and Tara were carefully dismantling the altar, cleaning and storing away its contents. Dawn sat at the table and watched them without saying anything, this time not asking if she could help. She felt kind of strange, almost lazy and full—like she'd just finished eating a big plate of spaghetti and was sliding into a content food coma.

When everything was packed up, Willow and Tara joined her at the table. "How do you feel?" Willow asked.

"Okay, I guess." Dawn hesitated, then added, "Kind of sleepy or something."

Tara nodded. "When you do a successful blessing or a spell, it's a little bit of a psychic drain, especially when you've never done it before."

The teenager twisted her hands together and looked at the two witches hopefully. "So it really worked, then? I—we helped her?"

Willow and Tara exchanged serious glances, then Willow rested her hand on Dawn's shoulder. "As much as we could, Dawn," she said quietly. "The rest of the way . . . well, it all comes down to Buffy. It always has."

" 'Evening, gents," Spike said in a louder voice. "How's it going?"

The two figures turned and stared at them, but it was impossible to tell their reaction because of the wooden masks that covered their entire faces. The masks themselves were anything but attractive—both were cut from dark wood and had grotesque, one-sided parodies of a smile with oversize eyes and a nose twisted toward the right side. The lips, eyebrows, and eyes were painted in darker colors reminiscent of something an evil clown would wear. Long dirty hair flowed unevenly from behind the wood, but it was impossible to tell if the hair was attached to the demon or to the mask. Tied here and there at the edges with rawhide strips were stained little bags closed with drawstrings. The edges around the wood were frayed and splintered, sticking out in thin, dry strips like kindling.

"If those are earrings, you guys have some pretty bizarre taste in jewelry," Xander noted with a half-hearted smile.

"Those are tobacco bags," Giles said out of the side of his mouth. "If I remember my history correctly"—he tossed a withering glance in Spike's direction—"each bag has a turtle-shell rattle inside it."

"Go away," said the figure nearest them. His—its?—voice was muffled behind the wood. "We're not looking for company."

"Pretty odd place to just be standing around, right in the middle of nowhere, so to speak. Maybe you're waiting for someone. Cigarette?" Spike held out his crumpled pack as an offering.

"What arc you, insane?" demanded the second, recoiling. "We don't smoke—our faces are made of wood!"

For demons, these creeps were pretty up-to-date with the language skills; of course, they'd been around for a couple of hundred years, and while a demon might not be able to change his eating preference, a lot of them could learn to communicate quite well. "There is that," Spike said. He gave them a buddy-buddy grin. "So the story in the neighborhood is that you guys are the ones in the know as to where we could get a little, uh, high-end meal. Speciality stuff—you know, the sort of munch-meat that isn't exactly sold prepackaged in grocery stores."

"What makes you think we know anything about that?" asked the first one. His voice was outright belligerent. To Xander, only the colors of their shirts—both in tacky, vaguely cowboyish patterns—made them distinguishable from one another. "We have wooden masks for heads. We don't chew."

Spike folded his arms. "So what? The word I get is that you guys go for the blenderized version and use a straw."

"Okay," Xander mumbled to Giles. "I don't know about you, but my disgust level just went through the roof."

"What difference is it to you?" Mask-face number one tilted his head, but it didn't help alleviate the strange of trying to hold a conversation with someone—or some *thing*—that had utterly no facial movement. Xander thought he could finally appreciate the phrase *wooden expression.*

Spike gave them another congenial grin. "My friends here and I would like to make a little purchase of our own. But we want the meat to be ultra-fresh."

"As in still alive," Giles put it.

"Well . . ." said the second demon, looking slyly at his companions. "I think we could figure that out."

"So maybe you could hook us up with your supplier," Spike said. "He could get an extra sale, we could get what we want, maybe you guys could get a little bonus."

Behind their masks, the eyes of the demons glittered. "Like what?" asked one.

"Like staying *alive,*" Spike growled as he morphed instantly into vamp-mode. One hand snapped out and his fingers hooked under the jawline of the nearest mask; he yanked it forward with enough force so that everyone there heard the *rrriiiiipppp* come from behind it as the wood pulled partially free of the demon's face.

The demon screamed and tried to bat away Spike's hands, but the vampire's grip was solid. Caught by surprise, Spike easily yanked the creature back and forth, aggravating the injury more with each pull. "I guess you want"—he pushed to the left, then pulled back to the right—"to help us *out.* Before I end up working this piece of firewood right off your face!"

"Let him go!" The other beastie yanked a wicked-looking hunting knife from a leather sheath at his belt, but Giles and Xander had him by the wrists before he could do anything with it. Giles pulled the demon forward until he bent, then banged the hand holding the weapon against his knee until the blade fell to the ground.

Spike was still pulling on the face of the first one. Some sort of goopy-looking yellow stuff was starting to ooze from beneath the edges all around the mask, making the ratty-looking feathers adorning it stick. "Are you gonna talk to us or do I have to pull this thing all the way off and show an unprepared world what you *really* look like?" Spike demanded.

"Owwwwww!" the creature howled. His hands were flapping wildly in the air each time Spike tugged. "What do you want—I can tell you anything. Just please stop pulling my face off!"

Spike stopped the side-to-side movement but didn't relinquish his grip. "That's better. Cooperation is your friend. Isn't it, guys?"

A few feet away Giles and Xander were struggling to hold down the other masked demon. It was really quite strong, at least for the two human men. "Let's not chitchat, shall we?" Giles gasped. "Get on with it!"

"Oh, yeah, right." Spike gave his prisoner a little shake. "Well?"

"We're supposed to meet a guy here," the demon whined reluctantly. "His name's Dunphy. Said he had a special treat for us if we could pay enough, a human woman who used to be a demon."

"Anya!" Xander exclaimed.

Spike's mouth twisted. "Figures it'd be Dunphy."

"Or Anyanka, whatever," the demon continued. He

gave an experimental tug to see if he could get free and got a painful pull for his trouble. "Hey!"

"If you don't want to get hurt, quit beating around the alley and keep talking," Spike said calmly. "You aren't finished yet."

"What are you guys, desperate for food?" snarled the demon that Giles and Xander were pressing mask-first against the ground. "I have five dollars in my pocket—take it and go to a restaurant!"

"Shut up, splinter-teeth," Xander snapped and jammed his knee into the demon's back to keep him from wriggling free. "I think your buddy is going to be more helpful than you."

"Yeah, fine, all right," said the other one. His voice was high-pitched, still at whine level. "That Dunphy guy, he's a fish-demon, right? He's got some scavenger in him, 'cause he said all he wanted was a few cuts of the meat after we carved it. He's supposed to bring Anyanka here—"

Xander had the arm of his prisoner twisted backward, and his grip tightened enough to make the demon below him groan. "She'd better be alive when he gets here!"

"She will be," said Spike's prisoner hastily. "We specified a live catch—we don't scavenge like him. He's a pig—he'll eat anything, alive, dead, or died last week."

Spike gave the monster's mask a sharp yank. "When?"

"He ought to be here in another few minutes," the demon told him. "That's what he said this morning when he was scoping out the 'hood and looking for a buyer."

"Marvelous," Giles said. His face was grim. "And what do we do with these two in the meantime? It's not likely they'll follow our instructions to go away quietly."

"If you'll just let go of my face, I'll be more than

happy to take off," said the demon Spike still had hold of. "No problem, no grudges. Really."

Spike cocked his head to one side. "Tell you what, my friend. Why don't we make sure you want to be anywhere else but where we are?" Before the demon could fathom what was going down, Spike used his free hand to pull his lighter from his pocket. He thumbed the strike wheel and pushed it close to the fraying edges of the mask, then let go of the demon as the splintered wood all around its face burst into flames.

The demon screamed and took off at a dead run down the alley, while his companion went into a near frenzy as Spike approached. He bucked and twisted, trying desperately to free himself from Xander and Giles. "No— *no!* I'll leave, I swear! You'll never see me again! I'll—"

Spike didn't bother to let him finish. Before either of the two men could decide what to do, the vampire reached down and set the flame to the second demon's face mask, at the same time jerking one of the dirty tobacco bags free. Giles and Xander yanked their hands away as fire encircled the creature's face and, howling at the top of his lungs, he bolted after his fellow demon. In no time at all, they were both out of sight and the alley was empty.

"Well," Giles said. "That was a bit cold, even for you, Spike."

Spike shrugged. "Hey, since I can only be mean to demons without getting a mallet thump inside my skull, I have to enjoy it where I can." He pocketed his lighter. "A little singeing will do wonders for their attitude, and besides, a good face-first fall in the wet grass'll put 'em right out."

Xander leaned over and picked up the hunting knife that had been left behind. It was a wicked looking thing with a curved, eight-inch blade and a cream-colored handle. He peered at it. "What is this, ivory? Don't those jerks know that elephants are endangered?"

"Oddly enough, I don't think they care," Giles said dryly.

Before Xander could stop him, Spike reached over and took the knife out of his hands. "Better give me that before you hurt yourself."

"Hey," Xander said. "I told you once already—I use tools every day that could make you into an altogether new and much more interesting shape." Still, he wasn't particularly upset to hand over the blade to another person.

"Someone's coming," Giles said in a low voice. Sounds floated down the alley and the three of them quickly backed up, each finding some nook or shadowed alcove into which to hide. It wasn't long before they recognized Anya's voice and heard the undertone of panic in it.

". . . ransom," she was saying. "Haven't you ever heard the term? There was even a movie made with that title. I think Mel Gibson was in it. See, there's this whole concept of getting paid enormous sums of money for the return of abducted people. You should read up on it." Her words were tumbling over each other, cut with little gasps as she apparently tried to catch her breath.

"Would you stop trying to pull in the other direction already?" The other voice, wet-sounding and unpleasant, had to be a demon's, probably Dunphy's. "You're just delaying the inevitable—can't you just accept that you're going to be dinner and quit arguing?" They could see the demon now; he had Anya's arms tied behind her back and was pushing her forward. For every three steps he managed, she found a way to go backward one.

"You didn't answer my question about the ransom thing," Anya repeated insistently. She never stopped her struggles. "Haven't you ever watched it on television? Or seen it at the movies? I just told you, there was this great flick with Mel Gibson trying to get his son back—"

"I saw it already, and life does *not* happen like stuff in the movies," Dunphy ground out. He shoved Anya hard enough to make her stumble, then changed his tactic and attempted to drag her. She yelped when her knees hit the ground.

From his hiding spot, Xander made a sound in his throat and started to move out, but Giles stopped him. "Not yet," the Watcher whispered. "Let him get closer— we can't let him get away. We don't know his arrangement with Celina, and we can't take the chance that he might warn her."

"But he's hurting her," Xander hissed.

"Down boy," Spike said in a barely audible voice. "Remember his market. Dunphy won't damage the groceries too badly. If he does, he thinks he won't get paid."

"Oh, I'll pay him all right." Still, Xander eased backward again, forcing himself to wait. His hands were gripped into fists and his expression was rigid.

Fifty feet away Anya struggled to her feet with Dunphy's prodding as the demon clearly decided it would be better if she walked on her own. "There's never any good ransom in something like this because the bad guy—that would be you—is always too stupid to plan properly," Anya told him. "Now, if I were you—"

"You're *not*," Dunphy snapped. "So shut up already!" This time he stepped behind her and used both hands to propel her bodily down the alley, and Anya had no choice but to go with it or risk falling face first onto the dirty concrete.

She said something else just as they started to pass in front of where the three men were hidden, but the words were lost in her gasp of surprise when Spike stepped casually out of the shadows. "Hey, Dunphy," he said casually. "What's a disgusting demon like you doing with a nice-looking human girl like her?"

Dunphy jerked to a stop and pulled Anya back against him almost like a shield. She squirmed and made a sound of disgust. "Let me go, you putrid piece of leftover fish food!"

"Shut up," Dunphy said, but he was more concerned with watching Spike. "Hey, I remember you from the bar—what the hell are you doing here?"

Spike shrugged. "Oh, just hanging out. Meeting up with some friends. You know, the usual."

"Yeah, well take your 'usual' somewhere else," Dunphy ordered. "I'm meeting some people here myself, and you don't want to be around when they get here. They'll eat you up and spit out the vampire pieces."

"Really." Spike gave him a dark grin. "I think they're gonna have a little trouble with that." He held up the tobacco bag he'd ripped from one of the face-mask demons and let it swing casually from his fingers. "Look familiar?"

Dunphy's bulbous eyes widened when he realized what it was, then he swallowed loudly as Giles and Xander stepped from their hiding places and flanked him.

"Xander!" Anya's expression melted into happiness, then went just as quickly into a scowl. "Xander, he's had me tied up all day and he hurt my wrists. He was going to sell me for a piece of my—for *butt* steaks!"

Xander started forward. "Time to let her go, baitbreath."

Dunphy swung to face him, yanking Anya around and keeping her in front of him. "Not so fast, human. What, you beat up one or two of the guys I was meeting up with? Maybe even killed him, huh?" Dunphy laughed wetly. "You think you're so smart?"

Xander circled to his left, and Dunphy tried to turn with him, but his movements were jerky and uncertain—he was obviously having problems keeping track of both Giles and Spike at the same time.

"So you're implying there are more of your 'friends' on the way?" Giles asked.

Dunphy swiveled toward the Watcher. "Oh, you bet. They—"

Spike sent the hunting knife end-over-end into the scrawny muscle of the demon's right thigh.

"Argggh!" Dunphy's hands flew up, and he grabbed at his leg at the same time Xander leaped forward and hauled Anya out of his range. "Awwww, what'd you have to go and do that for?" He staggered sideways and went down with the blade still stuck firmly into his leg, writhing on the ground.

Giles grabbed Xander and Anya by the arms and urged them in the opposite direction. "Come on, Spike," he said urgently. "We need to get out of here."

"What's the hurry?" Spike regarded the ugly-looking Dunphy. "I'm thinking we should finish him off first. Maybe carve him up like he was planning on fileting Anya." He stepped forward and grabbed at the handle of the knife. The demon gargled as Spike yanked it free and held it up. "Look, we even have the tool."

"But not the time." Giles pointed to the other end of the alleyway. "Look—I think the rest of the tribe is arriving."

Spike and the other two followed Giles's finger and saw a cluster of shadows moving at the far end, slipping from one spot to another at an alarming rate. "Time to travel," Spike said a little too cheerfully. "I vote we leave Dunphy for the masses."

"That sounds about right," Xander said.

"You're going to just *leave* him?" Anya asked in astonishment. "You're not going to at least . . . *beat* him up or something? Xander, he was going to sell me to cannibals—or whatever they were!"

"Are," Xander corrected. "And they *are* on their way here." He pulled her along behind Giles and Spike, glancing over his shoulder as they left the demon who'd kidnapped her still rolling in pain on the ground. "Believe me, Dunphy'll get his. In really short order."

Irritated, Anya squinted back in the direction he'd been looking. "What are you talk—*oh!*"

When Xander followed her gaze, he heard Dunphy scream and saw his prone form literally disappear beneath a wave of moving darkness, probably a dozen or more of the mask-faced demons. "Bleh," he said as they hurried away. "I'm not even sure *he* deserved to be eaten alive."

"Oh, I'm crying inside," Spike said. "They kill him off first, I'm sure. And trust me, the world is better off without one more foul-smelling monster."

Xander glanced at him. "And you would be what?"

Spike's chin lifted. "Hey, at least *I* bathe!"

"True," Anya said. "Most vampires tend to be a lot like what they were in their former lives. So—"

"Vampire facts and figures later, shall we?" Giles suggested. "Right now perhaps our time would be better served by going to the cemetery and seeing if we can provide Buffy with some assistance." He glanced at each of them as they left the alley behind for good and Dunphy's cries abruptly ceased. "After all, the night is still young, and our Slayer has yet to face one of the most formidable opponents of her life."

Chapter 14

ELSEWHERE IN TOWN, YES, BUT HERE . . . COULD THERE be such a thing as a beautiful night in the death-soaked ambience of a cemetery?

Only in my world, Buffy thought and actually smiled a bit as she wandered among the gravestones. She'd never mentioned it to anyone, and it was even something she really hadn't thought about, but she'd spent so much time in this place, quality and unquality time, that she'd come to appreciate the simple, cold beauty of the statues and monuments, the way the moonlight could turn the most inexpensive of these into a thing of bluish, ethereal elegance.

She'd left Angel behind at the main gate nearly a half hour ago, allowing herself only one glance backward as she'd followed the path that would lead her to the heart of the graveyard. That look behind her hadn't been so much to make sure he didn't outright follow—she trusted him implicitly, knew he would be there when he was supposed to and not be there when he shouldn't—

but for reassurance. Unlike Lot's wife, there would be no penalty for her curiosity, no damning curse to spend eternity as a figure of salt because of her desire to see what she left behind. No, should she fail, what awaited her in eternity was far more corrupt.

Now and then an owl's soft hoot cut through the darkness. Walking along at night on patrol, she'd always wondered where the birds went—presumably they were high in the trees, nestled deeply in the leaves and branches where they could safely enjoy whatever dreamland birds had. The only birds she ever saw in the cemeteries at night were blackbirds or crows, and she didn't like either, at night *or* in the daylight. Maybe she was superstitious—God knew she had enough reason—but somewhere along the line she remembered being told that if you saw three of them in a row, it meant someone you loved was going to die.

Buffy stopped by a particularly tall grave marker and stared up at it. It was very fancy, an oversize angel made of white marble shot through with green, although the wings had been carefully carved of flawless, snow white stone. Its eyes were looking to the east, in the same direction to which its hands were outstretched. She'd always wondered about these graveyard angels—did they possess a ghost or a spirit, hold something inside themselves and protect the soul of the person who rested in the grave beneath them? This one looked almost apprehensive, as though its task was to search the horizon each morning and make sure the sun came up. Buffy couldn't help wonder what, if anything, this tall, stone guardian would do if that anxiously awaited sunrise never happened.

She'd be the first to admit she'd had to learn to pay better attention to that special Slayer "sense" that would let her know when a vampire was sneaking up on her, whether it was from the bushes three yards off or standing six inches away. Tonight Buffy made sure that all systems were definitely on go, and so she knew right when . . . *something* was coming, something *bigger.* Maybe it was because she was meeting Celina and the vampire had once been a slayer herself, or maybe it was because she had so much more riding on tonight than just a confrontation. Tonight's battle was for a lot more than just Anya—it was for herself, her sanity, her *soul.* All of these things had come into question at one time or another in the chaos that had become her existence since she'd been called as a slayer, and Celina's very existence was a travesty to everything Buffy was, a slap in the face of all she had ever fought for. To say she was fighting for these things tonight sounded almost inconsequential, overused . . . except that it wasn't, now or *ever.* Especially tonight, *this* night, because the worth, the *righteousness,* of all three of those elusive but oh-so-precious things came together and depended on the outcome of the next quarter hour.

Right versus wrong.

Light versus dark.

"I know you're there," Buffy said to the quiet darkness.

She turned and saw nothing but the silent monuments and memorials, thinly leafed trees still hanging onto their summer foliage. A breeze came up, cold and crisp, and . . .

Celina rose from behind an ornately carved double headstone.

"I've been watching you," the vampire said.

"I know."

They stared at each other, one Slayer sworn to fight against the very thing the other had become. Facing each other like this, in the hush before battle, felt oddly like forming a bond. They both knew it, could see the similarities between themselves if not in appearance, in spirit. What was it they shared . . . a slayer's soul? Or its essence, something that went even deeper than the normal human spirit? In Buffy, perhaps, but in Celina that had been forfeit long ago. And once lost it would likely never be regained.

"We found out who you are," Buffy said. She didn't move and neither did Celina. "Cassia, isn't it?"

Celina smiled and Buffy had a moment to be amazed at how beautiful she was—the texture of her hair was like silk despite the false coloring, her eyes were clear and bright, her skin had remained without a single blemish or scar. Still so perfect after five hundred years. It was heartbreaking that such beauty could only be preserved through the most vile of acts, while letting a soul go naturally on to eternal peace left its shell to rot and disappear forever. It didn't seem fair.

"I haven't been Cassia in a very long time." Celina ran a slender hand up the side of the gravestone next to her, and Buffy imagined she saw a hint of the same appreciation of its somber elegance that she herself sometimes felt. "I left her behind in Greece. I think it was a million years ago."

"Did you lose her?" Buffy asked softly. "Or is there something of her still left inside you? You were a Slayer, someone special. One of a kind. Does that really ever die?"

Celina stared off into space for a few moments, thinking. "Parts of it did—*important* parts. But other parts . . ." She grinned, but it wasn't a pleasant thing to see. "Those are the feelings and abilities that stayed alive, yes. But they *changed*." Her eyes narrowed. "I don't think you fully appreciate the difference, Buffy. It's almost like a metamorphosis—the changing of something pretty but pathetic, *weak*, into something else that's stunning and immensely strong—*glorious*. A colorful but useless butterfly into, say, a sleek and deadly tarantula hawk wasp."

Buffy grimaced. "Not the simile I would have chosen."

Celina chuckled. "That's because you don't have a true understanding of what lies beneath *everything* in the world—prey and predator. As a slayer in Greece, I was prey, and it didn't matter how strong I was. As a vampire now, I am predator." A corner of the vampire's mouth turned up. "You, I'm afraid, are still prey."

Buffy moved to the left slightly, and Celina paced her; the two were unconsciously circling each other. "Why?" Buffy asked. "Why did you come looking for me? I mean, you had it down pat, didn't you? The Council didn't even *know* about you until we figured it out, but you can bet they've got the info by now—my Watcher's made sure of that." She frowned at the other woman, trying to understand. "News like that—it spreads like smoke on a windy day—you couldn't stop it now if you wanted to. You had the walk and the talk, could have stayed hidden forever, but you blew it. It's like you *wanted* to be found out." She stared at Celina, then asked again. *"Why?"*

Celina gazed at her thoughtfully, and Buffy had to give the vampire credit for not thinking that the current Slayer would fall for a shallow lie or a tossed-off excuse. "The truth is I didn't realize how hunting you down would get out of hand," she admitted. Celina actually looked a little perplexed. "It happened so quickly. A slayer isn't supposed to have *friends,* you know. Or lovers, ex or otherwise. We're supposed to live and work alone, die the same way. Do you have any idea how lucky you are? You're just a puny mortal, but you've had every chance I lost . . . or never had to begin with." Her mouth twisted. "All that opportunity and you don't even appreciate it. You're just an immature little *girl,* taking your slayer powers for granted and making a mockery of both the light and dark worlds. You're an *embarrassment* and a caricature of the very concept of a vampire slayer, an *insult* and a hypocrite besides to fall in love with the same kind of creature you're honor bound to kill."

Buffy shook her head, still mirroring Celina's graceful movements. They were like two lions sizing each other up, working up to a fight for their pride and their lives. "Maybe you were never the kind of person who deserved friends or love to begin with, Celina. As for the rest . . . times change. This isn't the world you were born into—we have things like electricity now. And communication."

Celina chuckled. "There is that. It makes such a difference. I always thought I could adapt to anything, but even I'm beginning to have trouble keeping up. I've bounced from country to country and century to century, traveled to places you can only dream of, like England, France, Germany, Spain, South America, even Alaska and Finland. Thailand and Malaysia . . . Oh, there was an era." Her eyes had gone dreamy for just a second, but then they hardened again. "Like a chameleon, I keep changing my appearance . . . but now the animal I would kill knows about me and my whereabouts before I get there."

"I assume you're referring to me," Buffy said.

"No offense."

"None taken. I've been insulted by better demons than you."

This time Celina didn't smile. "But I will be the last." She leaped.

Buffy was ready for her and she wasn't there when Celina's boot would have caught her in the midsection.

Her self-satisfaction was short-lived, however; she'd back-stepped and intended to hammer a good punch of her own right into the vampire's jaw when Celina dropped her foot, but that opportunity never came. Instead of dropping, the vampire's kick continued, driving forward in a single, smooth motion—her fists were up to protect her face while she literally *followed* Buffy forward in a move that was almost like dancing.

The kick that shouldn't have connected took Buffy right off her feet and sent her tumbling a good eight feet backward. She had a moment to be grateful for a solid routine of ab workouts—if her abdominal muscles hadn't been conditioned, her belly button would've touched her spine on that one—then she was up and again facing Celina. She was stung and a little breathless, surprised, but not hurt. This time.

Celina was through talking about things. She came after Buffy like a whirlwind, hands and feet flashing, making moves faster than Buffy had ever seen anyone do before. Buffy blocked, blocked again—then kept blocking the blows and kicks that seemed to come from everywhere. Every now and then she'd take a stinging crack to the ribs or the jaw when she didn't get a hand up in time, or fold in to go with a kick she couldn't avoid, but she was totally unable to go on the offensive—the vampire was far too fast ... and *way* more skilled than Buffy had ever been.

Buffy dodged behind a headstone and got an all-too-short respite. She grabbed the chance to draw in a couple of deep breaths, knowing the vampire didn't need any such break—she didn't require air in her lungs or oxygen in her muscles, and she wasn't going to loose steam before Buffy.

"Come on, *Slayer*," Celina taunted. "You're way

overdue to die—why don't you spare us both the annoyance of a fight and just face your end gracefully?" She followed the words by twisting around the headstone and doing a switch-kick that Buffy vaguely remembered from a long-ago Thai boxing training session—a split-second move made Celina's lead leg move to the back, and it was a darned good thing Buffy ducked, because the boot that cut past her head had full body weight in it. Celina swung through with the kick, and even if Buffy had been able to throw one of her own, the vampire's other leg came up to block on the return.

Buffy scrambled backward on her rear end, anything but graceful. She was in way over her head here—five hundred years had given Celina way too much time to train in methods of fighting that Buffy simply hadn't lived long enough to learn. She *had* to stay out of her reach or she could easily end up pinned in that pretzel-like hold Celina had used on her the last time they'd fought . . . except this time the sunrise was too many hours away to save her.

Buffy spun in a high crescent kick and got lucky— Celina had gotten a little too used to her being on the defensive and lowered her expectations. Buffy's kick caught her on the right side of the jaw, but it wasn't hard enough to do any real damage. It did buy her enough time to put ten feet between her and the undead vampire slayer, and that ten feet gave her two seconds, and that two seconds was just enough time to let her slide a hand into the pocket of her pants.

Her fingers closed around the velvet bag Willow had given her, and she yanked it free. Whatever knot her friend had used to tie the bag shut came loose instantly as she drew it out. Willow had whispered to her that she needn't do anything but get the tiniest portion of the contents of the bag to cross Celina's vision, but Buffy wasn't taking any chances. Celina was already moving toward her, and Buffy swept her arm across the rapidly disappearing space between them. Her jerking movement sent a shower of something dark and dusty into the air, and the vampire walking right into it as Buffy automatically back-stepped out of its flow.

For the briefest of moments, the air was filled with a crimson-colored sparkle. It was gone as quickly as it came, but Buffy paid for the second that she'd been distracted by it when the left shovel hook Celina had sent her way connected with her rib cage. The blow lifted her off her feet and sent her sprawling sideways, gasping with pain and hoping she didn't have a broken rib—or three—on that side. To add to her misery, she whacked her right cheekbone on the edge of the base of a statue, that same angel she'd admired only a few minutes before Celina had shown up for their confrontation. So much for feeling protected.

Buffy tried to pull herself upright and get out of the way as Celina came toward her again and found a spike of pain in her arm where she'd landed on it wrong. Celina set up for one of those deadly front kicks of hers—

—and missed.

The vampire spun and righted herself instinctively, but there had been a microsecond where Buffy had seen the bewildered expression on her face. Buffy leaned sideways, and Celina kicked again—

—and missed.

"What the hell?" This time Celina hesitated, then danced backward a few feet, still moving lightly on the balls of her feet.

"Having a little trouble with your eyesight?" Buffy

righted herself, then got to her feet, circling Celina once more but still being careful to keep a safe distance away.

"What did you throw in my eyes?" Celina demanded.

"Just a little something to help you see," Buffy replied. "We figured that since you've been working on both sides of the fence all these years—the light *and* the dark—you ought to be able to see on both sides."

Celina blinked furiously, but Buffy wasn't ready to move in for the attack, not yet. She wanted to make damned sure that Willow's powder worked, that it *really* took hold, before she put herself within Celina's reach.

"So to fight me you had to get help from someone else," Celina said bitterly. "You didn't believe in yourself enough to do so on your own."

"I may not be as old as you, but I'm not a fool," Buffy retorted. "I'm a real quick study and all I needed was that one lesson. Besides, what fun would it be for you if I was just another less-than-challenging human for you to defeat? Your end ought to at least be interesting."

"*My* end?" Celina lunged at her with a series of rapid punches. She had incredible speed, and Buffy took a few of them as sturdy hits . . . but still, she was able to deflect most of them—she knew the vampire was seeing two of everything and having a harder and harder time deciding exactly where Buffy was. "You're a coward," Celina snarled. She swung at Buffy again, but the Slayer simply wasn't there. Her frustration began to show as every strike she made became unsure, a less-than-powerful flailing at the unknown. "A typical human weakling!"

Buffy laughed. "Big talk for someone who can't even find her target! To hear you say it, I thought you were up for any kind of battle. Now all I hear is a bunch of whining about how I'm not playing fair. You thought I was just a human weakling? You've been alive—well, sort of—for so long, haven't you ever heard the expression 'All's fair in love and war'?"

"It doesn't matter," Celina ground out. "I could defeat you blindfolded!"

"You mean if *I* was blindfolded," Buffy shot back. She paid for her sarcastic remark, however, when Celina sent a spinning kick in her direction. It missed . . . but the vampire followed it with yet another spinning kick, this one a reverse hook in the *other* direction. As she reeled backward, it sank in that even though handicapped, Celina was still going to take some effort to defeat. Buffy couldn't help feel a grudging admiration for her. Still, despite her own "big" words, Buffy knew it was never good to assume you could take an opponent, just as it was always wiser to accept help when it was offered . . . and you could accept it. She might not have been able in good conscience to let Angel fight alongside her, but the doubling powder that Willow and Tara had created for her just might turn out to save her life tonight.

Celina kicked out again, but Buffy was ready this time, and she wasn't going to be caught by the same one-two kick pattern. She swept the vampire's leg to the right, slipped to the left and leaped in a high scissor-kick takedown. Her left leg came up and across Celina's hips at the same time as her right came forward behind the vampire's knees; they went down together, but Buffy had the element of surprise on this one, and all Celina could do was grunt before Buffy had swung around to an upright position and was straddling her. Celina started an attempt to free herself, then froze when she felt the point of Buffy's wooden stake sink slightly into that very special spot in the center of her chest.

"Well, I'll be damned," the vampire said in awe.

"You already are." Buffy raised her hand for the killing blow on the end of the piece of wood.

"Wait," Celina said desperately. "It's not *fair.*"

"Are you going to start that again?" Buffy asked. Still, she hesitated. This wasn't just *any* vampire, after all. Monster . . . yes. Undead . . . yes. But Celina had once been a vampire slayer. A *slayer,* for crying out loud. And because of that, suddenly Buffy just *had* to ask. "Why?" she demanded. She pressed the point of the stake in a little further, heard her opponent's gasp of pain. "Why did you turn? You, of all people. *Why did you turn, Cassia?*"

Trapped beneath Buffy's weight, Celina suddenly became very still, and when she didn't answer right away, Buffy didn't rush her. She was finally in control here, not Celina, and she would give her the courtesy of being able to speak her last words with care.

"Because it wasn't *fair,*" Celina said, and at first Buffy thought the woman was simply repeating herself. Then, as Celina continued, Buffy realized it was so much more than repetition. Instead of staring at her, the vampire's eyes seemed to gaze right *through* her, seeing some great and distant secret that Buffy would never be privileged enough to know. "The vampires—they had everything, they *took* everything. My family back when I was alive—they were all killed, you know. By vampires."

"I'm sorry," Buffy said, and she meant it.

"No, you're not," Celina shot back. Buffy knew the other woman would never believe her, so she didn't bother to protest. Celina's gaze refocused on Buffy and her mouth twisted into an ugly line. "You're just *polite.* Why should you care about me, or about what happened to me almost six hundred years before you were even a babe in your mother's womb? I lost everything in my world to the vampires, and then, at the end, I was facing the ultimate sacrifice. And for *what?*" She laughed harshly. "A mankind who refused to believe that vampires existed and who would've burned me for a witch had I tried to tell them the ugly truth. I had no family, no friends, and a Watcher with all the emotion and understanding of a barnyard ass. For this I was supposed to *die?*"

Realization hit Buffy. Cassia Marsilka hadn't been forced into this. She had *chosen* it, weakened and gone *willingly* into the darkness. The concept was almost earth-shattering, and Buffy's hand tightened around the stake. "You were supposed to die for the side of *good,*" Buffy said grimly. "Instead you chose the coward's way out." She was angry, yes, and she managed to keep her face expressionless but still . . . she couldn't deny the twinge of regret she felt on behalf of the vampire on the other end of her weapon. Why had she caved? It was obvious, of course—she'd been on her own, too far alone. Without the support and guidance of Giles and the others, Buffy herself could have very well been lost a long time ago. Destined to be born in a time far more crude, floundering without love or help or support—Celina, or Cassia as she'd been way back then, must have been lonely and, indeed, lost.

"*Good?*" Celina spit the word out as though it were something bitter on her tongue. "Good is nothing but a state of mind. Think about it, Buffy Summers. Good is only what other people have been ordering you to do ever since they found out you had more power than they do."

Buffy stared at her for a long moment, then shook her head. "No, you're wrong. It's not like that at all."

"Isn't it?" A sliver of moonlight cut through the clouds overhead and made Cassia's eyes shine, then the clouds closed again and the night darkened. "What have they—your Watcher, the Council—done for you besides take over your life and tell you what you should be and what you should do? Day in, day out, they order you around—how much thought have they given about your dreams and desires? Your future?" The vampire's laughter had a bleak edge to it. "None, Of course. They haven't considered any of that, and you know why even though you fight the pain of facing the truth. *Because you have no future.* As a slayer the only reason you exist is to *die*—you have *no other purpose.*"

Buffy opened her mouth to protest but nothing came out. Giles had done his best to support her, had done everything he could to force her vampired-riddled life into normalcy. Ultimately his efforts had been futile. Too much of Celina's words were true—how many of her dreams had disintegrated because of her Slayerhood anyway? *All* of them—love, college, a career. Career? That was a laugh. First she'd let her studies slide, then she'd first modified the idea of college—goodbye Northwestern University—then scrapped it altogether when her mother had died. She loved Dawn, but in the deepest, most secret place of her heart, she could never deny that Dawn wasn't really . . . well, Dawn was a part of Buffy's life only because Buffy was the Slayer. If she hadn't been called, if she hadn't been *born* as one, what wondrous things, *human* things, could she be experiencing right this second? Instead she was on her knees in a graveyard, grappling with a beast the likes of which, as Celina had pointed out, most of the rest of the world wouldn't even admit existed. If the people of the world wouldn't do that, how could they ever truly appreciate what she gave up for them?

"Join me, Buffy."

Buffy blinked. "W-What?"

"Join me," Celina repeated. Her voice was soft, almost hypnotic. Buffy hadn't felt such a powerful pull since she'd faced Dracula himself. "Think of all you could *really* become —immortal, powerful, young forever. And think of the man you love, Angelus. Would you not want to be with him for eternity? Why allow the puny trappings of human mortality to keep the two of you apart?"

God help her, but suddenly Buffy couldn't think of anything else. Angel's handsome features filled her mind, the shaggy softness of his hair when he'd been sleeping on it, the scent of him—was it because he had a soul that made him smell so different from other vampires, so clean? It had been only that one time, but she remembered everything about the way his skin felt against hers, the way they had kissed on that one and only night when they'd been fully together.

"You could be that way again," Celina said, so softly that Buffy almost didn't hear her. "Never separated. A thousand years from now, ten thousand, when the mortals who would bend you to their will are dust—not even a memory—Angelus would still be at your side. You could have the best of both worlds, Buffy Summers. You could have it *all*."

With a vague sense of detached resignation, Buffy felt her resolve start to let go. She couldn't deny all the possibilities swirling through her mind—strength and immortality, the abandon with which she could finally wield her skill and powers . . . and, of course . . . Angel.

Angel.

For all her age and experience, there were things that even Celina did not know. But Buffy had not forgotten them, oh, no. On the ground only a few feet away was the now-empty velvet bag that Willow had given her. There were other powers in the world into which she, and her friends, could tap; if she became a vampire, could Willow use an Orb of Thesulus to restore her soul as she had restored Angel's?

It was such a sweet and darkly tempting idea.

If Willow could, *would* do this for her, Buffy could not only stay with Angel, but be *like* him, a vampire with a soul and a slayer besides. Together they could live and love forever yet battle evil, and even so, Angel would be all right—the good side of him would never let him attain true happiness in her arms. She *knew* Angel, and there would always be that small part of him that would regret her vampireness, that would mourn the loss of the humanity she had sacrificed to be by his side. That tiny bit of anguish would be the one thing that, even if they shared eternity, would never let him slip over the edge into ecstasy and once more lose his soul.

Then again, did she really need bother with a soul? Buffy wanted to pretend to herself; what was a soul anyway? A conscience, an intangible bit of . . . *something* that only restricted and burdened a being with guilt and never-ending regret. Look at Angel, the way that even with a soul he was constantly tempted and pulled by the darker side of himself. Buffy had that side, too—she'd been told as much by the First Slayer, reminded of it again and again in her dreams and memories of that encounter. Fate was such a funny, fickle thing . . . was she *really* meant to be a slayer? Or was she meant for a far darker . . . and possibly *greater* existence? She might even be able to rid Angel of his soul, and then they could *truly* be together, without having to worry about light and dark, good and evil. . . .Free of the responsibility of literally carrying the weight of the world on their shoulders.

So much to think about, yet it all went through her mind in an instant, the fate of herself and, quite possibly, the world. She could feel herself weakening even more, sense the darkest side of her soul trying to claw its way to the foreground. Still poised over Celina, still in place for the killing stroke, the sparse clouds overhead finally parted. The sweet, warm light of the moon poured through and slid over the vampire's beautiful features, like honey pouring from a jar onto something delectable.

Except . . .

Except that whatever was below the surface was bad.

There was beauty there, yes, but it was corrupt, *tainted.* During this whole thing—the battle, the conversation, Celina's very careful attempt to manipulate Buffy's thinking—the vampire had been extremely careful to maintain her human façade, to never, *ever* slide into vampire-face and reveal the true side of what she now looked like. But that was exactly what this human face of Celina's was—a *mask,* something she hid behind because the truth of what she was, inside *and* out, was just too ugly to show for any length of time, at least to the other things in the world that represented beauty. She was like the ultimate undercover agent—someone who had the makeup and the outfit and the mannerisms, but who could never truly fit in and relax in the enemy's territory.

And if Buffy gave in, if she *caved,* she would be just like that . . . no, *worse.* She would be an outcast among outcasts, hated by the humans she had once lived to protect *and* the vampires she had once lived to kill, a never-ending target. Her former kind would despise her even more than they hated normal vampires—if such a thing could ever be considered "normal"—because she had been weak; her so-called "new brethren" would never trust her and ultimately hunt her down.

The happiness that Celina was offering her was nothing but a lie.

And Celina knew suddenly that Buffy realized it.

She morphed and tried to pitch Buffy sideways. Distracted just enough, Buffy started to tilt and instinctively threw one hand sideways to try and maintain her balance. Celina shrimped back and forth and nearly escaped, but Buffy recovered a lot faster this time—there was no way she was going to allow the vampire to get her in some kind of bone-bending, tendon-snapping, tie-hold. Celina thought she had the upper hand when Buffy went over with her, but she didn't. She grabbed for the hand Buffy had outstretched, and Buffy let her have it, let the vampire start to pull her in tighter and closer—

Until the stake Buffy still held in place in her other hand sunk firmly into Celina's chest.

The woman who had once been a vampire slayer stared at the current Slayer. She had one very, very short second to make a single sound—

"Oh!"

And everything Celina had been came to a dark and dusty end.

For a long moment Buffy stayed where she was on the ground, looking at the pattern of dust that had fallen next to her. It didn't look anything like a woman, but then the creature that had lain hidden beneath the feminine exterior she had just destroyed hadn't been a real woman in a long time. She had been something different, something lifeless and evil and unspeakable, and when it sunk into Buffy just how close she had come to turning into exactly that, she felt herself shudder and pull into a fetal position on the cold ground. She felt like she had somehow pulled herself back from the edge of a great and endless abyss, and all she wanted to do was squeeze her eyes shut and never open them again. She couldn't think of anything that could make her feel more ashamed than she felt right now.

"Buffy."

She wanted to open her eyes—

No, she didn't.

She felt the air move across her face as Angel knelt next to her. Then his fingertips were brushing her face clear of the dust that had coated it, the last evidence of Celina's existence. He slid his hands beneath her shoulders and lifted her to a sitting position, and with her eyes still tightly closed, the sensation was a little like swinging through space. Hadn't that been exactly what she'd just done?

"Buffy, look at me."

This time Angel shook her a little, and the motion made her eyelids jounce involuntarily. She caught him first as a sliver of paleness against the darkness, then his face became a wider, white oval against the backdrop of the cemetery. "Angel," she whispered. "Angel, I almost—"

"Shhhh," he said and pressed a finger to her lips. "You didn't 'almost' anything. No matter what you think, there isn't any almost in what you faced and defeated tonight—you do or you don't. And you *didn't*."

"But I was so *tempted*, Angel." Her eyes searched his darker ones and found a gaze filled with night but still lit from within by some kind of shine, as though the presence of his soul put a glimmer of the stars in there, a hint of the goodness that would exist in him as long as he clung to that unseen essence.

"Everyone is tempted now and then," Angel told her. "If we never face temptation, how would we know if we're truly strong?"

Before she could think of an answer for that, excited voices floated along the chilly breeze that crawled past the gravestones and monuments surrounding them. Buffy let Angel pull her to her feet as the familiar sounds came closer, and by the time Giles and the rest of her friends found her and Angel, she was standing upright, back straight and proud, and she had brushed her hair back into place.

"Buffy!" Giles was huffing as he and the others rushed up to the two of them. "Are you all right—did you get hurt? Are you—"

"I'm fine," she assured him, and dug down until she found a smile she thought would be convincing. "Right as rain."

"Did you get her?" Anya demanded, pushing past Xander. "Did you get the evil ex-slayer?"

"She got her," Angel said firmly. He looked at Buffy and only she knew he reached around and squeezed her hand. "And she had no problem doing it."

Epilogue

"I THINK I'M GOING TO READ UP ON CASSIA MARSILKA A bit more," Giles told Buffy as they headed back to the Magic Shop. "I'll wager we find her watcher was less than spectacular. Perhaps even downright careless."

"Celina mentioned something about that," Buffy said. "I think she said she was cold and emotionless."

Giles looked at her in surprise as they walked. "You had a real conversation with her, then? You didn't just fight?"

"It was a short one," was all Buffy would say. "But very . . . insightful."

The rest of their friends were waiting at the Magic Shop when Buffy, Angel and the rest of the gang got there. It felt good to walk in there and see their worried faces break into smiles of relief, to hug her little sister when she ran up to her. "How did it go?" Dawn asked anxiously. "I hope you pounded her right into dustpan leavings!"

Buffy chuckled. "Yeah, that's pretty much how it went."

"That disgusting fish demon tried to sell me as a meat product!" Anya exclaimed. "I would *not* look good wrapped in plastic!"

"Interesting thought," Spike said with a leer.

Xander glared at him. "You just keep your rancid little thoughts aimed elsewhere, chip-head."

Giles cleared his throat. "Well, I'm certainly glad this entire matter is finally cleared up. I'll have to make sure the Council's records are corrected straightaway."

"It does make you wonder how accurate they've been all these centuries with the infallible quill and ink." Willow's voice was bland, but her eyes were mischievous.

"I hardly think one relatively minor error is enough to condemn centuries of record keeping," Giles said huffily.

"Minor?" Xander asked. He looked amazed. "As Council errors go, this one *ranked,* what, top ten?"

Angel, who'd been quiet up to now, suddenly sniffed the air. "What's that smell?"

"Smell?" Buffy looked around. "I don't—no, wait. Yeah, I *do* smell something. Like—"

"I think that's the sage and the herbs we burned in the incense bowl," Dawn asked without thinking.

Oops.

"It's nothing," Willow said quickly. "Incense—"

"Stop," Buffy said sharply. Her gaze flicked from Willow to Tara, then back to Dawn. "Tara, before I left I know you said something about a blessing, but this place definitely smells like there was full-fledged spell-slinging going on."

"Not a spell, just a blessing. Nothing major, honest." Tara was trying mightily not to sound nervous, but she just wasn't pulling it off.

"A blessing," Buffy said slowly. "And did you by any

chance get Dawn involved in this little *blessing?*" She fixed Willow with her stare.

"Buffy, don't blame them, I *wanted* to help," Dawn said in a rush. "It wasn't their idea—"

"Of course it was," Willow said calmly. She stepped forward, looking half-ashamed, half-proud. "I'm sorry, Buf. I know you don't like Dawn to be involved in any . . . magic or whatever. But we needed *three* to make the blessing work. White magic, I swear. We would never do anything to involve Dawnie in dark mojo."

"I don't want her involved in *anything* mojo," Buffy said harshly. "Not now, not *ever.* Understood?"

Willow nodded contritely. "Totally."

Buffy's expression softened. "Don't get me wrong, Wil. I'm not ungrateful. I just . . ." She curled an arm around Dawn and pulled her into a hug. "I just don't want her to get sucked into something that could so easily turn into big, bad, and ugly. I want normal for her. Boring, even."

She squeezed tighter, until Dawn started to squirm. "Hey, careful—the weaker sister needs air, remember?"

"Sorry." Buffy released Dawn and watched as the teenager went over and flounced down on one of the chairs. She looked so pretty sitting there, so innocent and untouched. But on the Hellmouth that could change in . . . well, a matter of seconds.

"No more magic involving her," Buffy said with finality. "Everyone needs someone to watch over them, and for Dawn, I'm it. I'm her . . ." She glanced at Angel and saw him give her a ghost of a smile.

". . . champion."

"It is *so* good to be back home," Anya said. She burrowed a little deeper beneath the comforter. "I thought I'd never get the stench of that disgusting thing off me.

Rotten fish—ewwwww. It permeated my clothes. I think I should burn them."

Lying next to her in bed, Xander grinned. "Let's just settle for throwing them out. Less trouble with the landlord that way."

"Really, Xander, you have no idea how bad it was," she complained. "Dirty and smelly, it was all dark and there were *bugs*—"

"I know I almost lost you."

She blinked at his suddenly serious tone, then felt a rush of warmth for him. "Oh, I know I made a lot of noise," she admitted, "but I really never had a doubt that you'd find me in time."

"That's not what I'm talking about." He wasn't smiling. "I know your ex-boss showed up with a job offer, Anya."

"How—"

"Give me a little Sherlock Holmes credit, okay?" Xander began ticking off points on his fingers. "Anya is fine one day. The next she goes all Anyankaish and starts playing interrogator on friends who've had to make life-changing decisions. There really weren't a lot of blanks to be filled in."

Despite his words, Xander didn't seem like he was ready to hear her answer, so for once, Anya stayed silent.

"So I'd like to know," Xander continued, "what made you chose me? You've talked dozens of times about how great it was to be a vengeance demon, how you could live forever and would go back to it in a heartbeat if you could. You finally had the chance you'd wanted for so long. So why didn't you?"

"Because I love you." She'd meant to just say it, but the words came out in a whisper. She saw his eyes brighten, and her voice found more strength. "Because living for eternity without you would just be . . . *empty*. It wouldn't be living at all."

Suddenly she gave him a deliciously wicked smile, right before yanking the comforter up and over both their heads.

"And where would be the fun in *that?*"

"What would you have done," Buffy asked Angel later, when they were alone again, "if I hadn't . . . made it?"

"I knew you were going to win," Angel said, instead of answering her question. "I never had a doubt."

"That's not what I asked," Buffy said insistently.

Angel's lips pressed into a thin line, then his mouth relaxed. "I would have done what you asked," he said simply. "I wouldn't have interfered . . . but I would have been your second."

"You would have killed her."

"Yes." There was a beat of silence. "And then you."

She inhaled, appreciating the crisp, cold scent of the night, the feel of chilly air going into working, breathing lungs and coming out warm. "Good."

Behind them, the windows of the Magic Shop glowed with light and the sounds of life and laughter—the celebration of her victory—drifted through the partially opened front door. They were all so happy now—Anya was safe, the *world* was safe, ding-dong, the witch was dead. How strange was it that they had no concept of how close their heroine had come to falling, to being the second vampire slayer *vampire?* The second, of course, provided that there were no others.

"It's time for me to go," Angel said softly.

"I know." Buffy gave him a sad smile. There was no sense arguing, no matter what the desires of her heart had tried to stir up. The way things were, the way they would probably always *be,* she and Angel had no future with each other. Their paths might cross, but beyond that . . .

She tilted her head upward, and his lips brushed hers, soft and cold, yet always with that connection that made his touch and taste warm her all the way to her heart. Then he was, as he had always been, simply . . .

Gone.

Buffy didn't see him go—she never did. But that was okay, because as hard as tonight had been, she had learned something important, something *vital.* Somehow, in all the things that had rocked her world over these past years she had never before picked up this one incredible lesson.

Lightside or darkside, she could be at peace with herself and with the world, because she would never, ever, be alone. She had Giles, and Xander, and Willow, and all the rest of her friends. Most importantly, she had Dawn.

And, of course, she would always have Angel.

Her champion.

About the Author

Yvonne Navarro grew up on the north side of Chicago and spent her youth making up stuff in her head and drawing pictures to go along with the stories. Her first fiction was combined with artwork and was a mockup of a newspaper with the headline "Dr. Seuss Dies in Fire!" somewhere around the second grade. While she drew pictures constantly, she always had a storyline to go with them.

She didn't decide to seriously try to write those strange little mental tales until 1982. She sold her first story in 1984 to *The Horror Show Magazine,* and as time went on, she wrote more and more. She's now written in excess of eighty stories, over seventy of which have been or are scheduled to be published. In 2001 she swept first, second, and third place of the Short Story category at the Illinois state level of the Mate E. Palmer Communications Contest with "Ascension," "Divine Justice," and "Santa Alma"; "Ascension" subsequently took first place at the national level.

Sooner or later she was bound to try her hand at something longer, and her first novel, *AfterAge,* an apocalyptic vampire novel, was published in 1993. Her second novel, *deadrush* (this time putting a new turn on zombies), was published in 1995; both were finalists for the Bram Stoker Award in their publication years.

In her third solo novel, *Final Impact,* she turned to a mix of horror and science fiction. *Final Impact* won both the Chicago Women in Publishing's Award for Excellence in Adult Fiction and the "Unreal Worlds" Award for Best Horror Paperback of 1997 from the *Rocky Mountain News.* She kept the storyline going in *Red Shadows,* then followed that with *DeadTimes,* a pure horror novel. Her first suspense novel, *That's Not My Name,* was published in June of 2000 and placed first in the both the Illinois state and national levels of the Mate E. Palmer Communications Contest.

In addition to solo projects, she's written a number of media novels, including the novelizations of *Species* and *Species II, Aliens: Music of the Spears,* and three other Buffy the Vampire Slayer novels: *Paleo* (an original), and *The Willow Files, Vols. 1* and *Vol. 2. Paleo* won first place at the Illinois state and second place in the national level of the Mate E. Palmer Communications Contest in another category.

She recently finished the first draft of a supernatural thriller called *Mirror Me* and has numerous other projects in the works, including a children's book collaboration, plans for a sequel to *AfterAge,* and several other novels which are already outlined. In her spare time (!!!) she studies martial arts, and very, very soon, she's finally going to run off to Arizona.

Yvonne maintains a huge web site at www.yvonenavarro. com with full info, including covers and good-sized excerpts, from all her books, both finished and in-progress. The site has pictures, books and t-shirts for sale, and lots of other fun stuff. She's also the owner of Dusty Stacks Bookstore (www.dustystacks.com). Come visit!

ANGEL™

INVESTIGATIONS:

WE HELP THE HELPLESS

"Los Angeles. It's a city like no other. . . . People are drawn here. People, and other things. They come for all kinds of reasons. My reason? It started with a girl."
—Angel, "City Of"

For a hundred years, Angelus offered a brutal death to everyone he met. And he did it with a song in his heart. A gypsy curse put a stop to his rampage, but his doomed love of Buffy the Vampire Slayer drove him from Sunnydale on his own quest for redemption.

Now, go behind the scenes with your favorite broody vamp for all of the exclusive dirt. Exclusive interviews with cast and crew, episode "dossiers," character files, notable quotes, color photo inserts, and more!

Everyone's got their demons.

THE CASEFILES, VOLUME ONE
by Nancy Holder, Jeff Mariotte, and Maryelizabeth Hart
Available in Spring 2002

From Simon Pulse
Published by Simon and Schuster

Everyone's got his demons....

ANGEL™

If it takes an eternity, he will make amends.

❖

Original stories based on the TV show Created by Joss Whedon & David Greenwalt

Available from Simon Pulse Published by Simon & Schuster

2311-01

Buffy the Vampire Slayer™

> "Well, we could grind our enemies into powder with a sledgehammer, but gosh, we did that last night."
>
> —Xander

As long as there have been vampires, there has been the Slayer. One girl in all the world, to find them where they gather and to stop the spread of their evil...the swell of their numbers.

LOOK FOR A NEW TITLE EVERY MONTH!

Based on the hit TV series created by
Joss Whedon